WARNER
BOOKS

LARGE
PRINT

JERRY B. JENKINS

HOMETOWN LEGEND

WARNER BOOKS

LARGE ⓦ PRINT

Published in association with the literary agency of
Alive Communications, Inc., 7680 Goddard Street #200,
Colorado Springs, CO 80920.

Warner Books, Inc., 1271 Avenue of the Americas,
New York, NY 10020

An AOL Time Warner Company

Visit our Web site at www.twbookmark.com.
For information on Time Warner Trade Publishing's online publishing program, visit www.ipublish.com.

Printed in the United States of America
First Large Print Edition: September 2001
10 9 8 7 6 5 4 3 2 1

ISBN: 0-446-52998-2
LCCN: 2001093432

Book design and text composition by L&G McRee

The Large Print edition published in accord with the standards of the N.A.V.H.

To Shawn Hoffman and Michael J. Patwin Jr.,
whose visual storytelling gifts
served as impetus for this book

Acknowledgments

Thanks to Bob Abramoff; James Anderson; Bev Bahr; Ron Booth; Rick Christian; Mary Haenlein; Shawn Hoffman; Dallas Jenkins; Tim MacDonald; Ken Meyer; Charles Musfeldt, M.D.; Michael J. Patwin Jr.; Leslie Peterson; and Rolf Zettersten.

Miscellany

1913 Paul William "Bear" Bryant born in Kingsland, Arkansas

1923 Athens City High School founded in Weeks Bay County, south of Foley, Alabama; football Crusaders finish 7-0—only new school to ever rank first in state

1927 American Leather Football Company founded by Benton Estes in Athens City

1935 Elvis Aron Presley born in Tupelo, Mississippi

1943 Gayle Eugene Sayers born in Wichita, Kansas

1947 Roscoe "Buster" Schuler born in Foley, Alabama

1961 Calvin Sawyer born in Daphne, Alabama

1969 Buster Schuler marries Helena Myrick of Kansas City, Missouri

1970 Jack Schuler born

1971 Buster Schuler becomes assistant football coach at Athens City

1973 Crusaders 8-1, ranked second in state under new head coach, Buster Schuler

1977 Elvis Presley dies; Crusaders 8-1 behind star sophomore receiver, Cal Sawyer

1979   Crusaders 8-0-1 ranked first in state for twelfth time; Sawyer all-state

1980   Sawyer to Alabama to play for Bear Bryant

1981   Sawyer injured; returns to marry Estelle Estes of Athens City

1982   Elvis Presley Jackson born in Kankakee Banks, Indiana

1983   Rachel Sawyer born; Bear Bryant dies

1985   Schuler wins one hundredth game

1986   Crusaders 13-1 under new play-off scheme behind sophomore quarterback Jack Schuler; win state title for fifteenth time

1987   Crusaders 13-1 behind junior QB Jack Schuler; win state title for sixteenth time

1988   Crusaders 12-2 behind Jack Schuler; second in state; Buster Schuler resigns

1989   Estelle Estes Sawyer dies

1

Name's Cal Sawyer and I got a story starts about thirteen years ago when I was twenty-seven. Course, like most stories, it really starts a lot a years before that, but I choose to tell it from Friday, December 2, 1988, when I'm sitting with my kindergarten daughter Rachel in the stands of my old high school. We're watching the state football championship in Athens City, Alabama, almost as south as a town can be without being ocean.

Estelle, Rachel's ma and my wife, is in the hospital dying of the colon cancer. I'm hoping Rachel doesn't know while knowing that she does and wondering what in the world I'm gonna do when the time comes, if you know what I mean and I think that you do. Rachel's about to see something just as bad, and even one tragedy is an awful thing for somebody her age. But don't let me get ahead of myself.

By the time we were sitting there, I was already a broken-down ex–football player with a blowed-out knee who nobody remembered but me. Well, maybe not exactly nobody. I suppose some rec-

ollect that I played three years under Buster
Schuler, the coach out there that night. I played
on one of his state champ teams, made all-state,
and even rode the bench for Bear Bryant at
Alabama before tearing up my leg and coming
back to marry Estelle Estes.

Yeah, that Estes. Her grandpaw Benton Estes
founded the American Leather Football Company
in Athens City. I came back hoping to assistant
coach with Schuler, but when you marry into a
factory family you work there and coach junior
league football if you have time, which is what I
did.

But I never missed watching a high school
game. Not with Buster Schuler on the sidelines.
He says I was the best he ever coached. I don't
know if that's true or he just says it but I know
he was the best *I* ever played for, including the
Bear (but they might as well have been twins).
Buster played at Bama years before I did, only he
didn't get hurt and he did well and all he ever
wanted to do after that was be just like Bryant.

This was one of those big rivalry games against
Rock Hill from up the road. We'd beat em for the
state championship at their place the year before
and were fixing to do the same that night at
home. Rachel had her little good luck plastic sou-
venir football that American Leather passes out

to everybody who tours the place, and I had more hair than I've seen in the mirror since.

I love these games. The night air, the concrete stands, the rickety light poles, the ambulance that stands waiting but had been used only for the broke arm of a visiting player two years before, the band, the cheerleaders, the banners, the scoreboard with "Home of the Athens City Crusaders" underneath it in white on red.

Schuler wore his trademark fedora, sports coat, and tie. He was smooth-faced with dark, thinning hair and a black mustache, and this was his sixteenth season as head coach.

All around us sat moms wearing corsages and elementary school and junior high boys whose dream was to play for Buster Schuler and wear the crimson and white of Athens City High. Coach Schuler's wife was behind us too, but she always sat alone. I never saw Helena so much as clap, let alone cheer.

Now here's why sometimes I think Buster's only saying it when he says I was his best. Everybody knows he'd lived for the day he could coach his only son, Jack—his starting quarterback now for three straight years. Number 7 was a beautiful specimen of a football player, a tick under 6'4", about two hundred pounds, and faster than a wait to face the principal. He could also throw the ball through a wall, but course he hardly ever got the chance. The whole time every game, Buster would run the Bama wishbone offense—that's where the quarterback runs with the ball until he has nowhere to go and then pitches to one of his two trailing running backs and commences blocking for him.

Going into that game the Crusaders had lost only once each season with Jack at QB. Oh, the boy could run, and he was a leader, but everybody knew that if ever there was a kid who resented that ancient offense and challenged the old man's authority, it was Buster's own son.

And Daddy wasn't happy. Jack would behave himself for the first quarter or two, long enough for Athens City to roll up a big score. But there was no corraling that colt, and Buster would wind up slamming his hat to the ground, benching his own son, and stomping up and down the sidelines like he was losing instead of winning.

Next game Buster would start the backup quarterback, they'd struggle till Jack was out of the doghouse, he'd come in and get the big lead, start improvising, and get himself benched again.

Somehow it all worked anyway, but Buster would say, even in *The Athens Courier*, that his son was no example of how he expected his team to play. Jack had his full ride to Bama already sewed up and everybody knew that the Crusaders and Buster—frustrated or not—would ride to their championship on Jack's back.

So anyway, we were there and I was amazed as always at Rachel's attention span. I mean, I was a fan at her age, but by the fourth quarter I was usually playing my own football game behind the stands somewhere. She always hung in there though, asked questions, studied the scoreboard, and pretty much knew what was going on. She knew most of the players too.

Rachel even knew a little about the trouble between Coach Schuler and Jack, so when this game got down to eleven seconds to go and us trailing 28-24, third-and-ten on their 35, she looked up at me when Buster called his last time out.

A field goal wouldn't do it, and Rock Hill could smell that championship clear as the shrimpy salt air wafting up from the Gulf.

"We're gonna hafta throw the ball, aren't we, Daddy?" Five years old and she's strategizing.

I smiled at her. "Rachel, Coach Schuler'd sell his firstborn child before he'd put that pigskin in the air." I honestly don't know why I said it that way, and don't think I haven't asked myself more than once in the years since. Jack was not just Buster's firstborn, he was his only-born. But I said it and there it was.

I was nervous as everybody else, and I could hear the crowd whispering the same thing Rachel was thinking. Surely Buster's got to let Jack throw that ball into the end zone. Nobody could keep Jack Schuler from throwing a TD in a do-or-die situation like this.

We were all standing, waiting, breathing only cause we had to. Coach Schuler was scribbling on his chalkboard and pointing at players. I could see from big Jack's cocked head, towering over the others, that he was upset.

The rest of the team shouted "Crusaders!" and hurried onto the field, but Jack stood there shaking his head as he jammed on his helmet. Coach Schuler spun and saw his son slowly getting ready to head back out, and it was clear he didn't like what he saw. He grabbed the boy's facemask and pulled him close. I'd been there enough times to know what he was saying. "I don't want any fool heroics. This team needs you now. You're gonna go out and block like a Buick!"

I looked for Jack to give his dad some eye contact and show he was getting with the program. Right or wrong, you do what the coach tells you and you do it with all that's in you. But Jack just pulled away. Coach Schuler smacked him on the seat and shoved him onto the field with both hands.

I shoulda known what the boy was gonna do when a couple of the players looked to the sideline as if what they'd just heard from Jack in the huddle didn't jibe with what the coach had said. When Jack stepped up over the center, he sneaked a peek toward his dad, who was locked on him like he was willing him to stay with the plan.

The ref cues the clock and Jack takes the snap. As the play unfolds I see immediately it's the wishbone again, Jack leading the way. He's supposed to find a hole to run through or pitch to a back and block, as his father always told us, like a Buick.

Jack runs to his right, then drops back like he's gonna throw. Coach Schuler slams his hat to the ground as Jack spins right and comes all the way back to the near side of the field, eluding tacklers, not to mention his own running backs. He fakes a pass then races upfield, switching the ball from right hand to left and stiff-arming Raiders as he turns toward the end zone. Rachel's toy football digs into my shoulder as she pulls herself up and stands on the seat next to me.

The clock has run out and the noise is deafening and I'm shouting "Go! Go! Go!" as Jack reaches the 10 and then the 5, where two Raiders catch him from opposite sides. One hits him high, the other low, cartwheeling him into the air.

We all fell silent, wondering whether he'd hang onto the ball and if his momentum would carry him into the end zone.

But Jack dropped straight onto the top of his head, his full weight on his neck. In that eerie silence, I swear I heard the snap of his spinal cord from fifty yards away. Jack flopped onto his back like a Raggedy Andy, the ball slowly rolling free, and I knew. I knew from the silence of the new state champions and their fans on the other side of the field. I knew from the body language of Coach Schuler.

I turned to lift Rachel down and hid her head in my chest. The crowd started to murmur and Coach called out, "Jack?" his voice pitiful.

I glanced over my shoulder to where Mrs. Schuler stood alone, staring, her hands clasped before her mouth.

As the teams gathered around the still boy and paramedics slid a stretcher from the ambulance and waited for their cue, Coach Schuler ran out from the sideline. Players on both teams made way as he brushed a ref aside and fell to his knees before the boy.

The crowd went silent again, staring, as the coach wailed, "Son?" He unfastened the boy's chinstrap. "Come on! Jack?"

He felt the boy's neck, then looked desperately at the stunned players. Shoulders slumping, he scolded his son, as if by challenging him he could force him to rise and defend himself. "Why didn't you do what I said?" he cried out, begging with his hands, his voice echoing. "Why didn't you do what I told you to do?"

He finally broke down, laying his cheek on his son's chest. His sobs made us turn our eyes away.

Rachel, still clutching her tiny football, tried to peek through my hands. "Is Jack going to be all right, Daddy?"

I was grateful for the crowd between us and the field, but I had never lied to her. "I don't know, sweetheart," I said. "It doesn't look good."

"Is he going to die?"

"I sure hope not."

The coach's wife marched down the steps past us, ignoring comments and reaching hands. "Miz Schuler!" I called after her. "Helena, wait!"

But she headed for the parking lot. I pulled Rachel along and trotted up to the woman. "Helena, let me—"

She turned on me, her eyes dark and narrow. "I've been a football widow for twenty years. And now, and now—unless you can change this, Mr. Sawyer, no, there's nothing I'll let you do."

She rushed to their light blue Mustang convertible, slid in, and slammed the door. As the car raced off into the night, Rachel stared up at me. "She thinks Jack's dead, doesn't she?"

I pursed my lips and shook my head, but Rachel was right. And so was Helena Schuler.

2

The boy woke shivering at dawn in the loft of his parents' ramshackle house in Kankakee Banks, Indiana. So he had slept! Last time he'd checked, it was just after four in the morning, and he knew Santa would not come as long as he was awake.

Now he crept to the landing at the top of the stairs, his tiny feet making the floor creak. He leaned over the banister far enough to see that the tree, which had stood bare in the living room for two days, had magically been trimmed.

At the bottom of the stairs he tiptoed toward the blinking lights, the strung popcorn, the shiny balls, the star up top. He had asked Santa for only one thing, and while nothing under the tree appeared the proper shape, he believed it was there. He could smell it even over the scent of the pine.

The boy moved to his parents' bedroom, a chamber so small they hung their clothes in a hall closet. The door wouldn't open all the way without hitting the bed, and he had been warned to never let that happen unless the house was afire.

He carefully pushed the door, and the light roused his father. "What'sa matter, El?" he said, his voice thick.

"Nothing, Daddy. Just Christmas morning, that's all."

His mother groaned while his father slowly sat up. "Be right with you, son. Get the Bible."

Elvis not only got the Bible, but he also found Luke 2, though he could barely read. The boy had memorized the books of the Bible, and he could almost recite this story by heart. There would be no presents until they heard the real story of Christmas.

He sat staring at the package, the couch cushion scratching the backs of his legs, his feet bouncing inches from the floor. "Get some clothes on, honey," his mother said, squinting, enfolded in her long robe. "It'll only take a second."

The boy bounded back upstairs and pulled on a sweatshirt, jeans, and yesterday's socks. Back downstairs his dad ran his hands through his hair and asked if he couldn't have a cup of coffee before they started.

"No!" the boy said, knowing his dad was kidding. "Come on, now! Read and let's go!"

Elvis knew Jesus was way more important than

Santa, and he had learned not to complain about how long it took to get to the presents. His gifts to his parents were crafts fashioned at school, but George and Eloise Jackson acted like they'd never seen anything so special. "A hanger painted gold," his mother said. "I'll use it for my winter coat."

"Paint wouldn't stay on till we scratched the hangers," Elvis said.

He gave his dad a lanyard, perfect except for two twisted loops. George hung it around his neck immediately and said he would look for his whistle later.

They made the boy save the biggest box till last, and the longer it took to get to it, the more he worried he might be wrong. Unless he was imagining it, the smell was stronger than ever. But would what he wanted come in a square box? Was Santa trying to throw him off? Surely he hadn't misunderstood and thought the boy asked for a basketball.

Finally he sat with the package on his lap and attacked ribbon and paper. "Who's it from, first?" his dad scolded, and Elvis searched through the scraps to see.

"Santa!" he said, and kept digging. The corrugated cardboard box had a drawing of an electric space heater on it, just like the one his mother used in the cellar. But there was no mistaking the smell of genuine leather. Finally he turned the box upside down and shook it until a smaller box tumbled out of the stuffing, brushed his knee, and hit the floor. This was no toy. It was a football, the real thing.

Elvis leaped and whooped and hugged his parents, smiling so big he could barely see. His dad helped him remove the cardboard casing. "Let me toss it to you," George said.

"Not in the house," his mother said, so his dad underhanded the ball to Elvis from a few feet away. The boy gathered it in as he dove onto the couch.

He lay on his stomach and turned the ball so he could read the imprint. "What's it say, Dad?"

"Let me see," his dad said, but the boy only tilted it toward him. He wasn't going to let go of it for a long time, maybe ever.

George Jackson stood over Elvis and read, "American Leather, Athens City, Alabama." He started to read the fine print, but the boy had heard enough.

"That's where Santa got it?" he said. "That's where they make them?"

"Looks like it."

The boy kept the ball with him all the time. It rested in his lap at the dinner table. He slept with it. And until he took it to school in January, he and his dad played catch in the snow every day until their fingers were numb.

3

My daughter Rachel says she knew when her mom died because I knocked on her bedroom door and nobody ever did that. I was stalling for time and for God to give me something to say. Time ran out and I'm still waiting for how to say it. Fact is, Estelle's mother called from her shift at the hospital—we traded off—and told me to bring Rachel. "She's gone then?" I said, barely able to speak. The cancer had won after all.

Rachel made it easy for me. She opened the door and hugged my neck so tight I had to ease her back so I could breathe.

That had happened only a couple of months after Jack Schuler's funeral, which his own mother didn't come to. Story was that the only way Buster could even hope to hang onto his marriage was to follow Helena back to her people in Kansas City, Missouri, and even then he was never able to keep her sober. He taught some school back there but never did any more coaching. Even though he wasn't an old man I guess he just put in his time teaching and fished every chance he got. People say Helena was in and out of the hospital for alcoholism but that was none of my business and it isn't like Buster and I were ever friends enough that he'd report that kinda stuff to me. When you play high school ball for a guy you don't become his pal. Least that's what I always thought until last fall.

I had an idea how Coach must've thrown himself into saving his marriage, cause I didn't know what else to do myself but keep working and make sure I was always there for Rachel. I didn't know Estelle had left me the football factory until I had to know it and I'm sure if she knew the grief it brought me she never woulda done it. But in a way it was good because with me being in charge I set my own hours. Her people never forgave me for her giving me the business, which I could never figure out. I woulda given it to them cept it was clear she knew what she wanted to do by the way she worded it, and there was no way I was going to go against the wishes of a dead woman even if she wasn't my wife and I didn't love her with all my heart, which she was and I did.

That caused more than tension, as you can imagine, so I was pretty much left without help raising my daughter, which turned out to be a good thing, in a way. Sure, I would've liked to have a woman in the house for Rachel's sake. Not for mine, cause even though I was still pretty young I couldn't imagine ever actually loving anybody but Estelle—at least up to recent—but I had to be both mother and dad to Rachel. Turns out that was good for both of us—well, I shouldn't speak for her—but basically I just did what I had to do because I had no choice. I got to be best friends with Rachel rather than just her daddy.

Since I was a young man I'd done every job at the factory from shipping and receiving to cutting cowhide to sewing and turning and lacing and even molding and inflating, stamping and painting. So except for in-law relations who resented me, everybody there knew I knew how to make a football and make the place work. They also knew I wasn't gonna be there till Rachel was off to school each day and that I would be going home in time to be there when she got back. I never woulda seen myself as a briefcase-toting kind of guy, but I learned to lug a slew of papers with me so when she was in bed I could keep the business of the place going and not have to get a baby-sitter.

In the summertime when she was a kid, Rachel came to work with me every day and played with other kids who came with their parents. I got some kind of award from the state for childcare innovation, but the truth is I couldn't see doing something I wouldn't let other workers do, so I let em bring their kids and made sure they were taken care of. Now if I just coulda kept my assistant Bev from wanting to spend more time around those kids than in my office ...What can I say? You can't change a person's basic bent.

American Leather is one of those small-town factories that's pretty simple and straightforward. We got one product that takes a lot a people to produce. It starts out as a pallet of stacked cowhides cut so clean off the animals that they look like they could be put back on like snug jackets. Our supplier in Chicago does the dirty work, cutting each hide in as big a single piece as they can, dyeing em and putting the dimpling on em, even embedding that tackiness that will make the ball easier to grip.

I'll never forget the first summer I worked there and learned what "top grain" meant. I'd always thought it described the outer layer of the hide, but it's simpler than that. The top grain is the top of the cow, the part that has the fewest blemishes (which we in the biz call "blems"), cause the side of the animal gets the most barbed wire nicks and parasite holes. Your best footballs come from top grain.

Cutting machines use a pattern in the shape of

a quarter of a football and chop as many of those out of every hide as possible. Course, the more experienced the cutter, the more sets of four pieces (number-stamped and kept together through the whole process) we get out of each hide. When all that's left of the hide are the tiny spaces between the cutouts, a smaller pattern gets us the little pieces that make keyrings and such.

Those four quarter pieces are sewed together inside out with hundred-year-old sewing machines, then the balls are turned inside out to put the stitches on the inside. The guys who do that turning—man, they're the stars. I mean, everybody has his place in the process, but a man who can turn hundreds of balls a day is a wonder of nature. (Our top guy, Lee Forest, when he was young and in shape and cooking, once turned a hundred balls an hour for eight hours straight. Bet he slept that night.)

Course after that there's inserting the bladder, lacing, inflating and shaping, stamping logos, and painting stripes. Like I say, it's all we do, but there's a lot a steps and a lot a people involved. I love the simplicity of it. You can do it cheap and careless or you can use the best materials and hire people who work with pride. Hiring's my favorite part. Laying off people is the worst, and

I've done enough of that the last few years to last a lifetime.

Doing what I had to do made me grow up quick. Though I was an age when I ought to have been grown up anyway, being a single father made me serious-minded overnight. I'd always been a churchgoer, a Christian since I was a little boy, and Estelle had really showed me what faith was—right up until the day she died. But I couldn't see ever being as devout as she was until I was sort of forced into it by being sadder and lonelier than a transferred fourth grader. All of a sudden God and church and other believers went from being something I sorta liked because I was comfortable there to being my very source of life. I needed Jesus for more than my eternal salvation then, and before you knew it I was praying more, reading my Bible more, singing like I meant it because I did, and dragging Rachel to church every time the door was open.

That was nothing but natural to her, because I was now the way her mom had been and Rachel had never known different. I had gone along before and been happy to do it, but I didn't know I would do it without living with Estelle's example until I realized I was at the end of myself without it.

Rachel, bless her heart, was just like her mama. She believed with everything in her that Estelle was in heaven and that someday we'd see her again. I wasn't intellectual enough to be a doubter, but it sure was comforting to know that the more of God I realized I needed, the more of Him I learned to know.

That's not to say that either Rachel or I were perfect saints or that we didn't have our all-night crying sessions. The best thing my pastor ever told me was that the Bible said we weren't supposed to grieve like the heathens do—without hope, that is—but we are to grieve and grieve with all our might. We did that all right and sometimes we still do, all these years later. But Rachel and me sorta grew up together. She's my whole life, and she knows it. And, oh, how she's grown to look like her mama, dark-haired and dark-eyed with perfect skin and a thin little voice. She's passionate about what she believes in whether it has to do with God or with saving her school or our town or the factory.

4

And now, a dozen years after we somehow numbed our way through two tragedies inside a few months, the school, the town, and the factory were in trouble. Most people traced the whole mess straight back to the day Jack Schuler died and Buster Schuler resigned. When you've lost your wife and your little girl's mama it's hard to place as much importance on football misfortunes, but it's hard to argue with the fact that when Athens City High School football went in the dumpster, the leading business in town (now mine) and the town itself weren't far behind.

Last fall Rachel started her sophomore year and became a Fellowship of Christian Athletes prayer warrior. She also heard the rumors that with the dwindling school population and the loss of business at American Leather, everything she knew and counted on was in trouble. I had tried to keep from her my pressures at work, but after a while there was no hiding that I had laid off nearly two-thirds of the three hundred employees we'd had when I first inherited the company. People without jobs tend to move away, so businesses were closing, the school getting smaller, and stories floating about what it all meant. The problem with the stories was that they were true.

Athens City High School was nearing a critical point where if it lost many more students, the county would shut it down and—horror of horrors—send our kids up the road to Rock Hill, which was closer to the popular retirement community of Fairhope (and its strong tax base) and closer to Mobile Bay and its seasonal but healthy tourist trade.

Every time we'd drive or walk through town and see more boarded-up storefronts, Rachel would tell me she and God weren't going to let the town die. "That so?" I'd say.

"I'm praying," she'd say.

I'd become a praying man myself, but I wasn't sure God cared that much about Athens City. Surely He had bigger fish to fry. But I didn't tell Rachel that. If her faith hadn't been crushed by the death of her own mama, I wasn't gonna try to threaten it by questioning God's interest in the things she cared most about now. And it was easy to see what she cared about because she was a pack rat, a collector, a—what's she call it?—a memorializer. Her mirror was covered with pictures and pennants and clippings. And on her dresser, under a yellowed newspaper with the headline "Coach Schuler Resigns," was the very toy football she had with her the night Jack Schuler died.

She'd never taken it to another game, but she'd never thrown it out either. We still never missed a home game. But, oh, that became a sad chore. The crowds faded to next to nothing and the team barely ever strung together two wins in a row. People talk about how amazing it was that Athens City had more than twice the state championships of any other team in Alabama. But to me the most miraculous statistic was that up until the Jack Schuler game, in sixty-five years the school had never had more than three straight losing seasons, and that had happened only once in the 1930s.

In Buster Schuler's sixteen years as head coach at Athens City, he had never coached a losing team. This previous fall the Crusaders, under their third hopeless coach since Schuler, had suffered through their twelfth straight losing season. The county school board had even talked us into changing our colors to blue and white, as if that would erase memories of the tragedy we'd seen on that field. The worst idea had been the Jack F. Schuler memorial scholarship, awarded every year to the Most Valuable Player. It paid one kid's way to Alabama every year, but choosing the best player on awful teams had become almost impossible. None of em had ever been good enough to make Bama's football team, but they got the free education anyway. I finally figured out that the only reason anybody ever came out for football at Athens City High anymore was that long shot chance at the Bama lottery. I guess it didn't matter to them how the team did as long as one kid stood out enough to win the prize. All I could do, Friday night after Friday night, was sit there and shake my head at the absence of team effort. Every kid with half an ounce of talent was playing for himself.

Rachel didn't drive yet, so she still rode with me to every game, but she had her own friends to sit with now. Usually she wound up sitting with Josie, another FCA prayer warrior. Josie'd been going with Brian Schuler, Buster's nephew, who was the hot new quarterback. The kid had talent, but he was clearly not a team player. He threw three-fourths of the time and though he had a strong arm and good speed, his stats were terrible. He was poorly coached, and the only hope I saw on the horizon was that the head coach, believing what he was hearing around town, had already announced he would not be back.

The search was on for a new coach, but who would take the job for what would likely be just one season? Nobody I knew, and that included me. I didn't even have time for junior leagues anymore. It was all I could do to keep the tradition of showing up for home games while trying to keep American Leather's business from going overseas and trying to let my daughter go while still hanging onto her for dear life.

Rachel said she was praying for a miracle for the school, the town, and my business. Well, she wasn't the only one. I was already getting signals from our biggest customer, The Dixie States Association of High Schools, that their long-term association with American Leather might be starting to unravel. That would do us in for good, them accounting for right around 40 percent of our business. I believed their president, Chucky Charles, was more than a client though. We'd been friendly over the years if not exactly friends, but that was only because of the hundreds of miles between my office and his in Little Rock.

So the Athens City Crusaders' 2000 season had been another cesspool in which they'd missed the play-offs for the twelfth straight time. Even I didn't know if I'd be able to stomach one more season, and I admit I sided with those on the county school board who said it might not be worth the expense and the trouble to field one more team, especially if they couldn't find a coach anyway.

But Fred Kennedy, chairman of the county school board, had decided that since I ran American Leather I must know everybody in the football world, so he'd asked if I'd try to find someone to take the final season. The board gave me till the end of the school year. All I could think of was to ask the freshman and jayvee coaches of neighboring schools if anyone wanted to get one varsity year under his belt before testing the waters elsewhere. I thought it was a decent idea, and I figured someone might bite. The board loaded me down with the films of all the games of the last season, which I thought might be better to burn or somehow misplace than show anybody.

But I never got the chance to ask around whether some bold young coach was even interested in talking about the job. I guess you could say Rachel's and my prayers, at least the ones for the football team, got answered.

5

So it's a little less than a year ago now and I'm sitting in my office at the factory with two things on my mind. The first is sorta never off my mind and if you've ever been responsible for a business and more directly lots of people and their livelihoods, you know what that is. I'm not a neat-desk kind of a guy and even though I own the business the only luxury I got is Bev Raschke, the kid-loving assistant who answers my phone before I do. (She, of course, really runs the place, which is the joke I tell every day and which isn't so funny or far off when you get down to it.) I don't even have a nice office. I've only got one window and that looks out past Bev's cubicle onto the floor.

Anyway, I'm sitting there noodling how to keep the place alive and not lay off any more people while still trying to meet the business we do still have coming in.

My chief financial officer thinks I ought to be spending more time schmoozing Chucky Charles, and she's probably right cause Chucky's told me he's been getting courted by the competition. Well, I don't know how we could be doing a better job for Dixie States, and anyway I think my workers need to see me looking out for them. I'm down to the really old and valuable veterans, some a which been with us longer than I have. But I've already got em overworked and underpaid and now I'm asking for overtime and they're taking it cause they know if they don't I'll find someone who will. So that's first and foremost, as old Benton Estes used to be fond of saying.

Second, I'm thinking about the short drive north to see Rock Hill in their first playoff game. I'd like to see somebody give em a decent contest. We sure hadn't. They'd shut us out for the third year in a row, cruising along toward their second straight state title, undefeated and not even outscored for one half in all that time. I hate em on principle. Maybe their snotty coach isn't as bad as he seems, but he sure likes to gloat. He's been around for twenty years and he's got to be enjoying his revenge against so many losses to Athens City in his early days. They're gonna play Beach, who might be able to give em a game; they'd beat us almost as bad as Rock Hill had, although that doesn't always mean much.

I had my eye on the assistant coach at Beach, who had to be looking for some other opportunity because the guy he was coaching under wasn't much older than he was and didn't look to be going anywhere soon himself. I couldn't imagine a coach in a good program leaving for the thankless job I've got to offer, but stranger things have happened and some guys'll do pretty much anything to get a head coach title on their resume.

I probably wouldn't have gone to the Rock Hill game if I hadn't wanted to scout this assistant. Rachel couldn't go cause of some deal at church and I didn't really want to go alone. I sighed, looking at another request from some school group that wanted to tour the plant, wondering if the kids would wind up disappointed at how small the operation had become or whether they'd be at all fascinated by the process. I still was, but you kinda gotta be to stick with it as long as I had. We'd been putting off the tours until we had enough requests that we could group em and run em through all in one morning or afternoon. Bev and I were the only ones with the time to take em through, and I'd just recently dumped assisting the Human Resources department on her too.

Bev was a handsome woman a couple years older than me who'd been with American Leather since she was in high school. She'd never married, but somehow we'd been spared too much of the getting-together suggestions that most other eligible ladies and I get from everybody, cause even though we go to the same church and work together, Bev's got a way of acting older than she is and sorta mothering me, so people just don't see us that way—at least I don't. Plus she's got two cats, and that's about all I need to know about a woman.

Now she's heading for lunch. "You want me to pick you up something from Carl's Jr.?" she asks. I tell her yeah, thanks, the usual, but she says no.

"No?" I say.

"No, sir," she says. "You eat one more of them grilled chicken thingies and you'll be clucking before you know it. Now you can't weigh a pound more'n you did when you graduated high school, so it won't kill you to have a little red meat."

"It might," I say, proud to have stayed in shape despite the scrambled knee—and halfway impressed that she noticed.

"Well, what say we find out? I'm bringing you back their biggest, meatiest, cheesiest burger with the special fries and you're gonna danged well eat it all."

"Can I at least have a diet drink with that?"

"You're hopeless," she said. "All right."

"And you've got to eat the same."

"Now, no! I'm only getting you that cause I can't. I'm up two pounds and just want to enjoy it, whatcha call it, vicariously."

I didn't see the two pounds on her but I wasn't about to say that. I just waved her off. "So you're gonna watch me eat, is that it, Bev?"

"No, but I'll smell it and know you're enjoying it. Now promise me you'll ignore the phone. I got it on the machine and the world will survive without you for a few minutes."

She was back in less than half an hour, during which I scoped out a new work schedule for the lock stitchers and obeyed her by ignoring a phone call. She plopped the greasy bag and Diet Coke on my desk, and I said, "There's one message waiting."

"I noticed. How'd you manage to ignore it?"

"Learning to obey, Mother," I said. I took a huge bite of the double cheeseburger while Bev checked the message at her desk. With the phone to her ear, she spun in her chair to look at me. Course the first thing I thought was Rachel and I was already kicking myself for not having picked up the phone. I forced the bite into my cheek and mashed the intercom button. "What?" I said.

"Might be a crank, Calvin," Bev said. "But you'd better listen to this."

I grabbed the phone. "Yeah, uh," the recording began, "I'm sorry I missed Sawyer, but this is Buster Schuler and I'd appreciate a call back." He left a number with no area code and a nearby prefix.

"Where's that number from, Bev?" I said, mouth still full.

"Was that really him?"

"I'd know that voice anywhere. That number local?"

"Fairhope, if I'm not mistaken." Bev was never mistaken. "Shall I dial it?"

I swallowed quickly and shoved my lunch aside, nodding. "Just tell me when it's ringing." I didn't want Coach Schuler to think I was so big-headed I had to have a secretary place my calls. Bev dialed, waited a beat, and pointed at me. I sat up and actually straightened my tie.

"Fairhope Rehabilitation Center."

"Um, yes, ma'am. I'm returning Bust—ah, Mr. Schuler's call."

"One moment, please." She covered the phone and I heard her calling out to him and telling him he could take it on the house phone.

"Sawyer?"

"Coach?"

"Well, nobody's called me that in ages, but how in the world are you?"

He'd never been one for small talk and I knew he'd appreciate me helping him get to the point. "I'm good. What are you doing here?"

"I'd like to come see you," he said. "But I'm not ready for people to know I'm in town."

"I'll meet you anywhere."

"Well, I'd like to see you there at your work, and maybe I'm kidding myself to think people would still recognize—"

"Course they would, Coach, but if you want me to tell em to leave you be and—"

"I'd rather no one even knows."

"You got wheels? Well, course you do. You know the place. Park in the alley between Shipping and the water tower. I'll be waiting by the door. You coming now?"

"Right now."

I stood and spun in a circle, wondering how I could tidy up the place fast. Bev, as usual, came to my rescue. "You have to eat," she said, hurrying in. "I'll scrape the crust off this place and he'll just have to accept the rest. Now sit and finish."

I sat and wolfed as Bev swept off my credenza, the top of which I hadn't seen in years, and dumped stuff into file cabinets and onto shelves. "It'll take him twenty minutes," she said. "And we're working with years of buildup here."

I finished ten minutes later and tried to help

her, but Bev just took my arm, pointed me and my fast-food trash toward a garbage can in the hall, and kept working. When I returned my office looked halfway livable and she was spraying something that knocked out the food smell. She pointed to my chair, I sat, and she picked up the phone and called reception.

"Ginny," she said, "keep an eye on the driveway and give Mr. Sawyer's phone one buzz when a car pulls in toward the receiving dock. No trucks, just a car. Thank you."

The wait seemed forever but I knew I couldn't concentrate on one other thing anyway. When the buzz came, I leaped from the chair and headed to the side door. On the way I said, "Bev, you're the best."

"Yeah," she said, winking. "I know."

There would have been no mistaking Buster Schuler, especially when he got out of his ancient blue Mustang. The mustache and sideburns had gray in em and the eyes were wrinkled like a man even older than the coach had to be by now. But he wore the same white shirt and tie and I daresay the same hat. I don't believe I have ever seen him without a tie, not in the classroom or on the field, even during practice. He looked pale and stooped.

He hurried up the concrete steps and shook

my hand, patting me on the shoulder. "Aren't you ever gonna get older?" he said, forcing a smile but having trouble maintaining my gaze.

"I was about to say the same," I said, leading him inside.

"You know I've never tolerated liars," he said, not unkindly.

Bev nodded to him and took his hat, then left us alone in my office. I know all that management stuff about sitting next to a guest rather than behind your desk so you even the playing field, but my office wasn't big enough for more than one guest chair. And when Coach Buster Schuler was in a room, *no* seating arrangement would level the playing field.

I sat, gripping the arms of my chair, tucked my chin, and looked at him with my eyebrows raised. We both knew this was no social call, so I just waited. He leaned forward and rested his elbows on his knees, then jerked a thumb over his shoulder in Bev's direction. "You and her?" he said.

"Nah."

He rubbed his palms together, clearly more nervous than I was. I knew he'd get to the point. He'd come this far.

"It's Miz Schuler," he said. "And I need your help."

"Anything, Coach," I said.

Coach suddenly looked stricken. "Where's my manners?" he said. "How's that little girl a yours?"

"That little girl's a sophomore at Athens City," I said.

"Rachel."

I nodded, impressed.

"And I was so sorry about Estelle."

"Thank you. I got your card."

He nodded, looking miserable. "I'd say it's been a lot of years," he said. "But, believe me, I know how fresh a loss like that feels."

I nodded, waiting.

"Miz Schuler never forgave me."

What could I say to that? I just pressed my lips together and shook my head.

"Most people don't know that she had a problem long before we lost Jack. Long before I killed him, is what she'd say."

"Oh, Coach, no. You know better."

He shrugged. "Sometimes I do. Sometimes I don't. She was an alcoholic long before that, you know."

I shook my head. I really hadn't known.

"Well, a problem drinker anyway. We had a tragedy early in our marriage, couple years after Jack was born. She always resented my obsession, that's what she called it. Football. She only barely tolerated Jack playing. Did people know that?"

"Some, I suppose."

"She wasn't supportive."

"I know."

"She made me pay by drinking more."

This was painful. It was so good to see him, but I hated how beat down he seemed. "Don't feel like you gotta tell me—"

"But I do, Sawyer! I'm here asking for help, and you gotta know why."

"I don't need to know anything but how I can help."

"Well, then I feel like I need to tell you, okay?"

"If listening helps, I'm all ears."

He looked to the ceiling, then breathed a heavy sigh. "I know everybody wonders why she didn't know what she was getting into when she married a football player. She was kind of a society gal. Prettiest thing I'd ever seen. I couldn't believe she'd look twice at me, and like a dummy I thought it was the jock stuff she liked. Turns out she saw potential cause my grades proved I wasn't as dumb as I looked or sounded. How was I to know she was on a mission to make a businessman outa me?"

I stared at him. What he was telling me was exactly what I'd been afraid of with Estelle when we fell in love. A lot of people probably thought she'd pulled me out of football and into the business. Truth was she took me the way I was and would have been just as happy if I was a coach somewhere. But I didn't think that way. I would have enjoyed it, but football wasn't my whole life. She was. And I'd wanted to give her a life that wasn't so far from what she grew up with and I'd wanted to prove to her family that she hadn't married so far below her class. I don't think I ever convinced them or me of that, but the fact is I never felt the pressure Coach was telling me about now.

"I loved her, Sawyer. I truly did. I still do. But it was unfair of her to try to change me and then to blame all this on me."

I agreed but didn't dare say so. I didn't know what he wanted to hear, but I wasn't gonna take sides against the woman he loved.

"What happened, of course, proved her right, at least in her mind. I haven't been able to reason with her since."

I couldn't imagine a dozen years of that. "I'm surprised you're still together," I said.

He snorted. "Wouldn't be if it was up to her. I can't tell you the number of times she's thrown me out. She sees Jack at the foot of the bed, says he's blaming her for letting him play football. You and I both know Jack loved the game. He was a rascal and I don't know if I ever taught him a thing, but I never made him play."

Coach was silent, as if waiting for a response, but I was still back on the ghost story. One thing I knew for sure and would never say out loud was that if Jack had played the way his dad wanted him to, he'd probably be an NFL player today. My mind was reeling.

"So, when she, uh, kicked you out, you left?"

"Counselor told me to. Said a woman who's lost a child is temporarily insane and you gotta do what makes sense to her for a while, even if it makes no sense."

I was lost. "So you'd leave and then come back?"

He nodded.

"She'd what, come to her senses for a while and ask you back?"

"Never. I'd just stay away a few days and then after school one day, I'd drive home instead of to the hotel. She wouldn't even comment, as if she hadn't noticed I was gone. A few weeks later she'd get it in her head that since she never saw Jack in the casket, he's still alive and I gotta go find him. I try to reason with her, she imagines a conspiracy, and out I go again. This here, this is almost a relief."

"This here?"

"What's happened to her now, which is what I came to tell you. See, I've had her in and out of alcohol treatment centers, nothing permanent. Expensive. Where I taught school they wouldn't cover it because they called it a pre-existing condition. It never helped anyway. When she wasn't drunk she was crazy, so I never got a break."

His voice was shaky and he drew in a breath. I wanted to cry too, but I didn't figure that would help. I didn't know what he was looking for, but it didn't seem like sympathy.

When he got himself together, he said, "I don't mean to put her down, Sawyer. I'm just trying to tell ya."

"I know."

"I still love her. I don't even know why. She's given me no reason for twenty years, but I was raised that you love your wife and you keep your commitments." He shook his head. "Course I always thought I could love her through this and get her better too."

"Maybe someday."

He looked down. "I'm past hoping," he said. "Anyway, this last year I can't keep her sober. Somehow she always finds booze. Lies, negotiates, finagles, you name it. Typical stuff, they tell me, but I've never seen anything like it. I finally got a doctor to tell me she's a full-blown alcoholic and could kill herself if she keeps drinking. Insurance where I am still won't cover it, but God gives me this idea. At least I think that's where it came from. I was praying and pretty soon I get this idea, so two and two equals four or whatever. I call Weeks Bay County and find out I worked at Athens City long enough that part of my pension includes coverage for this kind of a thing. Only hitch is, she's got to be treated here. Somehow there's a spot for her at Fairhope Rehab, and I'm in the car with her the next day, driving all the way from KC. Had to have her doped up and restrained just to get her here. Now she says I must hate her and want her dead so she hates me and wants me dead and she never wants to see me again if I don't get her out of there and all that."

"A nightmare," I said.

"A relief," he said. "God forgive me, I need the break."

I kinda knew what he meant, but again, I was just listening, not trying to advise him. "So, what're you gonna do, Coach?"

"I'm gonna do right by the woman I love."

It sounded so strange it was almost funny. After what I'd just heard I didn't know whether I was supposed to laugh or cry.

"I'm serious," he said. "I'm going to find a room, get me a job, visit her every day whether she wants me to or not—I mean, I'm not gonna make a scene, just be faithful and be there so she can never say I wasn't. And I'm gonna try to make a life for myself."

"Doing what?"

"I was hoping you could help with that."

"Me?"

"You said you'd do anything."

"But—"

"You run the biggest business in town."

"Coach, I—"

"I'll do anything, Sawyer. I'm not proud. Put me on the line. I might not still be strong enough to be a turner, but I can cut or sew or whatever you want."

"Coach, I've laid off two hundred people since you left town."

He smiled a sad smile. "That's my fault too?"

"It's just, how do I justify hiring on somebody new when so many old friends have had to move away cause I didn't have a spot for em?"

He stood quickly. "I understand," he said. "Really, I do. I don't know what I was thinking. It's not like you owe me anything. I'll find some-thing."

Now I was standing. "Coach," I said, forceful as

I could muster, "I want you to do me the favor of sitting yourself back down. Now, I mean it. I can't imagine telling you what to do, but you came in here willing for me to be your boss, I need you to listen to me for just a second. Please."

Coach sat back down and I moved around to the front of my desk, suddenly grateful for Bev and her clearing enough of a spot to where I could sit atop it. "One a the advantages of the position I'm in is that I don't answer to anybody anymore. If I want to put you on, and I gotta tell you, it'd have to be part-time, then I can just do that. I think I owe you more than you may think, and even if I don't, this town does. I might take some heat for it, but that's my choice."

"Sawyer," he said, "I preciate that, I really do. But the truth is I didn't know how bad things were here and I didn't know you had to cut the labor force and all. I couldn't ask you to do that—"

"But I want to."

"I understand, but it wouldn't be good for either of us. I don't need much. I'll manage. I was just checking possibilities and you seemed to be the place to start."

And then it hit me. I may not be the brightest bulb in life's marquee, as that guy Garrison Keillor says on the radio, but this one finally banged me so hard I had to smack myself in the head. Unless you're dumber'n dirt, you'd thought of it before me and probably did.

When I hit Buster Schuler with the obvious, he sat straight up, laid his palms on his knees, and looked me full in the face.

"Fred Kennedy's still school board chairman? Don't toy with me, Sawyer," he said, his voice suddenly strong and clear. "This isn't funny."

"I wouldn't," I said. "It's a one-year deal, you'd have to teach, and there's no way—no matter what—that Athens City High stays open past the next school year."

"Not even if you and I coach em to another state championship?"

I held up both hands. "Don't include me. This is all on you."

"No, huh-uh. No way I'd do it unless you did it with me."

"I can't, Coach. I—"

"Then neither can I. The game has passed me by anyway. People were saying that when I was still coaching. Kennedy for one. I haven't been to a live game since, you know . . ."

"You haven't?"

"How could I? The memories, the, the—"

"I can't imagine. Did it spoil the whole game for you? No interest?"

"Oh, no." He was coming alive. "I sneaked a peek on TV now and then, but it wasn't the same. You want the truth, Sawyer?"

"Course."

"I still strategize, plan, play with lineups, relive old games."

"Coach! Do this! Take this!"

It was as if it was too much for him, like a gift he'd never even dreamed of. "What would people say? I couldn't even let Helena know."

I invited him to the Rock Hill game that night and he threw a hand over his mouth, sucked in a breath, and began to sob. "I'm sorry," he said. "Forgive me."

I didn't know what to say or do. Had I made bad memories rise, offended him? "You don't have to, Coach. It was just a thought. You just think about the job."

He grabbed my arm and wiped his face with his other hand. "That's not it, Sawyer. I *want* to go. You don't know how bad I want to. Thing is, I can't think of anything I'd rather do. You'd really take me?"

"Nothing I'd rather do either, Coach. Meet me at the high school at six, we'll get us some dinner, and you can ride up with me."

"Whoo-boy!" he said, with a rush of air. "You are without a doubt!"

I sat there waiting for him to complete the thought like I hadn't heard him use that crazy expression a million times when I played for him. I was, without a doubt, what? But I knew he never finished the line, and he had used it when he was happy, mad, or whatever.

"I got some work to do," I said, "and I guess you got stuff to do too, eh?"

He stood and thrust out his hand. "This is better'n I could have hoped."

"I'm putting you down as our head coach for next year," I said.

"No you're not."

"Just tell me when I can let people know."

"When you're ready to be my assistant."

"Now, come on, Coach. You know I can't do that."

"That's the price," he said.

"You were willing to work for me, and now—"

"And now you gotta agree to work for me if this has a prayer of happening."

I couldn't keep it from Rachel. "Daddy! You've got to do it!"

"You can't coach unless you're on the school staff, honey."

"So teach geography. You were good in that."

"Who told you that?"

"You did. Were you lying?"

"Course not. But teaching?"

"The kids would love you!"

"Ah!"

She was rustling around in her room. "Take me to the school, would you? Just for a minute before church?"

"I guess," I said. "I got to get a key to the field house anyway. I want to give Coach Schuler those game films."

She came out of her room with her plastic football and the old newspaper. "Where's the garden trowel?" she said.

"Garage. What're you up to?"

6

When they parked at the school, Rachel took her armful of stuff and headed for the football field while her dad walked to the small field house at the other end.

She knelt in the end zone under the ancient weather-beaten scoreboard with the now white-on-blue sign beneath it reading, "Home of the Athens City Crusaders." A smaller wood sign hung from that one and read, "In memory of Jack Schuler, #7."

Rachel used the hand trowel to remove a thin strip of sod, then dug a few inches into the moist, dark soil. She pressed into the earth the old *Athens City Courier* with the headline "Coach Schuler Retires."

"Dear Lord," she whispered, placing her tiny plastic football over the paper and replacing the dirt, "we need a miracle. Grandmaw used to tell me there was three things worth believing in: God, cattle, and football, in that order. I look around and see everything's changed. Folks have a hard time believing in anything. This town has one foot in the grave and the other in a pile of cattle dip, and if You don't do something soon, there ain't gonna be nothing left." She paused and laid the strip of sod back in place.

"Rachel!" Her dad's voice from across the field. She loved him in his windbreaker and a cap that covered his almost gone hair. He looked just like a coach. "We gotta go, sweetheart!"

She waved and nodded, and he strode toward the parking lot. "So, God," she continued, "what do You say? It's about time You show up and show off."

Hearing her dad's car, Rachel stood and pressed the grass down with her boot. He was going to take the assistant's job, she just knew it. That meant Coach Schuler would be back.

7

I swore Rachel to secrecy, which is probably the only reason the Athens City stadium was empty when Coach met me. It was getting dark as he stood there, hands deep in his pockets. I told him I had the keys. "You wanna see it with the lights on?" He shrugged, but I knew he did so I flipped em on.

"Place has fallen into disrepair," he said, but I think he was just talking to cover his emotion. He looked over the whole place and walked slow down to the scoreboard with its faded blue and the sign for Jack. "I hate the new colors," he said. "And I *really* hate that scholarship deal."

"Me too."

"To give money for playing for yourself . . ."

I made a face and couldn't hide it. To me it sounded like he was putting down his own son.

"No," he said, "I just mean—"

"I know. Wanna take time for a peek into the field house?"

He followed me to the other end of the field

and around the fence where the place, barely big enough for the varsity, stood next to the concession stand and bathrooms. The double metal doors opened into a concrete-floored free-weight room that took up two-thirds of the space. The rusty bars and bells were strewn about. "Nobody supervises these boys?" Coach whispered. He stared at the long row of dusty team pictures hanging cockeyed on the wall. "They quit shooting em after '88?"

I shrugged.

A short corridor led past the showers and a wall-mounted first-aid kit and stretcher and into a small, dull, cream-colored room filled with white wire-mesh lockers and walls covered with a big green chalkboard, a bulletin board, and various signs. One read, "T-E-A-M." Another that had been there at least twenty years said, "Play Like a Champion Today." That had to mock the last dozen teams that changed clothes in there. The stench brought back memories.

Coach was silent when he noticed above the drinking fountain a glass case displaying his son's jersey. The shirt had not been cleaned or mended but it looked somehow noble and, I have to say it, too good to be looking down on the guys that had followed Buster's last team.

I figured that ought to be an alone moment, so I busied myself peeking into the training room and the coaches room, separated from the lockers by a window and Venetian blinds.

I moseyed on out under the "Pride" sign over the door frame that players had slapped on their way out for years. Coach soon followed. "Just the way I remembered it," he said.

Rock Hill didn't have much trouble with Beach that night, but it was sure fun sitting there with Schuler and seeing him come alive. On the way up into the stands he kept his head down, probably to keep anybody from recognizing him. Once we got settled in, he never took his eyes off the field. And he talked the whole time. He dissected every play, groused about the Beach Bearcat coach, his strategy, the laziness of his players, their lack of discipline, and Rock Hill's showboating, taunting, boasting. "I mean, they're good, maybe as good a high school team as I've ever seen, but what's with all that?"

"Wanna leave?" I asked him.

"I never leave early," he said. "Past your bedtime?" I laughed and shook my head. "Good, cause I'm up for more football tonight. I wanna see those game videos a yours."

"They aren't videos," I said. "We're still using the same movie camera from when you were here. Anyway, I saw the games. Believe me, you don't want to see those."

"How much worse can they be?" he said, gesturing toward the Bearcat side of the field.

"Coach, we made those guys look like pros."

"I'd like to take charge of either of these here teams for ten minutes."

I knew what he meant, but if he felt the same about Athens City after watching the films, well, maybe he'd been away from the game too long.

Late that night upstairs in my house, I fought to stay awake as Buster watched film after film on a clacky old projector. "Tell me who the seniors are," he said, and every time I pointed one out, he said, "Good. Glad he'll be gone. Couldn't play for us anyway, could he?"

"Couldn't play for *you*."

"Us," he said, not looking at me. "I'm not doing this without you, Sawyer, and we both know it, so I don't want to hear another word about it. There! Him! Is he returning?"

"Nope."

"Good! Lazy. Never'd learn the wishbone."

Except for Yash Upshaw, a speedy black receiver, and Sherman Naters, a rough-and-tumble linebacker, I thought the underclassmen looked as bad as the seniors. Coach kept shaking his head every time one of em either made a bonehead play or celebrated a good one. "First guy who so much as raises his fist cause he makes a sack will sit the rest of the quarter. Agree?"

"Course."

"That junior quarterback, number 40, who likes to launch the ball all the time—that's my nephew, right?"

I nodded.

"He's not gonna like the wishbone."

"None of em are, Coach."

"They'll like winning."

"He wants the scholarship," I said.

"If I know my no-account little brother, his kid *needs* the scholarship. He won't win it playing like that."

"Your brother know you're in town?"

Coach nodded. "He's the one renting me a room."

"He's making his own brother pay?"

"I told you. They need the money. I'd just as soon pay."

I was drowsy and rubbed my eyes, then looked at him. The flickering images reflected off his eyes as they darted about the screen. "Give me some speed and teachable kids," he said. "That's all I ask."

"It's a caretaking job, Coach," I said. "I'd be a liar if I said different. It's about putting one last team on the field and seeing one more kid get the scholarship."

I had finally got his attention. "How do you turn this blamed thing off?" he said.

"Just crank that to the left."

The room went dark. I turned on a light and we squinted till we got used to it. "You know I'm no caretaker, Calvin. If I'm gonna do this thing, I'm gonna do it with all my might. We're going out there with one objective. We're gonna win and keep on winning until we're state champs."

I couldn't muster a look that said I believed him, and you know he was searching my face for one. "I'm with you, Coach," I said lamely.

"You'll come around," he said. "You coach the way you played and you'll see."

"Well, I gotta admit, there are a couple of interesting things going for us. First four games are at home, and I guess somebody pities us for the end of our school, cause we get to host the state title game."

"Let's be rude hosts, what do you say, Sawyer?"

I just nodded and smiled. He wouldn't have wanted to hear what I had to say.

By Monday the whole town knew what was going on, and Coach Schuler liked to have drove me nuts. He was given a couple of hours of health to teach and allowed to putz around the field house and start planning for the next season. Fred Kennedy thanked me for my work and the school board let me off the hook on teaching geography till the next fall.

A few days after *The Athens City Courier* ran the headline "Coach Schuler's Back!" the national sports magazines picked it up. We'd never been so popular, and I worried that people would have so long to get excited about it that Coach Schuler would never be able to satisfy em. Course he thought we were gonna win one more state championship and wouldn't settle for less himself, so it was like I was the only one feeling the pressure.

Before you know it, he'd dolled up a new playbook he wasn't allowed to show any players till the next summer, but I got to read it every night, give him feedback on every idea, and work with him on the field, the stadium, everything cept the field house, which, as he said, needed to stay just like it was.

Rachel asked me one day, "Is he the miracle we need, Dad?"

I could never bring myself to tell her anything but the truth. "Sweetheart," I said, "this may do more for Coach than it does for us. The only thing that'll save this town is business improving, and I don't see it."

8

Buster sat with me in church that Sunday cause I probably looked lonelier than a skunk at a picnic. Rachel always either had choir or her class of girls to teach or her own friends to sit with, so I was glad for the company and of course a little proud to be seen with him. I asked him was he excited and could he hardly wait till next summer, but before he could answer I felt a hand on my shoulder and turned to see Bev sitting behind us with her friend Kim.

"Am I gonna have to separate you two?" Bev said. "Now hush!" We chuckled, but we also obeyed.

I'm usually pretty good about paying attention in church, cause I need it. But something was bothering me and when I finally got it surrounded in my brain, I realized it was Kim. She's a kind of a severe-looking woman, dark-haired and usually serious. She had a reason. She's in her late fifties and had raised a couple of boys by herself cause her husband left her years ago. And I know the church had prayed for her dad, who'd had Alzheimer's, for about ten years before he finally died.

But still, Kim kept her faith and she and Bev socialized a lot. She came in and met Bev for lunch now and then at the factory and they often sat together in church. I always tried to get a smile or a laugh out of her, cause that was so rare.

That morning, though, when Bev had teased us, it seemed to me Kim hadn't been amused. It was just a small thing, but it was like she was looking the other way and pretending not to hear. Maybe it was just my imagination, but it bothered me enough that after the service I made sure to greet her.

She nodded. "Calvin."

"You taught me in Sunday school when I was a tiny kid," I said. "You can call me Cal."

"As you wish."

I was having trouble keeping her eye. "Kim, you okay?"

"I'm fine."

I threw my arm around her and pulled her close. She was stiff. "C'mon, you're out of sorts. Tell me what's up. Kids okay?"

"They're fine."

So I wasn't making it up. "Kim, you mad at me?" She pursed her lips and shrugged, backing away.

"Kim! C'mon! You know I'd never do or say anything to bother you."

Everybody else was clearing out of the sanctuary. Kim stood there with her arms crossed, looking like she wished she could join em. "You really want to get into this right now?"

"Course! What is it?"

She studied the floor, then looked around as if to see if anyone else could hear. "You're a wonderful person, Cal," she said. "But sometimes you can be oblivious."

"Oblivious?"

"Blind to things."

"I know what it means, Kim. But what am I blind to?"

"Bev," she said.

"What's wrong with her?"

"Nothing."

"You're mad at me cause I'm oblivious to Bev, but nothing's wrong with her?"

Kim looked madder than ever and just shook her head.

"Talk to me, ma'am. I'm listening."

Finally she looked me in the eye. "Would you just try to be more sensitive to her? Could you do that for me?"

I raised my eyebrows. This wasn't the first time somebody'd said that. Lee Forest, my famous football turner and the oldest guy on the line, had told me more than once that I needed to look after Bev more. Lee's a crusty old guy with good ideas and loyal as they come, but I'd passed off what he said cause I figured he just didn't know better. How would he know how I treated Bev? She never showed me any attitude, and she'd got a couple of raises a year ever since she started working for me. Now *Kim* thought I wasn't treating her right?

"Is she saying things?" I said, knowing that was unlikely. It just wasn't like Bev. Maybe I *didn't* know her as well as I thought.

"Of course not," Kim said. "She wouldn't."

"Well, that's what I thought. So what's the problem?"

She motioned me to follow her out and by the time we got to the parking lot, we were among the few left. "You just don't really know her, Cal," Kim said. "And that's your loss, especially after all the years she's worked for you."

I had to admit Bev and I weren't what you'd call friends. We didn't go to each other's homes, didn't see each other outside the office or church. But that was the way I thought it ought to be. She worked for me and you've got to keep a certain distance, right? "I feel like I know her well enough."

"Well, you don't, and it's not right."

"So tell me something I ought to know about her."

"I shouldn't have to tell you. You should ask her."

"Ask her what?"

"Like what she does outside the office, Cal."

I shook my head. What was this about? I almost caught myself admitting I didn't care. I figure if Bev wanted me to know what she did outside work, she'd tell me. "I don't know that I'd ask her, Kim. Or that she'd tell me."

"Just as I thought. Why don't you try?"

I wanted to ask why. I shrugged and Kim gave me that look again.

"All right," she said, "do you know how much volunteer work she does?"

"Wouldn't surprise me," I said.

"But you don't know."

"I know she does a lot here at church."

"That's not the half of it. She's on the go almost every night, doing stuff for people."

"Well, that's good."

"Did you know she spent as much time in my guest room as she did at her own home the last six years of my dad's life?"

I felt stupid. I'd had no idea. "She was helping out?"

Kim was through with me. She got into her car and rolled down her window. "That's the understatement of the year, Cal. She saw me one day at the grocery store and noticed I was crying. She'd been praying for my dad, but she didn't know how bad he was. She came home with me that day and just started doing stuff without asking. Did a lot of shopping for me, talking with Dad, keeping an eye on him in the night. You never knew any of that?"

Bev worked in my office and I hadn't known she was doing night duty half the time with Kim's father. I didn't know what to say. "Who was watching her cats?"

Kim looked at me twice. "Her cats?"

"If she was at your place so much, I mean—"

"Does she talk about her cats, Cal?"

"She used to."

"But not for years, right?"

I shrugged. "I guess. I wouldn't ask after her cats. I'm not a cat guy."

"No kidding."

"It shows?"

"Bev's cats have been dead for years." I tried to look surprised but I don't think I convinced her. "Nobody expects you to care about her cats," Kim said. "But it seems you'd know something like that."

"Not if she doesn't tell me."

"She probably didn't think you cared. She was right." She started her car.

"Would you just tell me one thing, Kim? Is this something you've noticed, or does Bev feel like I don't really know her?"

"I told you, if you knew her at all you'd know she'd never say a word. She thinks the world of you."

"Well, the feeling is mutual."

"Calvin," she said, "you just proved that's not true."

9

I divided my time between figuring out how to keep the company running and working through plans with Coach. Finally, one August morning, it's time. I've got a printout from the school office that tells who's coming out for football—way more than we could keep, of course, but that's what that scholarship and a returning legend'll do for ya. I recognize most of the names, cept the newcomers, and I figure I'll get a bead on them today, the first day of try-outs. Just like Coach Schuler, he announces it for early in the morning the first eligible day, Thursday the sixteenth. People think it's cause he wants to see who's committed and ready to work, but I know he just can't wait.

I wake up in a bed damp from sweat and know that even after my shower, I'm gonna have that humid shine all day. Coach and I meet at Sweet Tee's Diner for early morning coffee. The owner, Sherman Naters's ma, Tee, is a big woman with a soft heart and a smile from the waist up. I'm wondering where she is. Shazzam, her on-again-off-again boyfriend, is holding down the fort and he's got the TV going full blast with some Hollywood entertainment show that's reminding everybody this was the day The King died at Graceland in 1977.

Shazzam, who always looks like he's got about a week's worth a beard and wears a full camouflage jumper and rubber boots, pulls from his bald head a grimy cap with fishing lures hanging from it and puts it over his heart. "I say he's still alive, boys! I seen him, I have!"

He pours us some tea and tells us Tee is setting up a little stand at tryouts. He becomes solemn all of a sudden. "An honor to have you back, Coach Schuler, sir. You'll remember I played for you, in a manner of speaking, when you was first head coach here."

Somebody hollers for Shazzam to change the channel, and he finds Sports Center. Next thing you know, our story comes on and the place goes nuts. There's a woman with a microphone strolling in the end zone under our scoreboard, telling our history and showing pictures of Buster in his fedora. Shazzam shushes everybody and turns it up.

The reporter, all serious, looks into the camera and says, "Athens City, Alabama, once the high school football capital of the south, sixteen state championships since 1923. Legendary University of Alabama coach Paul Bear Bryant once called it the mother lode of all-American football players.

"Nearly a hundred students try out for the Athens City Crusaders football team each year in hopes of landing the Jack F. Schuler Scholarship to the University of Alabama. None of those scholarship winners has ever won so much as a spot on the bench at Alabama, but as the town pays for the scholarship, the high school standouts get a free college education nonetheless.

"The scholarship is named in honor of the quarterback who was killed in the state championship game in 1988. Football in this town has seen better days. They haven't had a winning season since that infamous game, and county cutbacks have doomed the school for closure at the end of this academic year.

"If there was ever a glimmer of hope for this town, it comes in the name of coach Buster Schuler. The legendary coach who retired after the death of his son is now returning for Athens City's last year. When a legend comes out of retirement, the football world takes notice."

I look to see what Buster thinks of it all, and he's gone, like I shoulda figured. I find him waiting in the car.

We head over to the field and pull up behind the packed stands. Coach tells me to go on ahead

and make sure the guys are ready to pay attention and follow instructions and he'll be along in
a minute. Well, I knew that. I'd never seen him a
second late to anything, and he'd already waited
long enough for this moment. I want to say something profound or clap him on the knee or pray
for him or whatever, but he already has his eyes
closed and is rubbing his forehead. His clipboard
and whistle are on the back seat, so I just leave
him.

I pass by Rachel and Josie handing out flyers
for a meeting in the gym a few weeks later, something designed to somehow keep the school
alive and keep the kids from having to go to
Rock Hill next year. Josie says, "I don't know why
so many people come just to watch tryouts."

Rachel says, "One word: scholarship."

Josie says, "Two words: no life."

I spot Bev in the stands by herself and wonder
why she's here. Neither of us had ever men-
tioned the scolding I got from Kim, and I'm glad
she's nowhere to be seen this morning. I don't
wanna suspect everything Bev does, just because
of Kim's crazy ideas, but course Bev doesn't have
a relative on the field, at least that I can think of.
I tell myself she's just showing support to her
boss. And the town. And the school. Course.
That's it.

Tee Naters has a folding table and a bunch of pitchers of her famous tea set up under a sign that offers it for a dollar a glass. Rachel makes a beeline for her, passing people who appear to be trying to move as absolutely little as possible. Hardly a head is hatless, and the men's caps have heavy sweat rings.

Tee is watching her son on the field. "Show em what you got, baby! Let the bone roll!"

So she's done her homework. She's trying to earn points with Schuler, wherever he is.

Rachel greets Tee and asks if she can put a stack of pamphlets in the diner. Tee's warm smile fades. "Sweetheart, it's a dead end, and I don't want my customers to have a daily reminder of it."

"Aw, come on, Tee, you've been here forever. This town's given you a lot. What're you gonna give back?"

Tee cocks her head and pours Rachel a free glass of tea. Rachel purses her lips. "Thanks."

I amble across the track to the field where the players show curious interest in me. But we all know who they're looking and waiting for. Stocky, olive-skinned Sherman Naters looks up and waves to his mother. "Hi, Mama!"

Yash Upshaw, the lanky black receiver I'd coach personally if we were employing a passing game instead of the wishbone, says to Naters, "She dress you this morning too?"

Sherman pushes a ball into Yash's gut. "I'll see you when we do tackling drills, huh?"

Abel Gordon, the biggest kid on the team at about three hundred pounds, lumbers by and grabs Sherman and Yash in headlocks. "None of y'all gonna be laughing when I win that scholarship, boys!"

Brian Schuler, the coach's squinty-eyed nephew and returning quarterback, says, "Whoa, whoa, whoa, Abel! Before you throw it out, give me a little puffy puff on whatever's making you hallucinate!" Brian carries himself with the confidence of a senior. He licks his fingers and snaps off a long pass.

Suddenly the crowd falls silent. The players stop, and everyone looks to the tunnel. Buster moves from the shadows into the brilliant morning sunlight and stops, fighting a smile, just surveying the field. I can't believe the difference in the man. It's as if he's grown three inches taller and ten years younger. The shoulders are back, the chest out, the whistle in place around his neck over the tie, and those perfect teeth are showing out from under the shadow cast by the brim of his hat.

Cheerleaders stand still in their practice outfits, people quit moving in the stands, and players hurry into a makeshift line. I stand there at attention, finally accepting that this is really happening and almost as excited as Coach Schuler.

Buster approaches the players, then suddenly turns to address the crowd, removing his hat and holding it with his clipboard. "I want to thank y'all for your time and your spirit. But right now, I want anybody not wearing a jockstrap to get off my field! Don't want anybody out here but my dawgs!" Nobody moves. "I said get off my field now!"

The cheerleaders look at each other and scowl, reluctantly beginning to disperse. The crowd in the stands stays seated. The coach looks up and, with a wide sweep of his hand, says, "That goes for all of y'all too! Thanks for coming, now bye-bye!"

It's clear people are mad, but nobody's gonna make waves while their kid is trying to make the team that might win him a scholarship. They shake their heads and trudge down out of the stands while Schuler watches until the place is empty of everyone but football players and coaches. He turns to the players, replaces his hat, and hands his clipboard to me. "Coach Sawyer, line em up."

Once everyone's in place he unbuttons his

sport coat and puts his hands on his hips, striding to the front row of players. He wrinkles his nose and sniffs. "You smell that?" he hollers. Yash turns his nose to his shoulder and lifts his arm. "What is that?" Coach says. He squats and pulls up a few blades of grass, holding em under his nose. "Yeah, that's it," he says, rising. "Everybody on your faces!" A few of the veterans and a new kid in a red stocking cap drop to the ground. The others hesitate, and Schuler shows them who's in charge. "Down on your faces!" he shouts, and the rest drop. Sherman Naters whispers to Yash, "Old man's crazier'n we heard."

"Now breathe, deep! Do you smell it? That, dawgs, is the smell of death! Over a decade of dead hopes and dreams, buried right here! The curse of individualism grows like a weed on this field—the curse that we call the Jack F. Schuler scholarship!" He plants his foot atop a player's head. "I didn't say lift your head, son. Keep your face in the grass. The scholarship fosters visions of grandeur, dreams of personal glory! It guarantees disunity and prideful individualism! And worst of all—worst of all—losing seasons! Hear this, dawgs! I am the cure to this curse!"

I didn't know who was who yet, but course it didn't matter. Coach whispered, "Let's see if we can't get about three dozen of these pretenders to cut themselves today."

"Three dozen?"

"I'm gonna cut this group to forty-eight by Monday, and there's got to be near a hundred here."

I looked at my printout. "Ninety-nine, Coach."

"No sense cutting more'n I keep if I can get em to do it themselves. I can spot the druggies and the boozers from fifty yards, so we'll start there."

I knew what he was fixing to do. I'd been there with him and with Bear. You think you're a football player until you find out what kinda shape a real coach expects you to be in. We got those boys hitting, running, and whatnot, and before you knew it, guys were just flat leaving the field. They left with their heads down as if they didn't want to face us, but Coach didn't put em down. He called out to em, thanking for their time and their effort. "Just leave your equipment in the field house, and please support us in the stands this season, ya hear?"

Some guys were in good enough shape but just too small. When they went flying from some pretty good licks, Coach would pat em on the shoulder, thank em, and send em packing. "You play an instrument?" he'd ask. "Band practice is in the gym." One guy couldn't run the tires to save his life. Coach told him, "Soccer team needs help."

While Coach concentrated on weeding em out, I was looking for guys with promise. I knew Coach wanted tough, fast, hard workers. One new kid was pale enough to be a Yankee, so I listened for an accent. Only thing that worried me bout him was he looked a little light. He was cut and tough, but he seemed to take hits personally, his serious, light blue eyes glaring from under a sticking-out brow at whoever gave him a good shot. I liked the way he worked and sweat and moved, but I kept fearing Coach would see his size or his attitude and cut him on account of one or the other.

When the guys line up to hit the inflated blocking dummies, they're sposed to fire off and bang one, then hit the ground, roll past one and hit the next. Well, the sun was riding high by then and a lot a guys had staggered off to quit, but Yankee smacked harder'n a guy his size ought to have been able. He made the suckers pop and everybody kinda looked up. Danged if Schuler didn't stop the drill and get in the kid's face. "Son, thanks, but unless you can kick, I don't want anybody under one sixty-five." He turned to the rest. "This is varsity competition. I want boys raised on meat and potatoes."

As Coach moved away, Yankee grabbed his arm. That's a no-no sure as you're standing there, and I figured the kid was history. "I like my steak rare and my potatoes mashed," he said. A northerner for sure. "And I weigh one seventy-three."

As if he'd forgot he had just cut him, Coach took the boy's hand off his arm and said, "Son, don't ever, ever stick your paw in this cage. You're gonna pay for that in sweat." He nodded toward the stadium steps, and the boy took off. Far as I knew, that was the first player Coach ever cut and then welcomed back just so he could punish him. I watched the boy run up and down and up and down, never losing steam. I couldn't believe it. He wasn't six feet tall, but he ran with long, springy strides. When he rejoined the others, he led the way in push-ups, sprints, and loose ball drills. I got to dreaming we might've actually found us a player.

The sixty-five or so survivors were finally cut loose to head for the field house. "Pads off and don't get a drink till after you've been weighed," Schuler said. "I'm not recording no water weight."

I told the boys to line up in alphabetical order, which might sound kinda dumb when they didn't all know each other, but if you think about it, it makes a crazy kind a sense. It

forced em to talk to each other and it told us
which of em knew the alphabet. Gotta have
smart players.

I read names off my list, and if nobody stepped
up, I knew they'd already been cut or cut themselves. It was hard to see Coach cut boys for just
not weighing enough, and I found myself hoping
Yankee hadn't sweat off too much of his 173. I
mean, there was no way a boy that size woulda
lost more'n eight pounds, even in the Alabama
sun, but there was also no way that guy weighed
173.

When he was next in line, I was past the H's
and I's. I couldn't believe the next name on the
list. "Are you kidding me?" I said to Coach. "*Elvis*
Jackson?"

"That's me," the boy said, hands clasped in front
of him at the waist. "And yeah, the middle name's
'Presley.'"

"Says here today's your eighteenth birthday," I
said.

He nodded and stepped onto the scale and I
started sliding the bar. "Born on the anniversary
of the king's death," he said.

"That so?" I said, keeping my eyes on the scale.
I wasn't gonna let him distract me.

"My mama went to his last concert, and when
I was born on the—"

"Yeah," Coach said, "that's more than we need to know, son. Happy birthday and shut up now."

I was amazed to see that bar slide into the high 160s and then past 170. "One hundred seventy-one," I said, raising my eyebrows at Coach.

Elvis Presley Jackson smiled. "Your scale's reading light."

Schuler shook his head and studied the boy. "You are without a doubt."

Jackson stepped down and headed for a locker. I entered the figure next to his name then glanced up in time to see him pull a ten-pound barbell from under his shirt. I caught Schuler's eye and nodded toward the kid. Coach didn't turn. "I know," he said. "Anybody wants to play that bad is worth one more day."

Several boys later I called out "Sherman Naters!" and Tee's boy stepped on the scale.

"The Shermanater!" he said, flexing and growling, making both of us laugh. But the boy's face grew tense as I edged the bar past 160 and finally to 165. As if we would've cut him. He was still the most impressive defensive player on the field. Naters grinned and breathed a huge sigh. "That's right, baby!"

Later, on the way to my car I saw Jackson. "Where you from, boy?"

"North."

"Figured that. How far?"

"Indiana."

"Daddy get transferred?"

"Not exactly."

"Uh-huh." Another gold digger. Well, I for one was hoping he'd be worth it.

By Monday Coach had trimmed the squad to forty-eight, and Elvis Jackson was still with us.

10

Rachel sat on the floor with other "lady war-riors" at the Fellowship of Christian Athletes meeting. Some were painting fresh A's on game helmets, while another helmet was passed, from which the girls each drew a player's number. This would be the player each person would pray for during the season.

Josie sat looking miserable. "One small step for Athens City football and one giant step backward for women's rights."

"Uh-huh, sure," Rachel said. They'd been through this so many times. "Nobody's forcing you to do this. The girls who want to play sports are playing sports. The ones who want to pray for football players are here."

Rachel drew number 99 and passed the helmet to Josie.

"Oh, no," Josie wailed. "Number 40! Mandatory swap. It's article 3, section 2 of the ex-boyfriend manual!"

Rachel slumped. "So Brian's your ex-boyfriend again now?"

"I take a backseat to this lame game four

months out of every year. I'm not going to do it again." She sat holding the number in Rachel's face.

"I always hated blonde jokes till I met you," Rachel said, finally trading with her.

11

"The moment has arrived!" I announced in the locker room after the first practice following try-outs. I set the box of game jerseys on the table and the players cheered as I pulled out the first one—number 88—and fired it across the locker room to Yash, who snagged it. "Be bout the only thing I catch this year, huh?"

At least he was catching on. I smiled. "That's the way the bone rolls." I pulled out number 55. "Shermanater," I said, and the boy stood and gathered it in. "Wear it well, son."

The next jersey in the box was number 40, but as I lifted it out and called "Schuler," Elvis Jackson pounced, grabbing it out of my hands.

"Thanks, Coach Sawyer," he said. And as he moved past he looked over his shoulder, "I look forward to starting for you, sir."

Cause he wasn't looking where he was going, he ran right into Brian Schuler, who flashed a phony smile and said, "Well, welcome to Athens City." He looked from Elvis to some of his friends for support. "Uh, ever since I was little, I been looking forward to senior season. And ever since

I was little, I been wearing number 40. Tradition is real important round here."

Jackson kept hold of the jersey. "Do you have any idea who wore number 40?" he said.

Brian shook his head as if he didn't know or care.

"Gayle Sayers," Jackson announced. I was impressed. Who would know that about a player who retired long before he was born? Somebody named after a dead singer, I guess. He told Brian, "The way I figure it, the fastest man on the team should wear number 40. Tell you what. You prove you deserve this, you can have it back."

The veterans hooted like they couldn't wait to see what Brian was gonna do to this brash kid. I thought about making him give it up myself, but there's nothing wrong with a little healthy competition, something to shake things up.

"Hang on just a second," Brian said when Jackson tried to slip past. "You're new. I'm not. But I am one heck of a nice guy, so I'm gonna give you a little friendly advice. Don't tug on Superman's cape."

"I don't have to," Elvis said, yanking the jersey away as Brian reached for it. "See, I'm the one holding it."

Brian pressed his lips together and drew back a fist, and I started heading that way just as Coach

Schuler stepped into the locker room. The two boys stood nose to nose as Schuler said, "I forgot to tell you boys to make sure they know at home about the two-a-day practices this whole month." He started to turn away, then turned back, smiling faintly at Elvis and Brian. "And if I hear of any altercations in the ranks, well, Truman dealt more mercy to Hiroshima and Nagasaki."

As Coach Schuler left, I stepped between the boys. From the corner, Snoot Nino, our little kicker, called out, "*Who* dealt more *what* to *who*?"

"Study your history, doofus," Yash said.

12

As was their custom on the day the players received their game jerseys, Rachel and Josie and several other FCA girls stood in the parking lot, waiting to announce to each player who was his prayer warrior for the season. Rachel wasn't any more excited about being assigned to Brian Schuler than Josie would have been, but at least they had no romantic history. She was stunned to see Brian emerge wearing number 12. Abel Gordon followed, wearing the number 99 Josie had traded for. Josie's eyes lit up.

And there came Rachel's number 40. "Who *is* that?" she asked as Josie grabbed Abel's hand.

"Elvis Presley something," Abel said, telling of the jersey confrontation and warming to Josie's attention. The new kid apparently didn't know anyone and didn't have a car. He hurried past and headed toward town. Since Rachel wanted to try one more time to get Tee to put a Save Our School flyer in her diner window anyway, she followed number 40 from a distance. When he entered Sweet Tee's, she decided to make the rounds of other businesses and come back later. It wouldn't take long. Almost half the storefronts were boarded up by now anyway.

13

Elvis found the place deserted except for Tee, who was tidying up before closing. As he moved toward the counter, he heard a car door slam in the alley behind the diner. In came Sherman. He pecked his mother on the cheek and held up his new jersey. Then he threw on an apron, giving Elvis a knowing look.

Elvis sat at the counter, and Tee said, "Sorry, son, kitchen's closed."

"Can I just get a cup of hot water?"

She raised a brow and poured him one in a coffee cup. He squirted catsup into it and added salt and pepper. "That's all," he said. "Thanks."

As Elvis guzzled his concoction, mother and son glanced at each other with what appeared to be amusement. "Want some eggs?" the Sherman-ater said. "Something else free to go with your jersey?"

Elvis ignored him but wasn't about to pass up the offer. He looked at Tee, as if to ask if it was really all right. She smiled. "How do you like your eggs?"

"Four at a time," he said.

Sherman stood grinning at Elvis as if he couldn't believe his gall, but Tee smacked him in the chest and said, "Scramble a family."

While her son headed back to the kitchen, Tee turned and introduced herself. He shook her hand. "Elvis Jackson."

She seemed to fight a smile as she studied him. "Your folks out of work?" she whispered.

He shook his head. "I'm on my own."

She grabbed a clean towel and ceremoniously handed it to him. "We close down for football games."

A job here and dinner every night? He slung the towel over his shoulder. As soon as he'd finished eating he found an apron and got to work. Tee and Sherman removed theirs, and Sherman clapped Elvis on the shoulder. "Nice to be able to leave early. Good to have you around."

When they got to the door, Tee turned, as if unable to keep it in any longer. "Child," she said, "what kind of mama names her baby 'Elvis'?"

He smiled. "What kind of mama names her baby 'Sherman Naters'?"

Sherman looked pained, but his mother led him out the door, chortling and calling over her shoulder, "Lock it when you leave."

Elvis scurried about the diner, making sure everything was gathered up. He carried a tub of dirties to the dishwasher and loaded it. When he looked out from the kitchen, untying his apron, the diner looked tidy. But it also reminded him of an expansive football field. The tables were defenders he would have to elude on his way to the door. And his balled-up apron made a perfect football . . .

14

Rachel taped flyers in any window where she was allowed. When she reached the diner again, she taped one on the outside of the door and one on the inside, deciding to ask Tee's approval rather than her permission. Rachel called out for the woman but all she heard in return was a young man's voice.

"December 12, 1965! Chicago Bear Gayle Sayers makes football history with six touchdowns in one game!"

The voice grew closer, but Rachel had no time to get back out the door. With number 40's helmet in her hands, along with the rest of her flyers, she ducked under a table. And here came the new kid, a ball of red cloth in his hands, acting out a football game with his own play-by-play.

"Touchdown number one came in the first quarter, an eighty-yard screen pass!" He tossed the apron-ball into the air and caught it on the run, high-stepping to the other side of the diner.

"Touchdown two was a twenty-one-yard tear through four defenders at lightning speed!" He barreled back in her direction. "Touchdowns three, four, and five are vintage Elvis, juking— who's your daddy?—open field improv—oh, you are, Elvis! That's right!"

As the boy stiff-armed imaginary tacklers and strutted through the diner banging into tables and chairs, he raved, "Gayle Sayers, in his prime, wishes he could keep up with this wild buck!"

Suddenly he stopped, hands on his knees. "But the sixth . . . Oh, baby, the sixth and final touchdown is a thing of beauty—an eighty-five-yard punt return."

It was all Rachel could do to keep from bursting out laughing as the boy tossed the balled-up cloth into the air again, caught it, and smashed into tables and chairs. "Oh, he's got it! Touchdown! Oh, yeah, uh-huh, uh-huh, boom!" He slammed the apron to the floor and flexed, growling and grunting. When he finally knelt to retrieve the apron, he found himself face to face with Rachel and flew back on his seat, sliding across the floor.

Rachel felt bad for him. She blurted, "I, uh, was just looking for Tee, and she's definitely not under here."

15

How dare she hide there watching him? Elvis felt such a fool! He retied his apron as the girl stood and thrust out her hand. "I'm Rachel, your FCA prayer warrior." Elvis shook her hand quickly and reached for his helmet, wishing he could disappear. She pulled it away. "Uh, no, I keep your game helmet until Friday night. It's kind of a visual reminder than I need to pray for you."

He scowled, trying to punish her with his look. "I do okay on my own."

She shrugged and moved toward the door, then stopped and mimicked Scarlett O'Hara. "A gentleman would walk me home."

So she was that kind. He just wanted her to remember his anger and forget everything else. "Let me know when you find one," he said and headed for the kitchen.

"Elvis?"

He whirled around. *What now?*

She smiled. "I just wanted to make sure that was really your name."

He shook his head, disgusted. "Cute."

"Well, face it, *Elvis*. You're stuck with me for the

season." Then, barely audibly, "If you make it that long."

Why couldn't she take a hint? Why was she even still standing there?

"If?"

"I know why guys like you show up in Athens City. Hate to break it to you, but Brian—the guy whose jersey you commandeered today—is a shoo-in for the scholarship. He's coach's nephew, you know."

"I know."

"Every one of the Schulers has gone to Bama since the days of Bear Bryant."

How had she turned this around? She was the one who had embarrassed him. Now *she* was trying to put *him* in his place? "Till this year," he said, through with her.

She hesitated. "So, what should I pray for?"

He shook his head. If he told her, she'd pester him for the whole story. He just wanted her gone. "I don't care," he said. "Pray for green grass."

16

You understand I hadn't really prayed about it. It's just that when the young woman in the copy center who puts all the material together for teachers—even one-class wonders like me—seems friendly and talkative, I start thinking God's trying to tell me something or give me something, namely her. Don't ask me why. Maybe Kim telling me to pay more attention to Bev—which I have been doing for months and not noticing anything different—or maybe hearing Coach talk about his wife with so much love despite everything she'd put him through. I don't know. Maybe I was finally getting ready to move on, way past when most people thought I should've been ready.

Probably it was just that this woman was really something to look at. So call me shallow. Her name's Jacqui and she's a good ten years younger'n me. But she's real pretty with a nice smile and bright eyes, and she's the type who holds your gaze till you gotta look away or smile yourself. Well, I'm not gonna do anything half-baked so I make sure the first thing I ask her is if she's a Christian. Folks down here know that means more than just whether you call yourself one but also that you're a churchgoer and serious about it. Jacqui wasn't from my church but from another one up the road.

I found myself getting more and more stuff reproduced and having to come to school a little earlier every afternoon for my geography class at the end of the day. I spent a little time talking with her each day and we learned stuff about each other, like that she studied library science and wanted to be a librarian in one of those school districts that could afford one. I can't think of one in our area, but who knows what Rock Hill might be able to do when they combine our school with theirs?

We got familiar enough to ask sorta personal questions without being too bashful, and I found out she'd never been married, had a couple of serious guys in the past that didn't work out, and that some man from her church liked to sit with her but has never asked her out. I'm thinking if I'm gonna pursue this I got to invite her to my church. I mean, I'm not switching after all these years and a daughter with another year of high school, and anyway, if there's competition, I've got to divide and conquer. Won't break my heart if Mr. Timid finds out

Jacqui's visiting another church cause a fella asked her.

I'm getting to the place where I'm gonna do something about Jacqui, but I haven't told one soul and I feel like maybe I'm in over my head. So I go to the most logical person I can think of. Bev takes her break about a half hour before I leave from the factory for school each day, and then she's always back a few minutes before I go so she can be sure I'm up to date on everything. Since I'm not about to all of a sudden start asking her about her personal life, I think maybe if I open up a little about myself, she'll open up more too. So that Friday morning when she's in and out of my office with mail and whatnot, I say, "Bev, could you do me a favor this afternoon?"

"A favor?" she says, like a big sister. "Between nine o'clock and five o'clock I do what I'm told."

I knew what she meant and I knew she thought she was funny, but I just tell her, "This is more personal than work." She sat up like she was all ears and I said, "Would you mind spending your afternoon break with me, here in my office, so I can pick your brain?" She hesitated, looking like she had to think about it, so I said, "Course you could get your snack and bring it with you."

"Give up personal time for something not

work related?" she said. But there was a twinkle in her eye.

"Yeah," I said. "Totally up to you."

"I'll be here. Can I bring you something?"

"Coffee," I said.

"With sugar," she said, making a note. "Caffeine alone wouldn't give enough of a rush."

I figured the mystery got to her. She wasn't gonna say no if she didn't know what it was about, and I thought I noticed a little pep in her step the rest of the day. That afternoon she put the answering machine on, came in with our coffees, and shut the door. I leaned back in my chair and put my feet up on the corner of the desk as she sat.

"Need a little advice," I said, and I told her all about Jacqui. The whole time Bev sat there sipping and peeking at me over the top of her cup. When I quit talking I took a big gulp and waited.

"That's it?" she said.

I nodded.

"You wanna know if you should be brave and ask this exciting young woman to join you at church and see where it goes from there."

"I knew you'd understand."

"I understand all right," she said. "Finally admitting you're lonely? You just hit the big four-oh, you're seeing the end of the road with your daughter at home, and you're realizing what's ahead?"

"Guess I'm growing up," I said.

"Seems to me like you're not. You're regressing, or at least stuck."

"Really?" I sat up and put my feet on the floor.

"Listen to yourself, sir. You're like a teenager all goo-goo over a pretty girl. She sounds nice, but she's too young for you. She's gonna want a family, she's—"

"Bev! I'm not talking about marrying her. I just wanna get to know her."

"For what?"

"Well, yeah, okay. I wouldn't mind being in love again." I blushed, but Bev was too nice to tease me about it.

"You act like you're out of choices," she said. "It's not like she's the only eligible woman in town."

"Yeah, but—"

She sat forward and put her cup on my desk. "Yeah, but nothing, Boss. You haven't even dated. Find yourself a—"

"It's not like people haven't tried to set me up."

"You don't need that. Women round here know you. They know your history, your character. Find yourself somebody your own age who won't want to be out and about in twenty years when you'd rather sit on the front porch and read the paper."

"I hope that's not me at sixty, Bev."

"I'm just saying . . ."

Well, I had asked. I had thought she would be excited for me, tell me to go for it. Now what was I supposed to do? What if I showed up at church with Jacqui after getting Bev's advice?

"Thanks," I said, with maybe not enough enthusiasm.

"For nothing, eh?"

"No, I appreciate it."

"Wasn't what you wanted to hear."

"No, but if I wasn't prepared to think about it, I shouldn't have asked."

She nodded. "You got another minute?"

"Course."

"Still open to ideas to save the business, keep people on the payroll?"

"Always," I said. "You know that."

"You want to know what Lee Forest and the people on the line are saying? Most of it's critical or crazy or at least impractical. But some of the old-timers have it in their heads that there might be another market segment we could compete in."

"Market segment?" I said. "Lee is using management lingo now?"

She admitted he hadn't used exactly that term. "But he and some of the others believe they can do more than make footballs. They'd be willing to learn new procedures and see part of the plant retooled."

"To do what?"

"Manufacture baseball gloves."

I sat back. "I like that they're thinking," I said. "But think of the cost of new equipment, of training, not to mention trying to compete in a new market. How can I lay off dozens of people and then announce a new kind of operation a few months later?"

"I'm just telling you what I'm hearing," she said.

"You know most of the companies with the ball glove accounts are having their manufacturing done overseas."

She shrugged. "What else is new?"

"Better get me an appointment with Les."

"And his cronies? Those four with seniority tend to hang together."

"Sure."

She stood. "Well, I figure you're on your way to school to ask for a date."

"What, you think I don't take you seriously? Tell you what, I won't do anything today, and that'll give me the weekend to really think about it."

• • •

I gotta admit Bev kept me from doing something stupid. I go to school, excited cause I'm gonna see Jacqui but kinda relieved I've decided not to make any bold move yet. I'm also thinking how much fun practice has been this week.

So I get there a good half hour before my class and go to the copy center and trade smiles with Jacqui. She's got my job finished and seems free to talk, so we shoot the breeze and I start thinking that if I *was* gonna get brave and ask her to join me at church Sunday, today would be the day. And then she up and says, "You know, Mr. Sawyer, I really like talking to you."

"I really like talking to you too," I say.

And she says, "It's so good to have an older person to bounce things off of. I get a fresh perspective when I realize that someone like you has been through what I'm going through, only so many years ago."

My smile froze and I acted like I was glad I coulda been some help, but my cotton, how old did she think I was? It hit me that I had never told her. Either she thought I was another ten years older'n her or she thought ten years was plenty anyway. All of a sudden I'm feeling like grandpaw the sage and thanking God I didn't ask her out. What in the world would she have thought, or said?

Oh, it wasn't my imagination. She had been so nice and smiley to me—because I was an old man. I felt like an idiot the rest of the day.

"Dawgs," Coach began at practice, "Athens City football lives by Schuler's three commandments. Commandment one: thou shalt run the wishbone offense. Commandment two: thou shalt never fumble my football. And commandment three: thou shalt do it my way, all . . . the . . . time."

As we ran the boys through the paces, forcing them into a shape they'd never been in, Coach kept preaching. I could tell by the looks on a lot a faces that specially the veterans were wondering how in the world anybody could be MVP and win a scholarship under a coach so hung up on selflessness and teamwork.

"For the next four months," Coach hollered between whistle blows, "your lives will consist of two simple activities: you will crush with apocalyptic force anything that moves, and you will sprint like dawgs until you sweat blood!"

During one drill, Abel Gordon worked so hard getting that big body a his going that he threw up all over Schuler's pant leg. The Shermanater busted out laughing until Coach grabbed his shoulder pads and pulled his face toward the mess. Then Sherman vomited.

"The wishbone runs on gain and maintain, gentlemen! Gain yards, maintain position. Now go hard, or go home. You think you're gonna make the playoffs with this blocking I see before me? You got about as much chance as spit in a hurricane. You are without a doubt!"

Elvis Jackson stood out if anybody did, darting around the field with those fluid strides, able to change direction seemingly without stopping. You don't expect a running back to hit as hard as a linebacker, but he did. You'd never have guessed Coach noticed. He didn't favor anybody. I knew he liked the Shermanater and expected him to lead the defense. And I believe he thought he could rassle his nephew into running the wishbone from quarterback, even though it meant cutting out that awful passing he'd done the year before.

We ran the guys through the gauntlet, hollering for everybody else to not just attack and bang and tackle but to also try to strip the ball from the runner's grip. "Make that ball carrier violate my second commandment!" Coach would yell. "Make him earn the right to move that ball or give up his position to you!"

The guys were hitting and smashing and

spending more time on the ground than on their feet.

"Dirt and dust, dawgs! That is the marrow of the bone!"

During a water break, Brian Schuler picks up a ball and nods to Yash Upshaw to go long. Yash takes off and Brian fires a half-decent pass, maybe slightly behind Yash, who drops it right in front of Buster. Coach picks up the ball, smiles, hands it to Yash, and says, just like I knew he would: "Only three things can happen when you throw the ball, and two of em are bad. Any odds worse than a coin toss, I don't play."

We went on to Bull in the Ring, a drill I love. It's where us littler guys can show what we're made of. Basically everybody's in a circle with one guy in the middle. The coach calls out a number, and that player comes charging the guy. Whoever's left standing is the bull in the middle for the next call.

Eventually, Coach's nephew is in the middle, and he proves to be a tough kid, taking and giving pretty good till number 40 is called. Jackson comes flying in and just levels him. Brian jumps up and it's clear he's stunned.

Coach was thrilled. "Did y'all hear that sound?" he said. "That's the first big bang I heard all day! That's the sound of percussion! You a tough guy, Jackson?"

"No, sir."

"Say again?"

"No, sir, I just want my chance in the middle."

"You floss with barbed wire and gargle with gasoline, boy? You're in the middle now!"

Coach calls Sherman's number. This oughta be good. He charges. Jackson stays still till the last instant, then shucks the Shermanater into two other players. Schuler calls three numbers at once, and Elvis somehow handles em all. I'm liking this kid, and I know Coach can't ignore him. He calls a number from either side of the circle at the same time. Elvis drops one and sends the other flying into Brian, knocking him over.

"Awright, ladies, that's enough!" Coach says, and he and I start walking to the next drill area. I turn to wave the guys along with us, just in time to see Brian blindside Jackson, spearing him right in the back. Course they wind up on the ground, fighting. Coach hears the commotion, and we hurry back to break it up.

"Can anyone here tell me why two of my players are in a head-on collision?" Coach says. I know enough to say nothing. I been here before.

"Elvis started it, sir," a lineman says. "He—"

"Why, thank you, son," Coach says. "You can go home." The kid shoots him a double take. "You are off this team!" He shoves the boy. "Go on now."

Stunned, the boy staggers away. The other players look at each other scared.

"Anyone else wanna tell me what happened?" Schuler says. "Come on, now, fess up. Tell me the truth or I'll make you run from here to eternity."

Another boy raises his hand. "Brian speared him from the back."

"Son, thank you. Now we'd appreciate it if you'd get off our field. Get out!"

The team is frozen. "Any more traitors? No one? Is that the game we're gonna play? Silence is a lie, dawgs. It's a crime of omission. And in Alabama, crimes get punished. Follow me. Everybody!"

In his coat and tie, Coach jogs to the parking lot, puts me behind the wheel of his Mustang, and stands on the backseat. I slowly follow the team as they jog through town. And the strangest thing happened. The kids were mad and I'm sure feeling unfairly treated, but people in town didn't know they were being punished. They musta thought this was another drill by a tough coach, and they cheered as we cruised by. The kids enjoyed that, a course, and ran taller, faster. When we neared the school again, Coach had another idea. "Shut it down and mash the clutch," he told me. The guys had to take turns pushing the car the other way, but again, to the cheers of the townsfolk.

By the time we finally got back to the parking lot, it was dark and everybody was dragging. Coach and I hurried past the boys to the field, where we began picking up the gear. The kids straggled one by one through the tunnel and past us toward the field house, most not even looking at us. I couldn't blame em.

When Jackson jogged past, carrying his shoulder pads, Schuler called out to him. "Son! We both know why you're here, so why don't you save us both a lot of time and energy and limp on out of here."

Elvis stopped and stared. "I *came* here to *play* for you."

"No you didn't! You came here to play for *you*. That's why you view every man on this team as a threat. Every time I turn around, you're in somebody's face. You've got one thing on your mind, and we both know that's the curse, and that requires playing time. Let me make it crystal clear for ya. You are not gonna play one minute for me."

Elvis's face went red and it looked to me like he was determined not to be drove off. He turned and headed for the field house.

Brian jogged up and hopped over the fence. "Coach!" he called. "Uncle Buster!"

Coach got nose to nose with him, pointing.

"Listen to me! Nephew or not, you get treated the same as everyone else!"

"Coach, are you really gonna just run the old wishbone all the time? How am I gonna get a chance at the scholarship if I don't get a chance to throw the ball?"

"Never mind the scholarship!" Coach said. "Your last name is not more important than this team. If you didn't learn that from your cousin—"

Buster turned away, and when Brian ran off, I said, "Coach, your nephew would have been only six when Jack—"

"Not now, Cal. Please."

Later, when the players were gone, I heard the faint squeak of cloth on glass and poked my head out of the training room. Coach Schuler was polishing the trophy case that held his son's jersey.

He put his fingers on the glass real gentle and stood quiet for a minute. Then he pulled away, rubbed off his prints, and left without saying a thing. I waited about a half hour and then tried to call him, but his little brother's wife told me he was at the rehab center. "Miz Schuler," I said, "I'm just wondering, do you think I should offer to go with Coach sometime?"

"Go with him?"

"To visit his wife."

"What're you, kidding?"

"No, ma'am."

"She doesn't even want to see *him*, Mr. Sawyer."

"I know, ma'am. I mean just to be with him, maybe sit in the waiting room or even in the parking lot."

"You'd have to ask him."

"Well, have you and your husband been to see her?"

"Excuse me?"

"No?"

"Not on your life."

I wanted say I was sorry I asked but I just thanked her. No wonder he never talked about them. I just wished he'd talk about his wife once in a while and tell me how she was doing.

I was falling behind at work and so stopped into the office for a couple of hours. I tried calling Rachel, but got no answer. When I finally got home, Bev Raschke was parked out front and Rachel was getting out of her car. I pulled next to Bev and rolled down my window.

"These kids today," she said. "Find em wandering the streets and ya feel obligated to bring em home."

"I can't keep track of her anymore," I said,

smiling. "You wanna come in a minute?"

She hesitated like she maybe wanted to, but she said no. "Better call it a night."

So much for not taking an interest in her. I walked Rachel in. "Where were ya?"

"Just out. Bev gave me a ride home."

"I noticed. Got homework?"

She shook her head, looking puzzled. I never had to push her on her studies. She was a way better student than I'd ever been, which wasn't saying much. Rachel was one of those who does most of her work in study hall and the rest at home before she does anything else and gets straight A's. Obviously got that from her mama.

Just before I turned in I came out of my bedroom to get something to read and, not trying to, overheard Rachel on the phone. "He didn't even ask," she was saying. "I wouldn't lie to him, but I'm glad he had other stuff on his mind."

It was all I could do to not try to hear more. Rachel'd never given me cause to worry. And I trusted her. I didn't need to know everything. Course I didn't.

17

Sunday morning Coach and I were sitting at the end of our favorite pew when Bev came and stood right next to me in the aisle. "Got a date for this morning?" she said.

"No, ma'am," I said. "Right now I'm following your advice."

"Well, who'da believed it?" she said. "You boys scoot down a little and let me in here. I don't want you bellyaching about having no one to sit with in church cept a broken-down old football coach."

"What?!" Buster whispered as we made room for her.

"I never said any such thing," I said.

The following Friday, September 7, my geography class was so hard to control, I could tell the students couldn't concentrate. I said, "You'd think we were opening football season tonight," and everybody whooped and hollered. That didn't help.

The stadium was full when Coach and I

showed up that evening. The Beach Bearcats' bus was already there. I didn't know if Coach needed anything more to psych him up, but all he could talk about was Beach's smart aleck new coach and something he'd said in the paper. "Did you read it, Sawyer?"

"No, sir."

"He said he wasn't worried about an old has-been who hadn't coached in twelve years."

I smiled. "He's got a point."

"What'd you say?"

"He got to you, didn't he?"

"You honestly think I care what some rookie coach says about me?"

"Looks like it."

He waved me off. "Agh!"

The guys were so juiced that Buster told them, "Most coaching is done on the practice field, so there's really nothing more for me to say except execute the plan or the plan will execute you. You know what to do."

The guys hesitated, then jumped and yelled "Crusaders!" They charged out of the field house, touching the Jack Schuler display case, then reaching to slap the "Pride" sign over the door frame. Coach and I followed, and as we jogged together, I said, "What were you going for there, Mr. Lombardi?"

He said, "What *is* that thing about planning to fail?"

I laughed. "You mean 'If you fail to plan you're planning to fail'?"

"Yeah, that's what I was going for."

"You needed a 'Get out of platitude free' card, didn't you?"

"I sure did," he said. "And I had one in my wallet."

Probably cause I was nervous I couldn't quit jabbing him. "Use it next time," I said.

"All right, Sawyer, focus. You weren't cutting up like this when you were a white-knuckled young Crusader."

"Yeah, well, my coach didn't look like he was about to throw up either."

"It shows?"

"Does it ever."

"In fact, scuse me a minute."

"Now, Coach," I said, "don't. That's too much like a bad movie."

"Barfing on the sidelines in my big comeback game wouldn't give the right impression either. I'll be right out. Remind the boys about the refs."

"That the men in stripes have got a job to do too and all that?"

"You got it."

"That gonna keep you behaving on the sidelines, Coach?"

But he had ducked into the bathroom.

On the second play from scrimmage, one of the oldest refs in the league missed an obvious call. Schuler erupted, and I knew he was back in business.

"How could you miss the face mask?" he screamed, running up the sidelines with the ref. "You are still the worst ref in America! Your wife and children must be hiding their faces in shame!"

That was all it took—there came the yellow flag. But that didn't stop Schuler. "Oh, that's good! That's the first good call you've made in years! You are without a doubt!"

Coach was totally into the game, but that didn't help us much. Beach scored on its first possession. "Yo, line!" Schuler screamed. "The game is football! Let's act like we know it!" He was red faced and sweating, and the cares of life seemed far from him.

Once while he was pacing he bumped into Elvis Jackson, who stuck his face in the coach's as if expecting to be put in the game right then. I gotta tell ya, I wouldn't have minded seeing that. But Buster has a long memory. He gave Jackson a look that woulda put a wart on a gravestone, and I knew the kid wouldn't be playing that night.

So Jackson took to hanging around me. I learned to avoid his pleading eyes. A couple times he mumbled, "Even on defense. Come on, let me in there."

We might as well have. Our starters were tight on both sides of the line. The defense was on its heels. Our offense was pathetic. The wishbone takes patience and requires playing within your-self. Buster wouldn't, wouldn't, wouldn't let Brian throw, yet the ball spent more time bouncing around in our backfield than in the hands of our ball carriers.

At the half Beach was leading 21-0, and everyone knew it coulda been worse. Our offense smelled worse than the locker room. As soon as they got inside the door, the team was at each other's throats. Nothing Coach hated worse than blaming somebody else for your own fail-ures, so I shouted over their screaming and shoving, "Knock it off! How many times do I hafta remind you about maintaining your disci-pline?"

But Buster came in right behind me, madder'n a duffer three-putting from two feet. "That's all right!" he shouted. "You go ahead, fight with each other, feed the curse! Go on! You are without a doubt! I have bled every possible drop of sweat out of your bodies, so there's only one thing left to do. I'm gonna shoot straight with you."

The boys dropped onto the benches and hung their heads. "You are a pack of pathetic, curse-infested me-myself-and-I's," Coach began, "and you are gonna have the worst season in the history of football unless a knight on a white horse shows up wearing shoulder pads!"

He glared at one player after another until they looked away. I'd sat under that gaze. No one asked if there was some strategy, some adjustment that would put us back in the game.

"Who's finished?" he said finally. "Who's done? Anybody wanna go home right now?" Nobody moved. "Then git those heads up and git em up now."

One by one they seemed to sit taller, to get the picture, to catch their breath and get themselves ready. But the third and fourth periods were no better, and we fell behind 35-15 with less than a minute to go and Beach had the ball. Buster told me to have the Shermanater call time-out.

I said, "Coach, let's just let the clock run."

I was wrong and I knew it right away. "Sawyer, we owe it to our opponent to give em everything we've got till that gun sounds."

I got Naters' attention and had him call a time-out and hustle to the sidelines. The three of us tried to come up with some defensive solution, but when Sherman raced back onto the field, we were shocked to see Elvis Jackson out there.

"What's he doing on my field?" Coach yelled. "Get him outa there!"

But as I shouted at Sherman to use our last time-out, Jackson distracted him, screaming, "They called in the cavalry, Shermanater. Now play some defense, you pansy mama's boy!"

Naters was so mad I thought he was going to come out of his uniform. He growled and pawed the ground, and the Bearcats snapped the ball while we were still trying to get his attention. Naters blew past the line and straight at the quarterback. As Sherman plowed him to the ground, he let fly a dying duck of a pass in the direction of the only clean uniform on the field—Elvis Jackson's.

Jackson jumped higher than I thought a kid his size could and picked off that ball at our 20. With time running out, he started upfield. I knew this kid was in big trouble. Nobody goes in without Schuler's say-so, and he was gonna get it.

Well, I'd never seen anything like it. Jackson broke free, and I mean free. He made everybody else on that field look slower than a classroom clock. He scored the touchdown and came off the field with a big grin, holding the ball over his head. Brian batted it away. "We lost, idiot."

Buster and I hurried to the middle of the field where the Beach head coach shook his hand. "Nice try, Schuler," he said. "Breaks my heart, specially on your big return and all."

Coach was smiling too, just in case anybody was watching. "You sanctimonious punk," he said. "We're gonna eat your guts with a spoon in the play-offs."

Their coach, still smiling, said, "With that Stone Age offense? Not a prayer, you old bag of bones."

As we left the field, Coach Schuler caught sight of Jackson at the fence, handing his helmet to Rachel. Coach said, "Get that boy's tail in my office, now."

I jogged over there, but Elvis had his back to me and Rachel was seeing nothing but him. "Maybe next time you won't have to sneak into the game," she said. She handed him one of her flyers. "I want you at our meeting Wednesday night, no excuses."

"Jackson!" I said.

"Am I in trouble?" he said, following me.

I snorted. "What do you think?"

"But I made the play."

"Don't be naive."

I left him in the coaches room and stood

behind Coach as he talked to the team. He ran a hand across his head and let out a big sigh. "Right now I'm too upset to trust myself to say anything," he said. "There's twelve more games before the state championship, and it's gonna be held on our field whether we're in it or not. You wanna watch it or you wanna play in it?"

He was still talking state championship? No one even looked up. "I'm gonna study the film," he said, "much as I can't imagine wanting to see this again. And I'd better see a difference on the practice field this week or you're gonna see some wholesale changes in the lineup." He sat on the edge of the table and shook his head. "There's no substitute for teamwork. Go home and forget this game. Take tomorrow off. Rest of our season starts Monday at practice."

When Coach and I entered the coaches room, Jackson stood quickly. "Oh, now you're eager to please, eh?" Coach spat. "Sit yourself down."

There was nowhere for me to sit but next to the kid. I wished I could have told him what to say or not say to have a prayer of staying on the team. Buster tossed his fedora aside and took off his sport coat. He sat behind the tiny desk, looking tired, and folded his hands.

"Let me tell you something, boy," he said. "Maybe it's twelve years away from the game that has me sitting here at all, cause it sure as shooting ain't cause you pulled off a miraculous play. Coach Sawyer here'll tell ya that I have zero tolerance for insubordination."

I nodded, but neither of em was looking at me anyway.

"You act like you never played high school football before, Jackson."

"That's right, sir."

My head shot up, and so did Coach's. "Where you from, boy?"

"Kankakee Banks, Indiana."

"Never played the game before?"

"Not since junior league. Our high school was too small."

"No football there?"

"Um, well, yeah. They had it."

"But they didn't have a scholarship or any kinda competition that woulda got a superstar like you noticed, that it?"

Elvis cocked his head and shrugged.

"I'm onto you, ain't I, Jackson?"

The boy shrugged again and mumbled, "I dunno. Guess so."

"You keep looking at me, boy, cause this may very well be the last time you see me. I'm gonna give you one chance to tell me why I don't ask for your gear right now."

"I want to play," Jackson said, a tear in his voice. "I'm sorry."

"I *told* you you weren't gonna play a minute for me until I saw a team attitude in you! You think by sneaking into the game you're gonna change my mind? I'm incredulous!"

Jackson had nothing to say.

"I want to know something," Coach said. "Are you telling me you didn't play high school football till you got here cause the program there in Indiana was too small for you? Now, no, I'm not taking your fool shrugging for an answer. Tell me straight out!"

Jackson looked down and mumbled.

"Eye contact, boy! You're fighting for your life on this team. That is, if you care."

"I do."

"Then look at me when I talk to you and answer me so I can hear you."

"My dad wouldn't let me play!"

"Well, there you go. What was he, scared you were gonna get hurt?"

Jackson shook his head. "Wanted me to work."

"Help support the family?"

Jackson nodded.

"Why not now? What changed?"

"I came here."

"You ran away?"

"I'm eighteen. I left."

"Your parents know where you are?"

Jackson shrugged but then immediately shook his head, as if he knew he had to tell the truth.

"So you come all the way down I-65 to play here, and you're totally on your own."

"Right."

"Where you living?"

"I have a place."

Coach pursed his lips and looked at me. I didn't know what to make of it either.

"So you basically don't respect any authority at all."

"I respect you, sir."

"Don't start that. Why do you think you're sitting here? You don't respect me any more than you respect your dad, leaving him there to fend for himself when the family needs you."

"My parents are dead."

"You got to get your story straight, son." Coach looked at his watch. "I'm sitting here for five more minutes unless you can keep my attention longer. You tell me your story, you tell me the truth, and Coach Sawyer here'n me are gonna decide your future."

Coach sat back in the squeaky chair and put his hands behind his head. Elvis Jackson leaned forward and sucked in a breath. "My real mom and dad died in a wreck when I was ten. My grandparents were too old to take me and I guess no one else wanted me. I was put in foster homes, but I was mad and scared and everything, so nobody kept me for long, till this last one where I stayed four years. We lived in a double-wide and they had a younger foster kid too, a girl who's ten now." His voice caught and Coach and I looked at each other. "I guess they'd had a bunch of foster kids over the years. Anyway, I was fourteen and I was a year behind in school and angry, but they seemed happy when the county took me there, like they wanted me.

"As soon as the social worker left, though, the mom went in the other room to watch TV and Jenny—that's the girl—hid out in one of the bedrooms. The dad told me to follow him outside, even though it was the middle of January and below zero. I can't remember everything he said but I got the point. He told me I had one role in my new family and that was to do what he said, get a job, and give him the money. I thought I was a tough guy and said something like, 'And what if I don't?'

"He grabbed my stomach with one hand and squeezed so tight I could hardly breathe. I tried to pull away and he just squeezed tighter and said, 'You think I don't know where to hurt you where it doesn't show?' I shook my head and he said, 'Make trouble and I'll tell em you molested Jenny.'"

Coach looked as angry as me. "You told someone, I hope," he said, his voice thick.

"I told the social worker as soon as I could, but she said my record was so bad no one was going to believe me. No one else had ever complained about the guy before. Everybody said he was poor but hardworking, a leader in the community and all that.

"Jenny was scared of him, so any time anybody from the county came over, she smiled and acted happy. She was a good actor. She fooled them like she fooled me at first."

"So, what about football?" Coach said. "You got some training somewhere."

"My real dad. Gave me a football for Christmas when I was so young I couldn't even hold it in one hand. I played junior football and later read everything I could about the game. I even worked out on my own and ran everywhere I could. The social worker finally convinced me to keep my grades up, and it was actually the foster mom who put me onto Athens City."

Coach flinched. "How'd she hear about us?"

"Well, she didn't exactly know about it, but one day she was watching TV and all of a sudden says to me, 'Football story's on.' I couldn't believe it. Usually she just kept to herself. She was scared of him too. I didn't even know she knew I liked football.

"I said, 'I can watch it?'

"She said, 'If you hurry. My show's coming on.' I hurried in there and saw the thing about you coming back. I recognized the name of the town from my football. I've still got it; brought it with me. Anyway, that's when I started making my plans. The social worker told me that once I was eighteen, I was on my own. I left a few days early because I knew tryouts started that day." He looked down. "I just wish I'd got Jenny outa there."

"Any real brothers or sisters?" Coach asked.

Jackson shook his head.

"Nobody ever helped you through the loss of your parents?"

"Everybody thought I was all right. Of course I wasn't all right. My mom'd named me for good luck and my dad had told me I could be the next Gayle Sayers."

Coach glanced at me, then back at Jackson. "Sayers was even before your dad's time, wasn't he?"

"He only went to one NFL game when he was like five or so. December 12, 1965."

"I was eighteen," Coach said, looking at the ceiling. "Wrigley Field. Sayers was a rookie when running backs also returned kicks. Six TDs."

"Were you there?" Jackson said.

"No, but every real football fan knows that game, son. Let me ask you something. You telling me the honest-to-God truth?"

"Yes, sir."

"Bout everything, I mean."

"Yes, sir."

Schuler shook his head and sighed again. "You want to stay on this team?"

"Absolutely."

"You know I gotta punish you for insubordination."

"I'll do anything."

"You'll do more than anything. You'll do everything. You'll run a mile tonight. You'll run two hours a day during the first three practices next week. Then you'll really face the music Thursday."

"The music?"

"You'll see."

"Thanks, Coach."

"Don't thank me, Jackson. Show me. And you're on a short leash. No more screwups."

"Yes, sir."

"And I want the name of that last family you lived with."

"Oh, I couldn't—"

"I'll leave you out of it, son, but you got to think about the girl in that home."

"That's what I'm worried about. What if he—"

"Just write the name and address for me, and then don't you give it another thought."

Jackson left to run his laps and Coach and I just looked at each other. "Story like that could make a nun swear," he said finally, studying the name and address.

Coach was gone by the time I walked out to see Jackson finish his fourth quarter-mile loop of the track. He didn't even look winded. He looked eager. "Almost lost your spot on this team," I said.

"Tell me about it," he said.

I followed him inside. "Can I do something for you before you leave?" I said.

"Sure. What?"

"Could I pray with ya?"

He shook his head. "You're a born-againer like your daughter?"

I nodded.

"You can pray *for* me all you want, but I won't be praying with you."

"Want to say why?"

"Not particularly."

"I *will* be praying for you."

"Suit yourself."

18

Rachel was waiting at home. "I was worried," she said. I wanted to say that was fair; I'd been worrying about her lately.

"Losing always takes longer than winning," I said.

"Want me to fix you something?"

I shook my head. "Thanks. What would Josie say about that?"

"You know I don't care. For all her women's rights flag waving, she's now going with Abel Gordon just to make Brian jealous."

"What's she want to do that for?"

"Says she's taken a backseat to football long enough."

"But Abel's a footb—"

"I know, Daddy. I didn't say she made sense."

I asked her how her school crusade was going.

"I'll know when I see what kinda crowd shows up Wednesday night. You'll be there, right?"

"I was just waiting for an invite."

"You were not."

"Maybe I wasn't, but lots of people would come if you asked em personally."

"You think?"

"I know."

And so Rachel did. Over the next two days she asked everybody she saw, including everybody at church. Lots of em told her they'd be there. I didn't want to pop her balloon, but I didn't expect much to come of it. "I invited the county school board," she said, "and it looks like they're coming."

That was a surprise.

Monday morning Bev had that meeting for me with Lee Forest and a few others off the line. They'd volunteered to come in for it on their own time but there was no way I was gonna let em do that. I told Bev, "Keep track of the time, add a half hour to it for each of em, and see it's reflected in their pay."

She looked funny, like she wasn't following. "Got it?" I said.

"Yes, sir," she said, but she didn't write it down till she got back to her desk. A few minutes later she took a call and asked me if I wanted to talk to a Mr. Seals from Malaysia.

"Who is he?" I said.

"Wouldn't say, but he's calling from there."

"Long distance?"

She turned in her chair and stared at me

through the window. "That would be a fair assumption," she said.

I smiled an apology, but I guess she hadn't seen any humor in my stupidity, which she usually does. "You reckon it's about manufacturing?"

"You reckon I'm clairvoyant?"

She wasn't mean. I was just dense. I pointed to my phone and picked up. "I'll get right to the point, Mr. Sawyer," the man said. "You can imagine what time it is over here and I can imagine how busy you are there, trying to keep your business alive." He sounded so friendly and sincere.

I said, "Fire away, Mr. Seals."

"I'm an American, sir, a southerner like yourself. I even played at Bama, like you did."

"You don't say."

"You're a straight shooter, I can tell. I'm probably not the first business owner in this part of the world to approach you, but I'd like to be the last. I don't want to waste your time, but just let me say I'd like the opportunity to show you how you could do your manufacturing here at such a fraction of your current cost that even with shipping your raw goods to me—I assume you get them from Chicago like the rest of us—and my shipping finished product to you, you would increase your profit per unit by more than 25 percent."

I didn't know what to say.

"Are you still listening, Mr. Sawyer?"

"Uh-huh."

"Good man. Now I know you're finding that hard to believe because that shipping cost would be yours, and you're wondering what you do with your equipment investment if you let us take over your manufacturing, though I'm guessing some of your machinery is more than a hundred years old."

Bev may not have been a mind reader, but this guy was.

"I'm also wondering what I'm sposed to do with loyal workers that have been with me for decades," I said.

"Everybody faces that, sir. But with the profits you'll be making, you could make them mighty happy with appropriate severance packages, couldn't you?"

Maybe I could, but I wasn't about to start saying yes when he was talking about something I'd been fighting for years. "Some of my best accounts—"

"Let me guess," he said. "Those include certain leagues and bowl games that count on you for instant turnaround and for specially packaged kicker balls."

"Exactly."

"We can match and maybe exceed the quality of your top-of-the-line product and set you up with sufficient inventory to where you could always be prepared to ship overnight to those clients. And if you want to keep your equipment and your top half dozen tradesmen, you can keep a boutique operation there for specialty products. Am I making any sense here, Mr. Sawyer?"

"Some, sure." I didn't want to say too much. I don't like being bowled over. "I've been giving some thought to expanding our product line."

"Like any good entrepreneur. Other kinds of balls? Or gloves?"

He had me. "Gloves."

"You have clients. You know your market. But don't invest in new manufacturing hardware until you hear our prices on those as well. We both know the moneymaking part of your business is selling to retailers. Your good name stays on your good product, but we do the dirty work. I can tell you're a thinking man, Mr. Sawyer, and that you don't make snap judgments. I am prepared with two alternatives. Three of my partners and I will be happy to visit you and discuss this personally, and I will guarantee none of them will be Asian."

What was that sposed to mean? "I got no problem with Asians," I said.

"But you must admit that if an entourage comes to visit and any one of them is Asian, it could tip off your troops."

"I see," I said, and he was probably right, but it still sounded rotten to me.

"Or," he said, "and frankly we prefer this, I am prepared to bring you and a loved one or one of your associates here, first class, all expenses paid, to put your mind at ease about our workplace, quality control, and ability to handle your work."

"That's certainly generous of you, Mr. Seals. But I—"

"Does either of those options sound better than the other at first blush?"

I cleared my throat. "I spose if I was ever gonna consider something like this, I would need a certain comfort level with your operation."

"We'd love to have you and . . . Is there a wife, Mr. Sawyer?"

"No, sir."

"You and anyone you choose—and if you wanted to bring others, we would work with you to find the most thoroughly economical way to bring them. Do you have your calendar handy there, sir?"

"Well, we're getting a little ahead of ourselves here, Mr.—"

"I would want this to totally be at your convenience. Of course there's no better time than the present. I mean, if this is right for your business, that means that every day you delay—"

"I'm certainly not going to rush into anything, Mr. Seals. This company has a long history—"

"Absolutely, and that's the reason I'm calling only you, sir. We're not interested in manufacturing for just any—"

"You wholesale yourselves, then?"

"Well, no, sir, but we work with only the finest—"

"What other stateside companies would you be manufacturing for, if you don't mind my—"

"Now, Mr. Sawyer, you understand that that would be highly confidential, proprietary information. You would enjoy the same level of confidentiality as any of our clients."

"But I wouldn't be able to sell a product without 'Made in Malaysia' on it, would I?"

"Unfortunately not, but as you know, that is a requirement of the United States government, not of Malaysia's."

"Our government wants people to know when they're buying other than American-made goods."

"Right, Mr. Sawyer. And while that used to connote lesser quality or cheap labor, the sheer number of widely known brand names who manufacture here has taken away much of that stigma. Now, with your raw goods coming from Chicago and being assembled here under your specifications, you might want to consider another option. You might want to have the final process handled right there in Athens."

"Athens City."

"Right. You might want to lace there or to inflate and mold."

"And what would be the advantage?"

"To be able to stamp 'Partially Manufactured in Malaysia with American Goods' on each and every product."

"Uh-huh."

"Now, when can we schedule you and someone of your choosing? I suggest now only because I assume your specialty manufacturing for the season is likely finished and it's just a matter of stamping the correct team names and logos on the balls for bowl games. Surely the head of the company doesn't need to be there for that."

"Some days I feel like I *ought* to lend a hand on the line, Mr. Seals."

"That bad, huh? I knew your work force had been decimated the last few years, but I can only imagine how tough things are getting."

I had the phone pressed against my ear and

both elbows on the desk. I rubbed my eyes. "All due respect, sir, but most of the people in this town, when they're not blaming me for our predicament, are blaming companies like yours."

"Oh, believe me, I understand. That's our biggest public relations challenge, Mr. Sawyer. But I hope you can see that we're here to help. It just doesn't make sense to pay more than you have to for production when margin is the name of the game. We cut your cost and improve your margin."

"And shut down my operation."

"That's one way to look at it. But if I had a facility costing me more than it needed to, I'd seriously consider shutting it down."

I leaned back in my chair and stared at the ceiling. "Mr. Seals, to tell you the truth, I'm a patriot. Sometimes I wonder why, but if it comes to selling American-made and me worrying about who gets enough work to keep their families fed, you gotta know I'm gonna look out for my friends and neighbors first."

"That's admirable, Mr. Sawyer. But you're bearing the entire cost. You do everything you can to keep your business alive, and as it dwindles, you get blamed anyway."

"True enough."

"So what better time than now to come and see the possibilities?"

I told him I was coaching and that the rest of the season would give me time to think about it. "But I don't want to waste your time," I said. "I gotta tell ya, this is a long shot. I don't know if I could keep living in this town if I sold out to—"

"Oh, Mr. Sawyer, don't refer to it as selling out. We don't want to buy your business. We want to help you to stay in business."

That conversation was ringing in my ears as the clock moved toward the meeting with my old-timers. I sorta wished I'd told Bev to listen in to the call, cause she's a good sounding board and I wanted to know if she thought I'd been wimpy. She was sitting there sorta spacey again. I mashed the intercom.

"You okay in there, lady?"

She turned slow and looked at me. Bev had been so low maintenance for so long that I knew something was up.

"How much longer till Lee and the others come in?" I said.

She sat there for a second, then checked her schedule. "They're all on eleven to seven today."

"I know," I said. "But they're coming in early to see me still, right?"

Bev stood quickly and bent over her desk, like she was trying to cover that she was sick or hurting. "Yeah," she said. "Course they are. In half an hour or so. Oh!"

She stood straight up and pressed a hand on her abdomen. I closed my eyes and opened em slowly. Bev hadn't wanted me to hear or see that, I was sure. I mean, if she didn't even tell me what she did on her own time, she sure wouldn't want me to know about her, you know, female, feminine, women whatever.

"Mr. Sawyer, I'm not feeling well."

I couldn't remember her ever leaving work. She'd called in sick now and then, but once she showed up, I never had to worry she was gonna change her mind and go home. I felt like a jerk sitting there when I could see she was out of sorts, so I got up and went into her area. "Sit down for a second, Bev. You okay?"

"I don't know," she said, looking pale. "I don't think so."

"You need to go home?"

"A little dizzy," she said.

"You want me to call someone?"

"No. Let me see if this passes. I'd like to make it home on my own."

I looked at my watch, feeling like a clod. "You

need me to run you? We can get someone to carry your car home for you later."

"This is so embarrassing," she said.

"Nothing to be embarrassed about," I said. "When you're ready, you tell me, and I'll take you home."

"I don't want you to miss your meeting. I'll get Ginny to sit in here for me."

"I can have you home and be back here in time," I said.

She called Ginny and told her she was feeling under the weather and needed her to fill in for the rest of the day. "Would you rather she take you home?" I whispered. I wasn't trying to get out of anything. I just didn't want her feeling self-conscious.

Bev shook her head and hung up, then stood slowly. She put both hands on the edge of her desk. I didn't know where to look or what to do. "I don't think she could help me if I fainted," Bev said.

Fainted? What was I supposed to do if she fainted? She reached for her bag, carefully slung it over her shoulder, took a deep breath, and moved away from the desk. I could have offered her my arm, but I didn't want her to feel—oh, face it, I would have felt conspicuous. I musta been blushing, following her down the hall and out to my car, praying nobody was watching. It woulda been easy to explain, a course, but you don't think about that kinda thing at the time.

"You wanna take some medication or something?" I said, opening the passenger door.

"Better not," she said, hesitating and straightening again. "Since I don't know what this is."

For some reason, that made me feel better. I didn't know what it was either, but I didn't have to worry it was something I didn't want to talk about. I settled behind the wheel while she tried to buckle herself in, but that took two hands and she kept wanting to press the one against her abdomen. "I don't think you need that belt for just a coupla miles," I said.

"I'd feel more comfortable with it," she said, looking at me, and I knew I was gonna hafta help. I held the receptacle in place but still she couldn't turn enough to get the clip into it. I grabbed that, but the belt had caught and tightened, so I had to let it snap back to the starting position. Now she was holding herself with one hand and keeping the other out of the way, so it was left to me to lean past her and do the whole seatbelt thing myself.

She held her breath as I did it, and so did I, but there was no way I was gonna avoid incidental contact, if ya know what I mean. So I just buckled down and buckled her up, didn't look at her, started the car, and got real serious about the rearview mirror. It hit me that I had worked with the woman for years and years and had never touched her, even by accident. I figured she was as embarrassed as I was.

"Thank you," she said quietly.

I drove slow through town, not wanting to look at Bev to see how she was doing. So instead I looked at all the closed businesses. I think they made the town look sicker'n Bev was. "Ever had appendicitis?" I said.

"No, and this is in the wrong spot for that." She was so quiet she hardly sounded like herself. "Must've been something I ate. This is so embarrassing."

"Think nothing of it." I was embarrassed enough for the both of us.

I pulled all the way up the drive so I was just a few feet from the front door of her little house. She kept one hand on her pain and unbuckled the seatbelt with the other, but the thing started sliding across her and then just stopped. She looked at me. I grabbed the clip and shook it a little until it rolled back into place. Then I sat there like a doofus.

"I hate to ask," she said, "but could you walk me?"

"Course!" I said, as if I hadn't considered anything else. I jogged around the car and offered my hand. She's a smallish woman, but she had trouble getting leverage. She seemed even unsteadier once she was standing. What I shoulda done, I knew, was put my left arm around her waist and let her hold my right hand with hers, but I couldn't get that coordinated soon enough. I just offered her my elbow and we slowly made our way to her door. She hung on like she was really hurting.

"Key?" I said.

"Haven't locked my door in twenty years." She reached to open it. I didn't know whether to help her in or what. "Think I'm okay from here," she said, giving me her car keys.

"Call if you need anything at all, 'kay?"

She thanked me and shut the door. I shoulda offered to call the doctor for her, taken her to Emergency, something.

19

I got back to the factory just in time to pull in behind Lee Forest. "I'd like to trade for your hours," he said, looking at his watch.

I held the door for him. "No, you wouldn't."

The three other older workers—Dave, Carl, and Belle—were waiting near Bev's area, chatting with Ginny. They kidded Lee the way he had me—"Glad you could make it," and all that. Ginny was full of whispered questions about Bev as I pointed the others into my office. Ginny had thought to add folding chairs.

"I'll let her tell you," I said. "Meanwhile, get a couple guys from maintenance to run her car home for her. They can use mine as a second car." I gave her both sets of keys and joined the others in my office.

The four people across from me represented the oldest long-term workers American Leather had ever had. Carl reminded me he remembered when my wife was born. Past that, he and the other two were with Lee just for moral support. As usual, he did the talking.

"Mr. Sawyer, we ain't the kinda people who

have a problem with young people being our boss."

"I know and I appreciate that."

"We go back as far as Estes himself, and it'd be easy to criticize anybody who came after him."

"Used to do that myself," I said. Every time he had a problem, a question, or an issue, he started the same way. My mind wandered as I sat taking in the signs of a lifetime of leatherwork in the arms and hands before me. Belle had mostly run the cutting machines and done lacing and inflating and molding. But the men had been turners in their younger days, using a straight or curved metal rod to help muscle the balls right-side out before the finishing process, and their biceps and forearms were massive and rocklike. Their fingers were orange, their knuckles big and bony, and nobody but their peers would dream of arm-wrestling em.

They were all in less strenuous jobs now, running the sewing machines or inserting bladders. But they were still eight-hour-a-day piece workers. They had seen the place humming and been there when the records were set that now faded on banners in the rafters.

"I know you can't do nothing bout the past," Lee said. "What's done is done, and no matter what anybody says, we know you held out long as you could before letting anybody go. But you know well as we do that we're down to where you just can't cut anymore and stay in business."

"Well, that's my problem, Mr. Forest," I said. "If more trimming can be done, I'll find it."

"I'm—we're not trying to tell you your business, but we been around long enough to know when you're at the limit."

"Getting close anyway," I admitted.

"It's down to just Wilson and us manufacturing stateside, ain't it?" he said.

"Yeah."

"How long before they go overseas?"

I shrugged. "They're fighting it tooth and nail like we are."

"We need something new," Lee said.

"Baseball gloves, I know," I said.

"That got to you, did it? Well, bless Bev's little heart." He paused. "You know, sir, you and her . . ."

"I'm studying ball gloves," I said.

"That's all we ask," he said, and the others smiled. "Glove leather is softer, easier to work with. More steps, but we can learn it. We can do it better'n anybody in the world, just like with the footballs, and we'd love the chance to prove it."

"Not thinking about retiring?"

Lee threw his head back and clapped both palms on his knees. "Retirement's for old people."

We chatted a few more minutes and I wasn't sure I was doing more than paying homage to loyal people. But they seemed happier after getting a little a my time. I didn't promise anything, but I saw in their eyes that they'd give it all they had if I was to add ball gloves to the line.

We were saying our good-byes when Ginny interrupted. "Sir, Alejandro is on your line and I think you'd better take it."

"I rang the doorbell and then I knocked, wanting to give Miz Beverly her car keys," the young man reported. "I thought maybe she was in the bathroom or asleep and couldn't get to the door. Stu said to just put the keys inside the door where she could find them, but when I pushed it open, I saw her on the floor."

I froze. "Was she, is she . . . ?"

"Stu went in with me and she looked okay, but her breathing was real shallow and her heartbeat was weak. We called the hospital."

"Good!"

"She's there now."

"Memorial?"

"Yes, sir. We're on our way back to work."

Why hadn't I seen her all the way inside and helped her lie down? How long might she have been on that floor if they hadn't found her? I told Ginny to call the school and tell em I might miss my class and to tell Coach Schuler I might be late for practice.

I jogged out to the parking lot, but course my car was gone. I spun around, and Ginny was at the door. "You let them use your car, sir." It was bad enough being an idiot. I hated that it showed. Luckily, here came Stu and Alejandro.

Twenty minutes later I slid to the curb at Memorial. Bev had already been assigned a room, and by the time I got there she was looking better. I wouldn't say perky, but she was okay enough to start apologizing. "You didn't have to come," she said.

I wished I hadn't. The sickening alcohol and cleaning supply smells were already starting to overwhelm me. Any time I got close to a place like that it reminded me of Estelle's awful final year. But I couldn't just bolt.

"What're they telling you?" I said.

"They drew blood and are running some tests. They might have to use a scope. They're guessing some kind of infection, bladder or intestinal, something."

"Serious?"

"They don't think so. See? Not worth any fuss."

After what I'd gone through with Estelle, I stayed away from hospitals as much as I could. Even when Rachel was a tomboy and needed patching, I was in and out of there too fast for memories to start kicking in. I had panicked when it looked liked something could be seriously wrong with Bev, but now I just wanted out of there. I guess she could tell.

"You go on now, Calvin. I'll get back to work as soon as they'll let me."

I stood in the doorway, lightheaded and miserable. "Take your time and take care of yourself," I said, trying to cover my restlessness.

I don't guess I succeeded. She waved at me with the back of her hand, shooing me out. I was grateful.

The players didn't say anything about Jackson running laps all during practice. I can tell you he didn't just put in his time, half running, half walking like most would have. He jogged at a pretty good clip, and every once in a while he would sprint a hundred yards or so. Then he would run the stairs. Nobody told him to do that. Coach pretended not to notice, but I know he did.

He spent most of his time hollering at the kids and talking about what he'd seen in the game film. I had watched it with him and was amazed that it looked even worse than I remembered in the live game. I couldn't even talk with him about it, it made him so mad. He got angrier every day, and I hate to say it, but we didn't see any progress on the practice field.

"I'm worried about myself," he told me as we left practice. "I don't even want to talk to this team anymore."

"There's plenty to say."

"It's just that the more I study that film, the more I see how far we've got to go."

"So tell em that."

He shook his head.

"Coming Wednesday night?" I said.

"Nah."

"You don't care?"

"I don't, Calvin."

"But if the kids somehow pull this off and the school stays open—"

"Ain't gonna happen and you know it."

He was right.

"Anyway," he said, "I'm seeing the wife tonight."

"Oh, sorry."

"Me too."

I didn't know whether to ask, so I did. "No progress there either?"

He shook his head and I left it alone.

I had learned to go to public functions separate from Rachel. She never seemed to mind being seen with me, but I knew not to push it. We were already pretty close for a dad and a teenager, but she was energetic and had her own mind and didn't need to have me with her all the time. I was as scared as any other dad that maybe I only thought I knew my little girl, but we'd had the talk—you know what I mean—and I trusted her. I know parents always think their kids are perfect, but if she was fooling around while also going to church and praying and reading her Bible and living like a Christian, well, she'd have more to answer to than me. I don't wanna be blind or naive, but, no, I'd've known.

Rachel and her friends had decorated the gym with a huge flag behind a small platform that had enough chairs for the school board. In front of that was a small wood lectern facing a couple hundred folding chairs, and the whole place was decked out with saving-the-school banners and posters.

I found a spot four or five rows back, across the aisle from where Rachel sat in the front row with Elvis Jackson. When no one sat near me I remembered how unpopular I was with people who had had a friend or relative lose his job at the factory. Even those who still worked there didn't want to rub it in by looking chummy with me. I glanced around and no one met my eyes cept

Bev's friend Kim, who was sitting near the back. I kinda wished I'd noticed her on the way in so I could tell her about Bev. But the way she looked at me made me figure she already knew.

Pretty soon everybody hushed and Principal Ferris stepped up and read a note:"We regretfully inform you that the members of the county school board will be unable to attend tonight's meeting. Please accept our apologies."

All of a sudden the mood changed. People were mad and griping out loud. Everybody seemed to be looking at the back of Rachel's head, including me. I don't know what kind of a program she'd planned, but I knew it was pretty much for the benefit of the county board. Her hope had been to get some sorta commitment out of em. Elvis whispered to her; she nodded and went to the podium. I was nervous for her.

Rachel smiled shyly when people applauded, and she pushed her hair behind her ear. I could only imagine how self-conscious she felt. I woulda been even worse.

"You know," she began, "if the county's not gonna support us, we have to do it ourselves." Many clapped."A lot of people have been leaving this town over the past few years, but the people in this gym love this town . . ." Now they were cheering."... and they love this school! And some of us students don't want to be bused to some other school. Everybody is always saying to put your money where your mouth is. If we show we are willing to do our part, the county board will know we're serious."

Shazzam hollered, "Oh, boy, here we go with the money pitch! You're sounding like church now, girl!"

"No, no, no," Rachel said. "I'm not asking you folks for a dime. We've already got the money." That got everybody's attention. "It is called the Jack Schuler Scholarship Fund." People gasped and groaned. She had lost her audience. "There are thousands of dollars in it we could use toward saving our school!" But people were waving her off and standing to leave. "Now come on folks! Some of you have younger kids! Do you really want em going to Rock Hill?"

People were leaving in droves. Even Elvis Jackson stood and stared Rachel down. "We can help hundreds of kids instead of just one football player!" she tried, but people booed. Jackson rushed past her. She grabbed him and the mike picked up her saying, "Elvis, I'm sorry."

He turned on her. "Save your prayers. I don't need em. And I don't want a groupie."

She looked like she'd been kicked in the gut. I wanted to gather her in or punch out Jackson, not to mention everybody who'd walked out on her. But I just sat there so she'd know I was still with her. When it was finally just her and me, I said, "Need a ride home?"

We didn't talk till we got in the door. "I'm not gonna win this, am I, Daddy?"

"No. But I love you for trying."

"You want me to go to Rock Hill next year?"

"Course not. But they're gonna have one heck of a football team with our underclassmen."

"That's not funny."

"Sorry."

"They don't need our guys anyway," she said.

Couldn't argue with that.

20

Thursday Coach showed up for practice angry as I'd ever seen him. He wouldn't look at me, wouldn't look at anybody. I couldn't imagine what had happened. It had to be something at the rehab center. I mean, how long can you stay mad over a bad game, a bad game film, bad practices? Maybe he was finally getting it that high schoolers just weren't the same as they used to be.

I didn't even get a chance to tell him about Bev. He starts in the coaches room telling me to have the players sit in front of their lockers with their gear on the floor. Once I had got em set, he came in, ears red, barely able to control himself. He wrote on the chalkboard the score of the first game, put his hat on the table, and began soft. "The other team is not your enemy. The spirit of division—that's your enemy."

He picked up a football program and leafed through it. "Here is a vision of unity. Rock Hill. Undefeated for two years and, get this, not even outscored for one half in all that time! This team is a well-oiled machine, a Detroit V-8 screaming down the highway to the state finals. This team has mastered the fundamentals, but you dawgs have not. Now some of you may be joining them next year, but until then . . ." and he slammed the Rock Hill program to the floor, ". . . we are gonna do things *my way*! That means we start over again and go all the way back to the beginning when God created football."

Coach picked up a ball and waved it in front of the boys. "This is fifteen ounces of pure, gen-u-ine American leather, sewn around a rubber sack, eight laces across the top." He slammed the ball into Brian's lap, picked up his shoulder pads, and smashed them to the floor. "These are shoulder pads!" He grabbed a thigh pad and slammed it down, then a knee pad. "Thigh pad! Knee pad!" He picked up a helmet and pushed it into Yash's stomach. "Helmet!"

The players recoiled with every throw and shout. "Each one of those things has its own specific function, and you all are going to rediscover *your* own specific function on this team!"

He put his hat on, said, "Coach, I'll see you outside," knocked over a water bucket, and kicked a football on his way out. We followed him to the tennis courts. It was an old tradition at Athens City that independent players got their minds right there.

"First we crawl," Coach said. "Then we walk. Then we walk together. Then we run the bone."

The two courts were made of hard-packed dirt, with a fence separating them. Coach placed the ball down and told the offense and defense to line up. "Jackson," he said, "you come in at halfback. You want in the game, you're gonna learn the bone. We're gonna learn the old-fashioned way. Crime gets punished in Bama."

He put me in charge of the offense. "Call Formation Left 39 every time," he told me. The only way that play works is for the runner to turn upfield when he gets the ball and follow the quarterback and the blocking guard. Start improvising or get tempted by what looks like lots of daylight if you skirt past them to the outside and, well, the play breaks down and you're toast. On the tennis court, the fence either helps a runner avoid that temptation or becomes the price he pays.

The defense was inspired because Jackson was carrying the ball every time, and they were led by the Shermanater—who Jackson had tricked into letting him stay in the game. Time after time Naters let his teammates key on the blockers while he shot through and drove Jackson into the fence.

"No, no, no!" Coach would scream. "You're running thirty to gain five! Trust your blockers! Turn upfield! Follow them! There's nowhere to go out here. Those dawgs are working to make a hole for you. Your job is to follow them and when you get there, trust the hole's gonna be open. You ignore them, they become useless. Line up and do it again."

Again and again and again. "Trust your blockers. One more time!"

After one smash into the fence, Coach grabbed Jackson's facemask and pointed him first to his left, then upfield. "Not that way! That way! Gain and maintain!"

Jackson bled, arms shredded. Finally I whispered to Coach, "You always said we squeeze coal to make diamonds, not tear it to pieces."

"We got a colt needs breaking," he said. "Do it again."

After a bunch more times getting blasted into that fence, Jackson couldn't get up. Coach said, "One more time." Jackson didn't stir. Other players bent over, sucking wind. Buster stood over Jackson and hollered, "Water break!"

Elvis started to stir, but Coach put a foot on his shoulder pad and held him down. "Not for you, dawg. Until you learn to trust your teammates, you're not good enough to drink with em." He knelt and knocked on Jackson's helmet. "Whatsa matter, Jackson, you on empty? Is that all you got? I don't need a quitter. Turn in your gear."

Coach stood and stepped back, and Jackson came flying to his feet. "No!" he shouted. "This is not over! I am not off this team! Do you hear me? One more time!"

Coach, squinting, shot me a glance. Jackson ran back into position. Coach blew his whistle and announced, "Let's go home."

21

Rachel waited for Elvis after practice, determined to confront him. But as he limped past ahead of Abel, he didn't even look up. "Elvis!" she called, alarmed at his wounds. "What happened?"

"Tradition," Abel said.

Rachel would not be put off. She followed Elvis on foot but lost him a couple of miles out of town as he jogged through a cotton field. She found herself at Orville Washington's farm, holding her nose at the sweetly acrid acres of manure spread amid the crop. She had sweat through the back of her blouse and it stuck to her.

There was no sign of Mr. Washington, a generous-sized black man who lived alone and tended the farm with a passel of day workers. Rachel crept between the barns and outbuildings and was soon forty or fifty yards from the farmhouse near a rickety stable, clearly past its use.

She jumped when she heard Elvis. "You're trespassing. Now go away."

Rachel stepped inside the stable and peered up at the loft. Elvis was silhouetted against the dim light. "Unless Mr. Washington knows you're here," she said as she climbed planks nailed to the wall, "you're trespassing too."

Elvis busied himself with a bucket of water and a rag, dabbing his scraped forearms. His clothes hung on makeshift lines attached to the rafters. "What are *you* doing following me?"

"I was afraid you were hurt."

He rolled his eyes. "Ah. And let me guess—you wanted to pray for me."

"As a matter of fact, no," Rachel said, stepping close and staring into angry blue eyes. "I am not trying to steal your scholarship, and whether or not you like it, it is my job to pray for you, so you might as well get used to it."

He glowered. "Why don't you just admit you betrayed me?"

"Why don't *you* just admit you're acting like a three-year-old?"

"All right," he said, plopping onto a cot in the corner. "I accept your apology."

Rachel sat next to him. "Wow, this little groupie is just overwhelmed." He was clearly not amused. "I'm on your team, Elvis. Long before I laid eyes on you I thought we could use that money for the school. I didn't want to hurt you." She studied him. "What happened to you today?"

Elvis shrugged. "Good old Athens City tradition."

She took the rag from him, working on one of his deeper scratches. "You know, last time Coach Schuler was here, our school was the envy of the state. You could learn something from him." Elvis met her gaze, then looked away. "Listen," she said, "I'm not gonna say anything to my dad or anyone else about you living up here."

"Thanks."

"So why *are* you up here?"

No response.

"*Why* are you up here, Elvis?"

He seemed to realize Rachel wasn't going to let him off the hook. "This is my last shot," he said. "No money for college. This phony address could be my ticket."

"That's how you registered for school?"

He nodded. "Farmer scratches his head and writes Return to Sender on stuff from the school that comes in my name. I snag it before the mailman comes back for it."

Rachel handed the rag back and moved toward the ladder, wondering if her dad knew any of this. "Know what?" she said. "I believe there's more to you than you think."

He looked curious. "I've never met anyone who believes in things the way you do," he said. "What is it with you?"

Rachel hesitated. Elvis had made it clear he wasn't interested in prayer, let alone God. Maybe if she didn't push now, a better time and place would come. "I'm a Crusader," she said.

22

Coach and I stayed late to rechalk the lines on the field. The custodial staff had been cut deep, so we couldn't expect them to do it. It felt good doing manual labor again. Something about desk work had always bothered me.

I was surprised when I got home to find a note from Rachel. "Daddy, I'm sure you know Bev is in the hospital and not well. I'm visiting her. Her friend Kim will bring me home."

Not well? Someone must have got old information. But when Rachel wasn't home an hour later, I called the hospital. "We're unable to provide information to other than immediate family members," they told me.

"I'm her employer."

"You might like to come down, Mr. Sawyer."

"What's happened? I thought—"

"Really, sir, I'm prohibited by policy—"

I almost had to sit down. "She's taken a turn—?"

"Please feel free to come down, Mr. Saw—"

"Tell me she's still alive."

"I can tell you that, yes. But you won't be able to see her. She's in ICU."

I sped to the hospital feeling something I hadn't felt for a long time. I ran from the car, hurried past the desk, and took the elevator to the Intensive Care Unit. Rachel and Kim stood in the hall, their eyes red. Rachel hugged me but Kim seemed the same as she'd been Wednesday night. I explained that Bev had seemed fine and had told me to leave. "What in the world happened?"

"If you cared about her," Kim said, "you'd have stayed and you would know."

That hurt, but I didn't want to defend myself by telling her I had feelings I couldn't explain. Rachel gave Kim a sharp look but knew better than to correct an elder. "The tests found, um—"

"Diverticulitis," Kim said. "Serious enough, but treatable if caught early, and this was."

"So she's fine then?"

"Yeah," Kim said. "That's why we're here."

I didn't figure I deserved her being sarcastic.

"Daddy," Rachel said slowly, as if she knew she was about to embarrass me, "they found this diver-whatever with a probe."

"Okay . . ." I said.

Kim turned and walked into the waiting room. I looked to Rachel as if to ask what I'd done. Rachel shrugged. "They made some kind of a mistake. The scope punctured her colon."

The place was getting to me again, and that news didn't help. I needed to sit down, so I stumbled into the waiting room where Kim looked up from praying. I wished she'd pray for me. I didn't want to talk to her and was glad to see Rachel had followed me in. She sat next to me and took my hand.

Kim stood and stared down at me. "This is not about you, Calvin. Whatever you're feeling, Bev is fighting for her life. I'm surprised you thought her worth the trip."

How could Kim know what I was feeling when I didn't? She had lost her dad, but would she remember what my Estelle had died of? I didn't know if somebody whose doctor had poked through her colon was supposed to live or die. How did they treat diverticulitis and an injury like that at the same time?

I hadn't figured out yet why I'd felt so panicky when I heard the news. Was it cause here was another woman in my life with a problem in the same part of her body? Or *was* I being selfish, worried how I'd get along at the office without Bev? Ah, it was more than that. I had to know whatever I could know and do whatever I had to do to make sure she would be all right.

"Has the doctor talked to you?" I said. "Either of you?"

"Not for a while," Rachel said. "I'll see if I can find him."

"Leave him alone," Kim said. "Let him do his work."

"I won't keep him from his work, Miz Kim," she said, an edge in her voice.

"Feeling guilty?" Kim said when Rachel had gone.

"You're doing your best to make me feel that way."

"Calvin, there are no secrets in this town. Bev falls ill, you run her home—surprise of all surprises—and you're back to the office in time to stay on schedule. You have somebody else take her her car or she might have died in her own house. You come by here when you find out—another shocker—but again it was fortunate for Bev you were between commitments."

"I do have commitments."

"To a class and football practice, both of which would have survived without you."

I stood. "She didn't need me, Kim! What could I have done here?"

She shook her head. "You don't get it. After all those years of serving you, she wouldn't even ask that you sit with her a few hours. Did either she or you know what was wrong with her when you left?"

"They hadn't injured her yet, if that's what you mean. She said they were running tests. I couldn't have stopped whatever happened."

"Calvin! Listen to yourself. If you were Bev, wouldn't you have felt better knowing someone was standing with you, would be there when you got your test results? No, she couldn't have known something would go wrong, but it would have had to make her feel better to know someone was here with her."

"She told me to go."

"And you were glad to. I'll bet you couldn't get out of here fast enough. Did you even think to call me?"

"It crossed my mind. But I know you're busy."

"Not as busy as you, apparently. Calvin, she's my dearest friend. She stood with me for *years*, asking nothing while my father slowly died. You think I wouldn't have taken a personal day to sit with her a few hours?"

What could I say? I hadn't even known how much *I* cared for Bev until a few minutes before. Kim was not the person to tell.

"I'm sorry," I said. "I should have called you."

"More important, you should have stayed with her from the minute she started feeling bad. It should have been obvious this wasn't her period or the flu."

I nodded. "Maybe I learned something," I said.

"I would love to think so."

"Give me a break, Kim," I said. "You want me to learn from this or don't you?"

She stood and moved to the window where she stared out into the darkness. "Maybe I've given up on you after all this time."

"After all what time?"

"All the years Bev has invested in you and you've been oblivious."

"There's that word again. Well, if I'm oblivious to one loyal worker, I'm probably oblivious to a lot of them."

Kim turned to face me. "That's not your reputation. People love you, Cal. You've had to make some tough decisions, but they forgive you because they trust you and admire you."

"Everybody but Bev."

"I didn't say that."

"Then what are you saying?"

"She feels the same about you that everybody else does."

Where was that doctor? "So you're the only one who knows I'm a phony?"

"I didn't say that either."

"I wish you'd tell me what you're saying, Kim. I'm feeling pretty beat up here."

"Poor Cal," she said. "All right, sit down and

listen." I did. "Here's what happened. I was going to be late meeting up with Bev the night she got sick, and when I called to tell her, Ginny-somebody from your office told me what had happened. When I got here she had come back from the colonoscopy. Over the next several hours she had some pain and some bleeding, which I was told were not uncommon. But then she developed a high fever and wouldn't eat. Her pulse went up and her blood pressure down.

"The doctor kept telling me this could still be a diverticulitis flare-up, but when she became nauseated and her abdomen tender, he had to start paying attention. Next time he examined her, her abdomen was rigid and hard and I heard him tell someone there were nearly no bowel sounds. I asked a nurse what that meant, and she said infection and inflammation must have spread."

"From this divertic—"

"Well, they thought it was something called peritonitis and they did some kind of a CAT scan or something and found air in the abdomen. Calvin, she was lying there with her knees flexed and her breathing short like the pain was excruciating."

"Oh, man!"

"They did a quick exploratory surgery and discovered the hole in the colon. I knew they were upset by how long they feared she had infectious material in there."

I sat shaking my head. "Well, thanks for telling me, anyway, Kim." She just walked out.

Guess by now you can tell I'm not what you'd call self-analytical. I was sitting there trying to pray and more clueless than ever about what was going through my brain. The waiting room was far enough from the patient rooms that I ought not to have been bothered by the smells, but my nose must have a memory. The place was making me sick, but no way was I gonna walk out on Bev. For one thing, I wanted to know from the doctor exactly what was going on, and besides, Kim was right. This wasn't about me.

I don't like flower shops either cause I can't shake the memory of the smell at Estelle's funeral. But I know I'm not alone in that and you can't live your life avoiding normal places just because you took one in the chops years ago at a place that reminds you of this one. I mean, the smells just brought back bad memories. It wasn't like they were as bad as a locker room or even the Chicago cowhide plant I'd been to so many times. I had to decide to put up with the hospital smell. There was enough to think about without dwelling on

Estelle, and I told myself she'd want me to think about her in heaven anyway, not in a hospital bed.

Rachel finally dragged the doctor into the waiting room, and that brought Kim back too. He looked apologetic. "Like I was telling the young lady, I can give you a general update because you are apparently her closest support group here, but as for a specific diagnosis or prospects for recovery, I'd need her permission to share that with other than blood relatives."

I was glad to see Kim turn her guns on somebody besides me. "We already know about the diverticulitis," she said. "And we know about the malpractice too, so—"

"Now, ma'am," the doctor said, "if you're going to take that tone and go that route, you're going to find me unable to say anything. We have acknowledged our responsibility for a procedural error, but—"

"That's a nice way to put it. Some bozo turns an early-caught case of diverticulitis into a life-threatening situation, and—"

"So," the doctor said, "you'd rather talk with our attorney than with me."

"No," Kim said. "Trust me, Beverly is not the type to file suit regardless, so—"

"Oh, *that* will put our counsel's mind at ease. 'Her friend says she won't sue us.'"

"Okay, truce," Kim said. "Her parents are elderly and live in Virginia. If they can afford the flights, they might be here late tomorrow. In the meantime—"

"Kim," I said, "that's not an issue. Soon as we're done here, you tell em to book the next flight they can and American Leather will cover it. We'll even have someone pick em up in Mobile."

"You're American Leather?" the doctor said. "I thought I recognized you." He shook my hand.

Kim said, "Why, thank you, Calvin. I'll call them right now."

When she left I appealed to my new friend. "Doc, Bev's worked for me for more than ten years and she's like family. It didn't skip past me what you said there about prospects for recovery. Now I gotta know if that's just words you use or if you're saying there's some question about her even making it."

He pressed his lips together and stared at the ceiling. Then he glanced at Rachel and back at me. "My daughter," I said.

"The next forty-eight hours are crucial," he said, sighing. I felt that feeling of panic again. "We're keeping her in intensive care so we can keep an eye out for complications."

"She could die is what you're telling me."

"We certainly hope not and we don't expect that."

"But it could happen."

"It could. Now, if you'll excuse me . . ."

I dropped back down into a chair. At least with Estelle we'd known she was dying; we just hadn't known when. I reached for Rachel's hand and she sat with me again. "Prayer changes things," I said. "We can at least do that."

"I prayed for Mama," she said.

I looked at her. "You know she's better off."

She nodded. "I'm not gonna quit praying, Daddy, but I'm not gonna pretend we always get the answers we want. I'm praying for the school, for the town, for Elvis. You know I'm gonna pray for Miz Bev. You should've told me yesterday. I've been praying for her ever since I heard."

"How *did* you hear?"

"Kim."

"I didn't even know you knew Kim."

"Daddy! Everybody knows Kim. She was my Sunday school teacher once."

"Mine too."

"I know."

"But why would she call you?"

She let go of my hand and ran her fingers through her hair. "Cause Bev and I've been doing stuff together."

"Stuff?"

"Going places. Doing things."

"That's where you've been?"

"A lot of the time."

"You didn't think I'd want to know that?"

"She didn't know what you'd think."

I squinted at Rachel. "What were you doing that neither of you thought I ought to know?"

"Volunteer stuff."

"All right," I said, "I want more'n one sentence at a time. What're you talking about?"

She sighed. "Everybody loves Bev, right?"

I nodded.

"She visited the youth group one Sunday night last spring. She was just telling us her story, you know, how she was raised in a good Christian home but had to choose Jesus for herself."

"Just like you."

"Just like anybody. That's what got my attention anyway. She told us how when she got out of high school and started working at the factory, she kinda drifted. From the Lord, I guess."

"I don't remember that. What was she doing?"

"Nothing bad. Just kinda being a Sunday Christian is what she called it. Going to church but not really thinking about it the rest of the week. Not wanting people to know she was a Christian, that kinda stuff."

"I think everybody goes through that," I said.

"That's what she said. And she was trying to keep us from it. She said that even though she didn't do anything terrible, she felt like she wasted a lot of years before she really gave herself to God. She went on some kind of a college and career group thing and heard a guy talking about choosing up sides, making a commitment, deciding whether you're in or out. It just got to her somehow. She started really feeling nervous when he talked about being a Secret Service Christian, kinda covering your bases by believing the right stuff and going to church, but keeping your identity private, you know."

I nodded.

"Anyway, Daddy, she really put it to us. She said we were old enough to decide for ourselves whether we were really sincere, and if we were, it ought to show. She asked for kids to raise their hands if they wanted to get serious and start acting out their faith and making their lives count. A bunch of us raised our hands, but Miz Bev pushed even more. She said there were all kinds of things we could be doing for God, even though we were busy. She told us there were people who needed stuff done for em, old people who liked to be read to, sick people that needed visitors. I thought everybody got excited about it like I did, cause so many of the kids looked like they were really listening. I didn't expect to be the only one who actually started going with her a lot."

"Where?"

"Like she said, the old folks home, poor people's houses, the rehab center."

"In Fairhope?"

Rachel raised her eyebrows and nodded.

Kim rejoined us. "Bev's parents will be here midmorning tomorrow," she said, "thanks to you. Really, Calvin, that was—"

"Can we stay with her?" I said.

"Close by."

"What shift you want?"

Kim looked surprised. "I'll take first," she said. "You take Rachel home and get some rest, and then you can be here when Bev's parents arrive."

I got their information and left a message for Ginny to have someone pick em up and get em to the hospital. I told Kim I'd spell her at dawn. I couldn't believe how exhausted I was.

"Rachel," I said as we drove home, "tell me why I shouldn't be hurt that both you and Bev kept this from me."

She hesitated. "That was Kim's idea. She worried that you'd think Bev was trying to get to you through me."

"Get to me? For what?"

"Oh, Daddy."

"What?"

"Don't be dense."

"Too late. I'm lost."

"That's what's got Kim so upset with you."

"She thinks I don't treat Bev right."

"What she thinks is that you don't get it."

"All right, I'll bite. Bev's taking you away from me somehow cause I did something she didn't like or didn't do something she wished I'd done?"

"No! Not that kind of getting to you. She knew you'd like it if she got me really interested in helping people and doing something about it."

"You've always been that way. You got it from your mama."

"But Bev didn't want it to look like she was trying to impress you by showing so much interest in me."

I parked next to the house and Rachel reached for her door handle. "Just a minute," I said. "Bev already impresses me. She's the best worker I've ever had, does everything for me, takes care of me. And it *does* make me feel good that she's taken you under her wing. So what would be wrong with my knowing that?"

The evening was cool and Rachel looked like

she wanted to get inside, but I wanted to finish this. I'd never claimed to be a smart guy, but I've got enough a what they call street smarts to have kept a business alive longer than it shoulda kept breathing. What was I missing here? "Tell me," I said.

"Daddy, don't you have feelings for Bev?"

Well, *there* was some good timing, cause I didn't know what to think of how I'd felt when I thought Bev could die. And since I couldn't get any more optimism outa that doctor, I was still worried about her, and probably more than I shoulda been about someone not related to me. "Course I do," I said. "I appreciate her more than I can say right now, and her being sick has made me realize that."

"That's it?"

"For now."

"What's that mean, Daddy?"

"I'm just trying to figure it out myself is all."

"Have you figured out if she's got feelings for you?"

"I know she does."

"You do?"

"She takes care of me, Rachel. She's always been like a big sister. She listens. She tells me what she thinks. She knows the kind of stuff I like for lunch and break."

"Wow, isn't that amazing after working for you for ten years?"

Rachel wasn't sarcastic often. "Well," I said, "okay. But she's great, you know? I couldn't ask for better."

"You ever wonder why she's never dated?"

I shrugged. "Busy? Picky, probably. Knows her own mind, knows what she wants. Never found the right guy."

"Yes, she did."

"Well, see, there's something you know that I don't, cause you've been spending time with her. But course that'd be kind of an embarassing thing to talk about with your boss, personal stuff."

"You don't talk to her about your personal business?"

"Naw," but as soon as I said it I realized how short my memory was. It hadn't been that long since I told her about Jacqui. "Well, not much."

"Why? Cause it's not right to do at the office?"

"Sorta."

"Why not take her out and talk personal stuff?"

I shook my head. "We don't see each other like that. She's older, and—"

"How much older?"

I was thinking six or seven years and almost said that when I thought back real quick. I had been a sophomore in high school when she was a senior. And it had been just a couple years since her big fortieth birthday bash. "She's, um, two years older, but see I see her as—"

"Two years is nothing for old people," Rachel said.

Now *I* was getting cold. She looked relieved when I got out of the car, and we hurried in to the warmth of the front room. She sat on the couch like she was ready to keep talking. I wanted her to get her sleep, and I hoped I could rest too, getting up so early.

"Daddy, you don't know what Bev thinks of you, do you?"

"I think I do."

"Well, I know I do, so you want to guess?"

"I think she likes working for me, and she always treats me with respect and I'd say even admiration."

"Admiration?"

"Some people find me admirable. Is that so hard to imagine?"

"Daddy, Bev is old-fashioned. She's not gonna make a move until you do."

"Make a move?"

"She's desperately in love with you."

Rachel couldn't know that. "Get off it," I said, trying to keep from smiling.

She stood and headed for her room. "You heard me," she said.

"You and Kim are dreaming," I called after her.

"No, we're not," she said. "We're listening."

I was supposed to sleep after that? I set the alarm and stretched out, my hands behind my head. Somewhere deep inside I had known where Rachel was going, but I couldn't let on. Trouble was, how bad was this? If I didn't feel the same, was I going to lose Bev as my assistant too? And wouldn't Kim love to hear me talking about that!

I admit I missed Bev when she wasn't there or I was traveling. I couldn't remember not wanting to get to work every morning, even when there was nothing but turmoil cause of the layoffs. What else would I be looking forward to than seeing her? Besides being great at her work, I always felt like she was glad to see me and happy to do whatever it took to make my work easier.

How long had she felt this way? Old-fashioned is right. Unless I totally insulted her by never picking up on it or treating her like a big sister instead of somebody I really cared about, she'd probably stay another twenty years and never, like Rachel said, make a move.

I rolled onto my side. A light from behind the

house shined through the edge of the curtain onto Estelle's picture. All I could make out was the shape of her shoulders and hair. I forced myself back to high school and remembered the eyes of a teenager. But I couldn't conjure the face of the woman I'd married. I stared and stared and worked at it, but the face in my mind was Bev's.

The panic, the concern, the shame over just dumping her at her house—I knew what that all was now. It wasn't selfishness. It wasn't worrying how I'd replace her at the factory. I didn't want to be without her. If she should die in the same hospital and from something similar to Estelle . . .

Well, that didn't matter at all. This had nothing to do with Estelle except that she'd been gone so long. Bev made me happy. Bev was a bigger part of my life, of me, than I had let myself think. I couldn't lose her. And for all my total embarrassment over the idea of even putting my arm around her the other day, all I wanted to do now was hold her. Who else would care as much? Who else should be standing with her now? I lay there praying for a good block a time between when I traded places with Kim and when Bev's parents showed up.

ICU rules and regulations or not, one of these days I was gonna get in to see Bev. She'd need her energy to get better and I didn't want to mess her mind with something we wouldn't even be able to talk about till later. But I wasn't gonna hide my feelings or pretend I didn't know about hers. If nothing else, I was gonna somehow let her know that nothing mattered to me more than her getting better. The reasons and the details could wait.

23

I was early, but Kim seemed relieved, and she brought me up to date quick. Bev had had a fitful night, but she never woke up enough for anybody to tell her Kim was there. The nurse said that whatever good might come from Bev knowing someone was with her would be outweighed by her need for sleep.

"Should she wake up today, Calvin, would you tell her I—"

"Course, Kim, and she won't be surprised. I spose she'll mostly be surprised that I'm here."

"I was about to say the same, but you are here, and that means a lot to me, so I know it will to her too. Do me a favor. If she asks why you're here, don't say anything, not one word, about work."

"Work?"

"Even if the reason you're here is because you think she's the best employee you've ever had, it'd mean more to her if she thought—"

"It's because I'm her friend. Give me a little credit, Kim."

"There's hope for you yet."

"You gonna be able to get a little shuteye before heading to work?"

"Probably not," she said. "But thanks for asking."

"You want me to call you if—"

"That'd be great. I'll probably go home at noon or so and sleep until evening visiting hours. Will you still be here or do you have to get to the factory?"

"I'll be here," I told her. "Praise the Lord for phones, huh?"

I couldn't believe how long it'd been since I'd seen the Raschkes. They'd moved out of Athens City about a month after Estelle died. I never knew em well, but everybody knows everybody in a town our size. One thing was sure, they looked their age. Course they probably hadn't slept and they were worried. I couldn't get anything but the simplest greeting out of the old man and I soon saw that he had some kind of dementia. The missus took charge, got the head nurse to bring the doctor, and she and her husband spent quite a while with him in a little office.

Mrs. Raschke talked to me like she thought she knew why I was there. "I've heard a lot about you, Mr. Sawyer, and we so appreciate how good you've been to Bev." She told me what the doctor had told her, which was what I'd heard the night before. When she talked to her husband she put her face right in front of his and held both his hands. He seemed like he was on the edge of tears the whole time and didn't understand much. Somebody told em they could go in and see Bev for ten minutes if they did their best not to wake her.

I watched them tiptoe in and go to either side of the bed. They carefully put a hand under each of hers. Bev didn't stir. I was so jealous I could hardly stand it. I wanted to go in there and slip my arm under Bev's neck and draw her to me, telling her she was gonna be all right, that I loved her and would always be with her. Talk about waking her up. That probably would've killed her.

It was all I could do to switch gears and think about football, but the Raschkes said I should go and fulfill my responsibilities to the team. I slipped away praying Bev would wake up soon but sort of hoping she'd wait till I was there.

We played our second and last nonconference game that Friday night, September 14, against the Plateau Pirates. In warm-ups and early in the game it was obvious they had a good club.

Just like in the first game, everything started out wrong, specially on offense. Our defense was getting chewed up too, but somehow we kept em out of the end zone. Brian couldn't get anything going when we had the ball. I didn't want to nag, but I kept looking at Coach like it was time to try Jackson. Coach kept throwing his hat down and rubbing his head every time we failed to move the ball and Snoot had to punt. Finally Coach shrugged and nodded.

I called for Jackson. He looked up from the bench like he was startled. I said, "Yeah, you!"

"You like running through fences, son?" Coach said. "Now's your chance. You run through the hole, boy, or your next practice is gonna be on a bed of nails."

At the half it was scoreless, but Coach was still mad cause the Pirates were making us look bad. "Hello, Crusaders," he began in the locker room. "Anyone awake? Can anybody explain how they can cut through our defense—except for Naters—like a hot knife through butter? Abel! I require a reply!"

"Coach, you told us that if—"

"If? If! If my mama was my daddy, I wouldn't be here. Why don't you go running. Go run and take Yash with ya."

He lifted them off their seats and pushed them toward the door. Yash said, "Coach, we're in a game!"

"Not anymore you're not. Now go!" They would wind up running laps the entire second half.

Coach whipped his jacket off and turned to his nephew. "Brian, what kind a sport is football?"

"Contact sport, sir!" Brian said.

"Contact sport? Everybody agree with that? Let me see a show of hands." Coach smacked every hand he could reach. "Wrong, wrong, wrong! Football is a *collision* sport!" He knelt before Brian and pointed in his face. "You're supposed to be a leader on this team, son, and you are running our offense like a fat man on a frozen pond!" He pointed at Elvis. "Now until I say otherwise, every play is gonna be a handoff to Jack!"

Everyone froze, including me. We'd all heard him call Elvis Jack, but I studied his face on the way back out to the field, and Coach never seemed to realize it.

The second half was Jackson left, Jackson right, Jackson up the middle. Coach roamed the sidelines shouting, "Let the bone roll!" But even with Elvis racking up over a hundred yards, we still couldn't punch it in for a score. With fifteen seconds left, it was still nothing-nothing, third and goal on their 4-yard line. We'd played a pretty lousy game overall, but it sure was fun to be in a close one and have the fans screaming.

I thought we should let Snoot kick a field goal, but Buster called time out and told Brian to send

Jackson up the middle. "Coach," Brian whined, "they're waiting for that!"

"Jackson up the gut."

But Jackson didn't run up the gut. When the hole closed he ran right, then circled back, got tripped up, and fumbled. Brian, who had stayed put like he was supposed to, picked up the loose ball. With time running out, he ran it in for the win.

The crowd and the team went crazy. Elvis ran to the end zone and jumped to celebrate, and a big lineman from Plateau sent him sprawling. The Sher-manater pile-drove the Pirate to the ground, and a huge brawl broke out. Three guys from our bench raced onto the field and got into it. Yash and Abel finally quit running and Yash joined the fight.

When it was finally over and the Pirates were on their way back to Plateau, Coach told me, "Remind the boys this wasn't much to celebrate. And I want everybody on the field once they're dressed."

I got em out there and Coach started grabbing guys one by one. "You," he said, pulling Brian and then Elvis out of the pack and pushing them onto the sideline, "and you, line up over there." He kept grabbing guys. "You, and you, and you, over there."

Finally fifteen guys were separated from the rest, and I think pretty much everybody'd figured out that he had picked all the ones who'd been in the brawl. He turned his back to the others and said to those fifteen, "I do not believe that fighting makes you tough." They looked down.

Then Coach spun and pointed at the rest of the team. "But I know, I *know* that standing on the sidelines watching makes you a coward. Now the rest of y'all don't know what it means to be a team, and I don't want to see you on my field again. You go on and go home. Go on!"

It was like the air went out of everybody, me included. Abel, who had watched from the sideline when Yash raced onto the field, said, "You've got to be kidding."

Coach turned his back on him.

I could hardly believe it myself, but I knew one thing: Buster Sawyer never said anything just for effect. He had just fired thirty-three guys off his football team. That just left Brian Schuler, Sherman Naters, Yash Upshaw, Snoot Nino, Elvis Jackson, and ten other guys who, as Coach said, knew what it meant to be a team. Well they'd really be finding out now.

Coach stepped in front of Elvis. "You fumble my ball one more time, and I will not give you a second chance." He paused. "See y'all Monday."

I spent every spare minute at the hospital, but now they were telling me Bev was intentionally being kept in a coma. The hospital wasn't saying much—covering their own tails if you ask me—but this was sounding more serious than I feared.

I sat outside Bev's room most of the day Sunday and finally went to church that night. After the service, where we prayed for Bev, Coach told me, "Got to face the music in the most public place we can."

"We?"

"You're not still with me?"

"Course, but I got enough enemies in this town. Former employees, for instance."

"So, I'm on my own."

"What are you asking me to do?" I said.

"Sit with me at breakfast at Tee's before school."

"That's pretty public, all right."

"That's the idea."

"At least Tee's boy is still on the team."

Back at the hospital that night, I told Rachel. "I'll be there too then," she said.

"Rachel ..."

"I *will*. Anybody with a brain knows Coach did the right thing."

"Cept the kids who got booted and their parents."

"They're wrong, that's all."

"Yeah, but the man kicked kids off the team for *not* fighting, Rachel."

"That's why I'll be with him and you tomorrow morning, Daddy."

I called Coach and told him.

"Well," he said, "she won't be the only teenager at our table. My nephew will be there too."

Next morning, Tee's was packed and people were waiting for tables. But like she'd known we were coming, Tee left one open, and Elvis pointed us to it when we walked in the door. The place went quiet, but Coach, cool as a poker player, ordered as soon as he sat down across from Brian.

Just over my left shoulder at the next table sat Abel Gordon, his dad, Andy, and Josie. Out of the corner of my eye I sensed Andy's hateful stare. He didn't say anything till our food arrived and we had just looked up from praying.

"Schuler's a danged lunatic," he said, loud enough for everybody in the place. Several obviously agreed. "You don't punish players for not fighting, especially during senior season when college is on the line."

"Pass the salt," Buster said quietly.

"And that assistant coach is softer than a Georgia peach with rain rot."

Now I'm a Christian, but I confess that's not what I was thinking just then. Rachel's mouth was thin and tight and her eyes had narrowed. I kept chewing, trying to be an example. Brian was looking between Coach and me, as if wondering who was gonna be the one to shut the guy's mouth.

"No wonder Schuler's own son—"

Rachel dropped her fork and it clanged so loud everybody jumped, and Big Mouth actually shut up for a second.

"Ain't it funny," Rachel said aloud, "how the dumbest people always have the most to say?"

Coach stared at her with admiration, and Brian looked like he was about to burst out laughing. Andy Gordon's chair scraped the floor and he stood. "You ought to teach your daughter to keep her mouth shut!"

I swallowed. There's a limit to what a man will take, and Mr. Gordon had just stepped past mine. I've had laid-off workers and their families call me everything in the book, but you say something about Rachel, you're gonna answer to me.

My heart was racing, and as I stood, so did Brian, but Coach stopped him with a gesture and he sat back down. Now all I could see was Andy Gordon's sneer. "Maybe you ought to watch your mouth," I said, and he stood there with his eyes locked on mine, hands on his hips. I'm afraid what I mighta done to him if he'd made a move.

Coach stood and whispered, "Sit down now, Sawyer. This is not the place for this."

He gave me an out, and I took it. But he wasn't finished with Mr. Gordon. "You know, Andy, if your boy had the fight you had twenty-five years ago, he'd still be on my team."

"My son belongs on that football team!" Andy's voice was shaky. "You just cost him his only chance at a scholarship."

"Oh, now there it is!" Coach said. "The trouble with you people is that you see me, you see this team, as a gate to greener pastures. But until you succeed right here, you don't deserve greener pastures. Your boy and I have different definitions of success. And I see where he got his."

Mr. Gordon slapped a bill on the table and walked out, Abel rising slowly to follow. He stopped halfway out and came back to get Josie, who sat there with a red face, tears streaming. As she stood she looked at Rachel. "This is why I hate football," she said.

That afternoon in the fading twilight, Coach and I stood facing the fifteen remaining players. They looked scared. On the way out, Coach had told me to say something inspirational.

"Inspirational?" I said.

"You teach Sunday school, don't ya? Give em

something from one a your classes, then I'll take over."

"Thanks for the time to think about it."

"More time I give you, Sawyer, the more you worry and look for reasons to get out of it."

I couldn't argue that. And now we were standing there, and he was looking at me. "Boys," I said, "Gideon went to war against an army of thousands with only three hundred soldiers, because they were the only men with the guts to fight and win."

As if we'd rehearsed it, Buster took over. "I can go to war with even less than what's right here in front of me. So if any of you are afraid of getting hurt, or of losing, you can leave right now."

They sat still except for Elvis Jackson, who got up off the bench and slipped past Coach and me. He stopped on the field, jamming on his helmet and fastening the strap.

Coach came alive. "You know, that's just what I thought! There is not one quitter on this team! Now the last one off this bench is gonna run laps. Let's go!"

The rest leaped up and whooped and hollered. They gathered around Coach and he barked assignments. He told Brian, "Outside linebacker," and Elvis, "Safety."

As Coach continued through the group, Brian

edged up to Elvis and pressed his facemask against his. "It's gonna take more than speed now, boy. You're gonna have to show some brains."

"Just call my number," Elvis said.

Coach finished and noticed Snoot Nino off to the side, sitting on his helmet.

"Snoot," he yelled. "C'mere boy!"

Snoot trotted over, but Coach reminded him, "Bring your helmet."

As Snoot was strapping it on, Coach said, "Outside linebacker and wide receiver."

Snoot shot him a double take. "You saying I'm gonna play? I mean, during the first three downs?"

Buster put a hand on either side of Snoot's helmet and pulled him close. "It's time to run with the big dawgs, son."

"But, Coach, I'm a kicker. I just kick."

"You line up on the outside, and if someone throws the ball, you catch it. Now, go!"

He turned to the rest of the team, held his hand out, and said, "Get a paw in! On three, Crusaders! One, two, three!" And I swear I saw more emotion in those fifteen guys than I'd ever seen on a full team anywhere.

I wished I could've told Bev about it. I spent time outside her door again, wanting her to wake up so bad I could taste it.

When I got home Rachel said Elvis had told her at school that none of the guys thought they'd win another game with just fifteen players.

I nodded. "Probably can't, but like you said, Coach did the right thing, so all we can do is the best we can." I thought a second. "How much are you seeing of Elvis?"

She looked at me funny. "Just around school. You know I'll tell you if I start seeing anybody serious."

I nodded.

"Mr. Kennedy called, looking for Coach."

"He's probably at the rehab center. What'd Kennedy want?"

She shrugged.

A few minutes later Coach called. "Kennedy get hold of you?" I said.

"That's why I'm calling. School board had a meeting tonight and wanted me there. Glad I was unavailable. They want to meet after school tomorrow in the gym."

"No practice?"

"Right. And what does meeting in the gym tell you? Bet everybody'll be there."

24

Word got around about the meeting, especially when practice was canceled, and the team wanted to be there. Coach told em absolutely not. He was sure some of the kicked off players would be there, and he knew a lot of their parents would be. Sherman Naters told him, "We don't have to be afraid of them. They're the ones who don't fight."

I was frustrated to where I wanted to burst. Only place I wanted to be was the hospital. Rachel said she'd go. "I thought I'd have to talk you out of going to the big board meeting," I said.

"Nah," she said. "They don't come to mine, I don't go to theirs. Remember every detail though, Daddy. Oh, I can't stay long at the hospital either because of a project."

I made the mistake of asking her if the project included Elvis Jackson. She held up a hand and looked me in the face. "Daddy, you've got to stop this. I would not be seeing a boy without you knowing it, and certainly not Elvis. If I tell you I'm running errands or on a project, then that's what I'm doing. You used to trust me."

"I'm sorry, honey," I said. "I still do. It's just that I

know he's got to be interested in you unless he's blind."

"Don't be so sure."

"Anyway, he's not our kind of a kid."

"What does that mean?"

"You said yourself he's not a Christian."

"He's more than not a Christian, Dad. He's anti-everything about it."

I was amazed how different the gym looked for the emergency board meeting from what it had looked like for Rachel's save-the-school deal—no posters and no big flag. And Coach was right. There were lots a parents there, and they weren't happy.

The board sat at a straight table in front of everybody, and the five men and two ladies, plus their attorney—Mr. Callman, shared four microphones. "We have just one agenda item, Mr. Schuler," Fred Kennedy said, getting right to it. "We're directing you to reinstate the thirty-three football players you suspended Friday night."

Buster, next to me on the front row, stood. "Is there some reason this directive could not have come to me in private or by phone?"

"I'll take responsibility for that, Coach," Kennedy said, and he was squirming. "I don't guess I figured you'd obey."

"And you thought by trying to embarrass me in public in front of the parents of the very boys you say I suspended, you'd get a different reaction to your directive?"

Kennedy started to answer, but Freda Slater, taking notes at the far end of the table, interrupted him. "Excuse me, Mr. Schuler," she said, "but are you implying that you did *not* suspend these players?"

"More than implying, ma'am. I did not suspend them."

"Then perhaps the reason for this meeting is moot."

"Perhaps."

"So they're back on the team?" Kennedy said. "This was just a temporary disciplinary measure?"

"Would that be acceptable?" Coach said, surprising the life outa me.

Kennedy looked like he could breathe again and started gathering his stuff like he was ready to adjourn and go home. "Absolutely," he said. "Everyone agree?"

The board members and the attorney nodded and a few parents even clapped.

"So you're saying," Coach said, "that if I suspended em for a coupla days, that's okay, but if I expelled em from the team, that's not okay."

Kennedy looked up and down the table. "Yes,"

he said, but he was kinda tentative, like he was afraid of some kinda trap.

"Well, then," Coach said, "you might want to deal with the fact that I did *not* suspend these boys. I booted em."

Kennedy cleared his throat. "You heard our directive."

"I heard you agree they deserved discipline."

Kennedy sighed. "It's wrong to fight, Coach Schuler. And thus it's wrong to be kicked off a team for *not* fighting."

"You said yourself the boys who watched were in the wrong."

"I, we, said nothing of the sort."

"I thought you just finished telling me that if I suspended em that was okay."

"Yes, but—"

"So you agree they were wrong and needed discipline."

"Don't put words in my mouth, Mr. Schuler. I—"

"I misunderstood you then, sir?"

"No, I—"

"So we're just debating the severity of the punishment?"

"Well, yes, I suppose."

"All due respect, sir, but my contract calls for autonomy in dealing with discipline on my team, even to the point of dismissing players."

Kennedy glanced at the board again. "Anyone have a copy of Coach Schuler's contract handy?" They shook their heads, including Attorney Callman. "Not having it in front of me, sir, I'd have to review that, but regardless—"

"Mr. Kennedy, are you telling me you asked me to cancel practice for my very shorthanded team to discuss my employment, yet you did not come prepared with a copy of my contract?"

"The purpose of this meeting was not to discuss your employment, Coach. It was to direct you to—"

"It's not? If I disobey your directive, you're not gonna take action on my employment?"

"We did not expect you to be insubordinate."

"According to my contract, *you* are in violation of our agreement; I'm not."

"Sir?"

"You're overruling my contract, usurping my authority to carry out discipline. Can the county afford the lawsuit I would file if you continue in this?"

Kennedy huddled with Callman. "To clarify, Coach," he said, looking grave, "if we force you to reinstate these players, you would quit?"

"Oh, no, sir."

"Then we understand each other. For you to continue in your current role, you are directed to put those players back on your team."

"I respectfully decline."

"Then we will be forced to ask for your resignation."

"Then I will be forced to sue for breach of contract."

The crowd murmured, and Kennedy asked for another few minutes with the attorney. When he turned back, he asked, "Mr. Schuler, did you bring a copy of your contract?"

"I would never start a game without a game plan."

"May we review it, please?"

Coach pulled his contract from inside his sport coat and delivered it to the table. Kennedy and Callman sat close, looking at it together. Coach said, "Page four, paragraph six, sub point B."

They passed the contract to other board members while Kennedy and the attorney whispered. Callman looked like he was really trying to be persuasive, and finally Kennedy announced, "We'd like a five-minute recess to confer as a board."

I half expected people to come up to Coach during the break and tell him that they either hated his guts or they were standing with him. But nobody did. I said, "What do you think's gonna happen?"

"Truthfully? I think I'm gonna get fired."

"Can they do that?"

"I'd beat em in court eventually, but Athens City would be merged with Rock Hill by then. What would that get me but a lot of expense and lost time?"

I hoped the board was wondering the same thing.

When Mr. Kennedy took the floor again, he said, "Mr. Schuler, we appreciate your helping us clarify this issue. We have acted with advice of counsel as follows. Miz Slater?"

She stood and read from her steno pad: "Moved by Mr. Little, seconded by Miss Jarvis, and carried unanimously that Mr. Kennedy be authorized to respectfully ask that Coach Buster Schuler consider the board's most earnest and sincere request that he reinstate to the Athens City High School varsity football team all thirty-three players dismissed Friday, September 14, 2001."

She sat and Kennedy stood. "Would you do me that personal honor, Coach Schuler?"

"Of considering your request? I surely will."

"And when might we expect the courtesy of your decision?"

"Oh, forgive me," Coach said, "but I didn't hear in that motion a requirement to report back."

Kennedy scowled and bent to Callman, who whispered to him. When the board chairman straightened again, he said, "I'm asking as a personal favor that you would report your decision to me within twenty-four hours. Can you do that?"

"Certainly. I can even save you the mystery and the time. I appreciate your couching your counsel in the form of a request rather than an illegal directive. In light of that, I'm happy to report that I've considered your request and will not be complying with it."

"Mr. Schuler!"

"I will, however, continue with utmost diligence to perform my duties as contracted and assigned. I will, to the best of my ability, make my priority educating and shaping young lives while hopefully also building a winning team that will make this city and this county and the school board proud."

"Now, Buster—"

"And I would also like to earnestly request that the board and parents and students—regardless whether they agree with my decisions—would do *me* the personal honor of continuing to support this team by showing up at the games and rallying behind the boys."

Someone yelled from the crowd, "I'll save *you* the mystery! Forget it!"

People laughed and applauded. "Well, that's fair enough," Coach said. "At least both sides got to put in their respectful requests. Now if there isn't anything further, I have a big day tomorrow."

A board member mumbled, "Move that we adjourn," but before Mr. Kennedy could even ask for a second or a vote, the board up and left. The crowd mostly booed. I asked Buster if he wanted to skip out the side door.

"They can mob me there as well as here," he said. "Let's go. Heads high."

We walked out with everybody else, and scared as I was, I noticed no one had the guts to confront Coach. Mostly they ignored us or talked to each other loud enough for us to hear. When we drove off, Buster let out a big breath and said, "I didn't know if I'd be back or not."

Rachel was already home when I got there. I told her about Coach's bluff and she smiled. "He's taking a lot a heat at school. Kids think he's lost his mind. There's gonna be petitions, kids boycotting the games, all that. There's gonna be a small crowd at homecoming."

"Too bad. First league game. Dickinson's gonna be tough."

"I'll be there."

"Well, figure the Shermanater's ma and her boyfriend, and that's three. How much noise can y'all make?"

25

Mr. Raschke slept most of the next afternoon in the waiting room. His wife, after thanking me too many times for their airline tickets, spent most of her time in with Bev. I was still not allowed in her ICU room, but through the glass wall I saw her with her eyes open for just a few minutes when she talked to her mama some. I wished I was in there, but when Mrs. Raschke took a break, she told me Bev wasn't making sense anyway. "Couldn't understand a thing," she said. "I don't think she even knew she was talking to me."

"Does she know I'm here?" I said.

"I thought she knew that already, Mr. Sawyer. I didn't say anything. I don't believe she was really awake anyway."

Rachel showed up after school and Mrs. Raschke held her close. "I'll never forget somebody singing that old Jimmie Rodgers song at your mama's funeral and you crying your eyes out, poor thing." Then she broke down for the first time and I figured she was remembering her own daughter as a little girl.

The floor nurse joined us and said, "The doctor

is hopeful the repair procedure was successful and they won't have to go in again. They don't expect her to be lucid until about midday tomorrow, but barring any other complications, she should be out of the woods."

I was so relieved I could hardly speak. "What about out of the hospital?"

"That may be another week, and she'll need bed rest at home too. But they're optimistic, provided she has a restful night and everything stays positive."

I thanked her and turned away. It'd been a long, long time since I'd cried. Rachel had to notice, but she didn't say anything. "God still answers," I said. She nodded.

I didn't know for sure when Bev would be conscious and really out of danger, but we had to talk. At least I did. Only thing I was afraid of was that maybe she hadn't really told Kim she cared for me. Maybe Kim was just assuming based on somethin else Bev said. What if I went telling her I realized I loved her and it sent her back into a coma?

The next morning I shaved, showered, ate, and was out of the house in twenty-five minutes. I was kinda surprised to find nobody waiting at ICU, but the night nurse, about to come off her shift, told me Kim had just left and the Raschkes were expected by mid-morning.

"The doctor says Miss Raschke should be awake today."

"No kidding! She doing all right?"

"He's encouraged. Her temp is normal. They've cut back on the meds, so she's sleeping on her own, and when her body tells her she's rested, she'll wake up."

"How long, you figure?"

"Not long. She should be back in a regular room tomorrow."

I pulled a chair next to Bev's door. The walls and the doors of all the rooms in Intensive Care were glass to give the nurses a good view. I turned the chair to face her and just sat watching. I don't think she moved for the first twenty minutes or so, but when the day shift came on, a couple of different staffers went in to check her charts and readouts, and I think she knew things were happening. She looked to be trying to turn over, then gave up cause of all the tubes and stayed flat on her back.

I was tempted to make some noise and wake that woman up. She had to get hungry though, didn't she? "What time's breakfast come round?" I said.

Nobody answered. I turned to find the nurses' station empty for some reason. That wouldn't last long, but this was my chance. I looked up and down the hall, then hurried in. Bev had those little plastic oxygen feeds in her nose, and her lips looked dry. Her right hand was bruised from the IV, and her fingers were the only things moving. If they'd cut back on her medication, she was gonna start feeling worse all over. Bev closed her mouth when she breathed in, and when she breathed out her lips made a little pop.

I found a clean washcloth in the bathroom, soaked it with warm water, and wrung it out good. Soft as I could I pulled it slow across Bev's lips. She pressed her lips together, licked em, and exhaled again. I dabbed her forehead, pushing her hair out of her face, then drew the cloth across each cheek and over her chin, folded it, and caressed the back of her hand on either side of the IV feed.

When I returned from putting the washcloth back a nurse was at the station, but she was on the phone and didn't seem to notice me. I stood at the foot of Bev's bed and watched her sleep, hisses and tones coming from the machines.

I hated that she was here. She had to feel miserable and uncomfortable. I missed her, mainly. For days I hadn't talked with her. There was a fragile quality about her I'd never seen. I moved to her side and slipped my hand under hers, careful to not touch the IV tube.

How could I ever explain how I'd missed what she meant to me? I wanted to cup her face in my hands and kiss her, but I had no right. Maybe Bev cared for me too, but I wouldn't steal a kiss while she was sleeping.

"Breakfast!"

I jumped and let go of Bev's hand. So this was how they woke em up. I figured I was about to get booted, but the aide chirped a good morning at me and started pushing buttons on the bed to make room for the tray. "You wanna get her sat up?"

"Excuse me?"

"Take her hand and put your other hand behind her head while I raise the head of the bed, 'kay?" I hesitated. "C'mon! Don't let her breakfast get cold."

The aide mashed a button and smoothed out the sheets near Bev's feet while I followed orders. Bev squinted, her eyes still shut, and put her left hand down to help push herself up.

"Morning, Miz Raschke!" the aide said. "Breakfast time, honey!"

Bev looked at her, bleary eyed. "I can eat?" she whispered.

"I'll keep the shades pulled and that light off till you're ready, ma'am. Just tell hubby when you can stand some more light."

I said, "Oh, it's, I'm not the—ah . . ."

Bev slowly turned to look at me. "I can eat?" she said again.

"Call us if you need us," the young woman said and was gone.

Bev's chin dropped to her chest and she shut her eyes again.

"Let's see what we've got here, Bev," I said, lifting the cover off a pitifully small bowl of oatmeal. Next to it was one piece of dry toast, cut in half.

She tried to turn her head to look at me again but all she could manage was to tilt toward me.

"Want me to help you?" I said.

"Time is it?" She sounded drunk.

"Seven."

"Morning? No dinner last night."

"You remember last night?" I said.

"Felt bad for you."

"Bev, this is Friday morning, September 21."

"No, it isn't."

I put her spoon in her hand and tried to curl her fingers around it.

"Rag doll," she said. "No muscles."

"May I feed you?"

"Oh, Mr. Sawyer, no—" She seemed to be coming around.

I put a finger under her chin and moved her face so she could look directly at me. "No more 'Mr. Sawyer,'" I said.

She tried to smile. "No? Then what?"

"Whatever you want to call me."

"Boss."

"I don't think that'll work either, lady."

"You called me lady yesterday at the office."

"You weren't at the office yesterday. Neither was I."

"I was sick."

"That was days ago. I don't remember calling you anything."

" 'You okay, lady?' you said."

"Did I?"

"Um-hm." She sighed. "Bite."

I took the spoon and scooped a small bit of oatmeal, touched the bottom of the spoon to my lips to make sure it wasn't too hot, and held it to Bev's mouth. "Wait," she said, laughing weakly. "What'd you do?"

"Checked the temperature. It's okay. You want me to wipe off the germs? You think I got cooties?"

She shook her head, looking weary enough to fall back to sleep. "That's how you kiss somebody with bad breath."

"What?"

"You kiss something else and touch their lips with it."

"I was just making sure it wouldn't burn you. Now, c'mon, open up."

"You don't wanna kiss me?"

There was nothing I'd rather do, but I had no idea if she'd even remember this.

"Don't," she said, "cause I need mouthwash first."

"Beverly!"

"You're embarrassed?" she said. "How'm *I* gonna feel?"

I put the spoon to my lips again, kissed it loud enough for her to hear, then fed her a bite. Bev seemed to have to remember how to swallow. "Plain," she said. "But good."

"More?"

"Mm-hm."

I held another small bite to her lips. "Check the temperature," she said.

I kissed the spoon and fed her some more. Four or five more bites, all with a kiss of the spoon, and the oatmeal was gone. "Toast?" I said.

She shook her head.

"Anything else?"

She nodded.

"What? What do you want, Bev?"

"Kiss, boss."

"You sure, lady?"

"Find me mouthwash first."

26

Needless to say, I couldn't wait for the next day, but there was this matter of a football game that night. We took a 1-1 record in nonconference games into our league opener, which also happened to be Homecoming. Actually, every game at Athens City was Homecoming, because not that many people left after high school, and if they did, it was cause they'd lost their job at American Leather and couldn't afford to come back anyway. Families and friends of the fifteen players were there, of course, and a bunch of students who didn't care one way or the other but came out of curiosity, I think, to see if anything would happen because of all the guys Coach booted. I didn't see any of the kicked-off kids, and a lot of their friends must have boycotted us too.

All that to say we had a pretty small crowd. The band and the pom pom squad were down too, and we'd lost one cheerleader whose brother was a benchwarmer who wouldn't have played anyway.

Otherwise it looked like Homecoming. There

were the usual banners, even one for the team to break through when we headed out onto the field. But the Dickinson Dolphins had to know something was wrong when they had as many fans at the game as we did.

Normally I don't let anything get in the way of my focus at a game, but when I looked to see where Rachel was, she seemed so happy I had to look again. She was motioning me to come see her. The band was setting up for the national anthem, so I jogged across the track to the fence in front of the stands. Carrying two boxes full of papers, Rachel hurried down from her seat near Tee. She was laughing. "Tee was wondering if you and Coach were gonna suit up," she said, but I think she could tell from my look that she coulda told me that later at home. "I'm sorry, Daddy," she said, "but two things real quick."

"Real quick," I said.

She opened the top box for me and there was a whole pile of signed petitions from people willing to see the Jack Schuler Scholarship go to saving the school. I could've told her that the people who hated Schuler for what he'd done to the team had signed those cause they didn't care if nobody got the scholarship now. But I didn't want to spoil Rachel's fun. She'd finally started seeing progress.

"Don't know what I think about that, honey," I said. "Now what else?"

"Elvis asked if he could take me to TAG."

"TAG?"

"The After Game," she said. "A little Homecoming dance in the gym and some snacks, that's all."

"It's like a date, you know."

"That's why I'm asking you. We'll be home by midnight."

"You want me to say no so you'll have an out?"

"I'd like to go."

"Be wise."

"Is that a yes?"

"Sure, but we're clear on this boy, right?"

"Yes, sir. I'm trying to be a good influence on him." The anthem started and I turned to head back to the team. "Thanks, Daddy."

We were awful. I don't know how else to say it. The whole first half it was Buster throwing his hat, kicking over coolers, throwing his clipboard. Nothing was working. Seemed like every series it was three failed plays and Snoot was punting. We never even got close enough for a field goal try, and the Dolphins scored 14 in the first quarter and 7 in the second.

I felt sorry for the kids. It wasn't like they

weren't trying. We were just asking too much of too few. Eight of em had to play on both offense and defense, and quick as they were, they hadn't learned yet how to make the adjustment without a break. Trying to give somebody a breather, Coach sent Snoot in on defense. The Shermanater pointed him to the line and set him up against a monster. Snoot stepped across the line of scrimmage, pointed in the guy's face, and yelled, "I'm gonna rip your head off!"

The monster threw his head back and laughed. And when the ball was snapped, he drove Snoot to the turf and rolled him over. The little guy had to be helped off the field, all the while hollering, "Leave me out there! I wasn't finished with him yet!"

With us down 21-0, there was nothing to say at half time. Coach just sat there staring, and I saw a look I hadn't seen since he came back. He would open his mouth to say something, then press his lips together, shrug, and shake his head. Finally he just pointed at me and I led the team back out onto the field.

The second half was even worse, and Coach was furious. At one point he swept everything off the table behind the bench, cooler, paper cups, and all, then tipped over the table. Dickinson's coach put in his scrubs when the game was out of reach, and we lost 34-0.

Our guys were so beat up at the final gun that they just collapsed on the field. Some sat, some lay on their backs, all yanked off their helmets and sucked wind while our little crowd clapped for em out of courtesy.

I stood waiting for em to get up. When they got off the field, Coach and I would give em their due. I thought. But when I turned to say something, he was gone. I turned in a circle and saw him marching out toward his car. I ran and caught him as he ripped off his whistle and threw it into the Mustang.

As he dug for his keys I said, "Coach! You can't just walk out on these boys."

"They won't listen," he said.

"So you're done?"

He reached for the car door. "I gave it a shot. It's over. It's what the board and everybody wants anyway."

"You're a coward," I said. He laughed. We both knew it wasn't true, but I had to get to him somehow. "When people don't listen to you, you quit. You did it twelve years ago, and you're doing it right now."

"Now, you watch it, Sawyer."

"No! What about not moving on until you succeed right here? What about 'The spirit of division is our enemy.' I believe those things. That's why I'm still here."

He got in the car. "You should have left years ago, Calvin."

"Look," I said. "All I know is that when you left, this town started to die. And this town, this team, Elvis, they need you. And you need them."

He shook his head. "Well, they don't get the wishbone."

"Then teach em something else."

"I don't know nothing else," he said, and we both had to chuckle.

"Coach, this team's like your Mustang; they're fast and quick. You can't keep driving em like they're a two-ton truck." He looked straight ahead, and I didn't know what else to say. "Would you just sleep on that?"

I never relax till Rachel's home, so I sat on the porch strumming some chords of my favorite John Prine stuff. I'm no picker, so the neighbors were probably glad when Rachel came up the walk just before midnight and I put the guitar up. I squinted past her and waved at Elvis Jackson. He saluted shyly and kept walking.

Rachel sat and laid her head on my shoulder.

"He'll be in love with you fore you know it," I said. "Careful."

"You've always trusted me, Daddy."

"It's not you I'm worried about."

"He knows enough to worry about you too," she said.

I laughed and told her about Bev. Well, not all about what happened, a course. Before she could start bugging me about it I changed the subject back to Elvis. "How was the, what'd you call it? TAG?"

"Boring. We went for a walk. I've been trying to get him to see the bigger picture. I took him to the train cars."

Three abandoned cars sat on a stretch of track about a block long at the edge of town. When Athens City had started dying, so had the rail line. The doors had been welded open so kids couldn't get locked in. The walls had graffiti all over em with names and years of graduation and stuff.

When Rachel was younger, she often asked me to walk her there and let her sit and look at the names. She'd run her fingers over the names and make up stories about the people. If I let her, she'd spend hours.

"That's as good a place as any to give a guy the bigger picture, as you say."

"I think he was impressed, Daddy. Hard not to be with all those memories on the wall. That boy's got memories he doesn't talk about."

I didn't know how much I should say. "Just between me and you, I checked with the registrar to see where he was living and he's listed at Orville Washington's address. Something tells me Mr. Washington doesn't know that."

"Why?" she said.

"Cause his boys played when I did and he used to come to the games. Don't you think if he was putting up a football player, he'd be coming again?"

Rachel shrugged. "Elvis washes his own clothes."

"That so?"

She nodded. "Could he use our washer and dryer?"

"He asked?"

"My idea. I haven't said anything."

"I wouldn't want you doing his wash for him."

Rachel laughed. "Neither would I! I'd just tell him he can use our machines."

I stood and she followed me inside. "So, is he open to anything you're saying?"

"He's listening. I promised to help him with history. I won't hold back, Daddy. I'm not gonna waste time on a guy who's against what's important to me."

"Atta girl," I said.

The phone rang. "Am I calling too late?" Coach

said. I told him it was okay and he said, "You got an offense that'll work with fifteen beat-up kids?"

"Yes, sir."

"I spose it's some sorta newfangled passing game."

"Yes, sir."

"Agh!"

"I can keep it simple and have playbooks copied by Monday practice," I said.

There was a long silence.

"Do it," he said. Least that's what I thought he said.

"Beg pardon?"

"You heard me, Sawyer."

"Need to make sure, Coach."

"I said, 'Do it.' Even saying that feels like swearing. Can I have em by tomorrow?"

"You're gonna call a Saturday practice after a loss on Homecoming weekend?"

"I spose not. Fact, I'm going to see Helena tomorrow morning."

"How early?"

"Early. Why?"

"I, uh, would just be happy to go along if you needed company, but course if you don't and you'd rather I butt out, I can do that too. I need to be back by late morning anyway."

Coach was silent a little too long. Then, "Why

don't you just come out and ask me what an old alkie looks like, Sawyer?"

"Now, Coach, you know me better'n that. I'm offering to stand with ya during a tough time is all. If you're no-thanking me I'd preciate it if you'd just say so."

Another long pause. "Calvin, forgive me. That was uncalled for. I apologize."

"Don't mention it."

"No, now I was out of line. I'm sensitive about Helena and—"

"I understand."

"Actually, I would appreciate some company tomorrow."

"Count me in," I said.

"Okay, but I'm still gonna need a copy of your new offense so I can start studying this heresy."

27

Morning came early, and on the drive to Fairhope Coach told me it was unlikely Miz Schuler would want to see me or even know I was there. "She doesn't even want me there," he said. "Doesn't want her*self* there."

"Is there a waiting room?"

"You can wait in the hall. Actually, I wouldn't mind you hearing how we talk. Or don't talk. Maybe you got some ideas. I'm out."

"She still mad at you?"

"I wish. She doesn't talk to me at all now."

We pulled in a few minutes later. "She sleeping?" Buster asked the receptionist, removing his hat.

"No, she's been up pacing already. She's in her room now, though."

Coach motioned me to follow, grabbing a straight-back chair from the lobby. He set it outside her door for me and went in.

"Hello, darling," he said, and I heard him slipping off his jacket and a chair squeaking. "Hope they're taking good care of ya and that you're getting some rest. Need anything? Nothing? I can get you what you want or call somebody for ya. Nothing? Okay.

"Teaching's going all right, but kids ain't like they used to be, ya know. I try to make it as interesting as history can be coming from a guy who looks like he was there when it happened. You were always good in history, weren't you? Well, you were always good in everything."

I heard nothing for a while and checked my watch. He sat in there more than ten minutes without saying a thing. I thought I heard him sniffling. Finally he says, "You ought to see Cal Sawyer's girl. Remember her? Rachel. She's a junior now, a beautiful young woman and a wonderful Christian." There was another long pause. "Well, love, I won't keep ya. Just wanted to check in. You let me know if you need anything, hear?"

She was still ignoring him, and his pain came over me so fast I could feel my face scrunching up to keep from crying. I lost the battle. But just as I heard him turning to leave, she spoke. Her tone was so cold it made me shudder. "You think I'm blind and deaf besides drunk and insane?"

"Of course not, Helena. And they tell me you're making progress."

"You think if you don't tell me you're back coaching, I won't know?"

"I'm sorry," he said. "I should have told you myself."

"Why didn't you?"

"I didn't want to upset you."

"So it's better I find out elsewhere."

"I apologize."

"Typical," Miz Schuler said.

"I'm sorry?"

"Typical jock logic."

"All I can say is I'm sorry, darling."

"Won't be satisfied until you kill someone else's boy?"

I don't know how Coach kept from responding to that, but maybe he didn't trust himself to say anything civil.

"You don't need to keep coming here, you know," she said.

"I come because I want to, Helena."

"You don't care what I want."

"Of course I do."

"Then you wouldn't come."

"I have to do what I think is best for you."

She swore at him, and again he said nothing. Finally, "I'll see you again soon."

"Don't bother," she said.

"It's no bother."

"It bothers me."

"I know. You said that."

"If you'll excuse me," she said sarcastically, "I need more sleep." And the visit was over.

In the car I said, "You want me to keep my nose outa this?"

"No, go ahead. Got an idea?"

"I was just wondering if she means it. How about not showing up for a while and seeing what she says? The staff would tell you."

"What? You think she'd start asking for me?"

I shrugged. "It's none of my business."

"No. It's a thought."

Coach took me home and I sent him off with a new playbook. He thanked me but left shaking his head.

An hour later I was leaving the house for the hospital when I took a call from Mrs. Raschke. "They tell us Beverly is out of danger, so Clifford and I are going to have to get back home," she said. "I wanted to thank you for every kindness." I offered to have them driven to Mobile, but she wouldn't hear of it. "I don't know if Clifford has another trip like this one in him," she added. "But I believe he understands she's on the mend now, and I'm glad they were able to see each other."

She told me Bev was to be moved to Room 316 by noon. I changed into a suit and tie. That would surprise her. I took a bunch of work with me in a leather portfolio, including some baseball glove catalogs. I got there early and found 316 empty, so I set my portfolio on the window ledge, sat in the visitor's chair, and started going through my stuff.

A nurse's aide showed up about half an hour later and made up the bed. "This room will be occupied soon," she said.

"With Miss Raschke," I said. "Right?"

She pulled a printout from her apron. "Right."

"I'll be feeding her lunch," I said.

"Oh," she said. "All right, then."

Pretty soon a techie rolled in some machines. "You waiting for Ms. Raschke?" he said.

"Sure am."

"Shouldn't be long."

The words were swimming on the page and I was almost dozing when two men and a woman, all in dark suits, stepped in. "Morning," I said.

"Hello," one of the men said. "You represent Miss Beverly Raschke?"

"That would be correct," I said, standing.

"You people don't waste any time, do you? You local?"

"I am," I said. "And you are?"

They all produced business cards. I took them and patted my pockets. "Didn't bring mine," I said. "Name's Sawyer."

"Mm-hm," the woman said. "I don't suppose

we'll have an opportunity to talk with Miss
Raschke."

I sneaked a peek at her card and noticed she
was with a law firm. "Not for a while," I said.
"Better give her several days."

"Days?"

"I'd make sure she's at her best," I said. "You
wouldn't want even more trouble, would you?"

They looked at each other, nodded to me, said,
"Mr. Sawyer," almost in unison, and left.

When Bev was finally rolled in and transferred
to the new bed, it seemed like forever before
everybody was gone. "Nice suit," she said, trying
to smile. "That good news or bad news?"

"We're not gonna talk shop for a few days," I
said.

"Yes, we are. I'm hurting, Cal, but I want out of
here."

"Slow down."

"I know, but I'm tired of lying around. And you
and I have to talk."

"We do?"

"Don't play dumb with me, cowboy. I had a
dream about you."

"Tell me."

"You wanted to kiss me."

"So sort of a nightmare?" I said.

"I wasn't dreaming, was I, Cal? Seems so long ago."

"It wasn't."

"I was so out of it. You caught me at a weak moment."

"I did?" I said. "You were the one making demands."

"What?"

I reached into the side pocket of my suit jacket and produced a huge bottle of mouthwash. She pressed both hands on her abdomen.

"I'm not supposed to laugh!" she said, gasping.

"Sorry."

"You are not."

"No, I'm not."

"Give me some of that," she said.

Bev was able to feed herself that day, but I sat close and watched. Once in a while she fed me a bite. I said, "Am I gonna catch diver-tickle-eye-tis?"

"You deserve it," she said. "But don't worry. I'd drive you home and leave you to fend for yourself."

"Ouch."

"Serve you right if I never came back to work."

"Ginny's doing fine."

"Calvin! Would you do something for me?"

"Anything."

"Fire her."

"How bout I just send her back out to reception?"

"'Kay."

The next day I whispered to Coach in church, "You read the playbook?"

"Of course, what do you think?"

"Okay, so?"

Coach pulled a pencil out of the pew back and scribbled on his bulletin: "The game has passed me by." I just shook my head.

Monday afternoon before practice I was excited. I sent the kids out and gathered up my stack of new playbooks. When I came out of the coaches room I found Buster standing there perfectly still, gazing at Jack's jersey. When he noticed me he straightened up and started chewing his gum again.

He pointed at the display case. "People say it was my fault, don't they?"

"Folks say a lot of things," I said. "That don't make it the truth." He looked at me, then back at the jersey. I held up my playbooks. "You ready for this?"

He fought a smile. "I can't tell."

"Coach," I said, "the Bear himself said football changes, and so do people."

He nodded but looked doubtful. "If I abandon the wishbone, you think God'll still let me into heaven?"

On the field the guys stared at my stack of books. Coach said, "Go on, pass em out."

I said, "Boys, the key to our new offense is how the receivers spread out. This'll give us more ways to move the ball and it'll give Brian a chance to throw to the whole field."

Brian grabbed his copy and started leafing through it like a madman. "Throw?" he said. "Throw?" He grabbed Yash's jersey and pulled him close. "Throw!"

Yash said, "As in pass?"

I said, "About thirty-five times a game."

"Not a lot of plays for halfbacks," Elvis said. "What happened to Coach Schuler's commandment one?"

"I play the hand I been dealt," Coach said. "You boys have five days to learn and execute every play in that book, so I suggest we get started. Now!"

It was a rough week, and as excited as the boys were, they still didn't catch on to the new offense right away. They missed passes all over the place. When they were open, Brian threw behind em. When he was on the money, they had butterfingers. Coach kept shaking his head, but I knew that when they got it, things would really come together. Buster would tear a page out of the book and hold it up, showing everybody the diagram, where they were supposed to be, what they were supposed to be doing.

Elvis found out that even though the halfback didn't run the ball much, he received passes out of the backfield a lot. Rachel told me she was helping him run through the formations in the diner after hours. "Even Tee gets into the act sometimes," she said, laughing. "You should see her, playing like she's Brian, hollering out the snap count and passing Elvis the ball by the front door."

On Thursday Yash missed a pass cause he ran the wrong route, and Coach tore out the page and mashed it into his facemask. "Don't show up until you know the plays!" he screamed. "I swear I'm gonna stick with the bone if we don't get this."

Rainbow 46 Gold was a pass to Elvis that Brian finally started connecting on. It called for a wishbone setup and Elvis going into motion as if he might take a pitch or make a block but instead sneaking through the line. Brian seemed to be able to tell with a glance where Elvis would go. I kept telling Coach, "That play's gonna work."

"I'll believe it when I see it," he said, and maybe I was dreaming, but I heard hope in his voice. Even Rachel and Tee knew the Rainbow 46 Gold and often worked on it with Elvis.

Friday, September 28, we showed up for our fourth straight home game with a 1-2 overall record, 0-1 in the conference, and a chance to even our record against the Fort Geneva Falcons. Coach and I were always the first ones there by a couple of hours. Normally Buster dolled up a game plan starting early in the week and we tweaked it till kickoff. This week he hadn't showed me a thing yet, and I figured it was because we were working out of the new playbook. I asked him a couple times if he wanted me to suggest a game plan based on the new offense, but he never picked up on it. Just like he didn't answer anymore when I asked if he wanted me to go with him to the rehab center again. "You been going without me?" I said, but he just gave me one of those looks and I left it alone.

Now we were sitting in the coaches office and he ceremoniously dropped a laminated sheet, plays typed on both sides, onto the desk in front of me. I don't know what made me so emotional all of a sudden, but I was so disappointed I almost cried. I just looked at it, read it, turned it over, studied it, kept my mouth shut, and looked up at him.

"It's all wishbone," he said.

"I can see that."

"You don't approve."

"No I don't," I said. "I thought you bought into the new offense."

"You know me better'n that, Sawyer. It's worth a try, but we're not there yet."

I shook my head.

"If you think I'm wrong," Coach said, "say so."

"I think you're wrong."

"Fair enough. But we're going with my offense tonight."

"You still wanna win the state championship?" I said.

"The state championship?! Calvin, the last time I looked we were 1-2 and 0-1 and outscored 69-27."

"That's right, and if we go 0-2 in the conference right outa the gate, we're gonna be in too big a hole to have a prayer of making the play-offs."

"Man," Coach said, "I really made a believer outa you, didn't I?"

He was making fun of me cause I had bought into his dream? Well, of course he was right. What was the matter with me?

• • •

We had even fewer fans that night, probably cause we didn't look like a good football team. Nobody likes to watch a loser. I gotta admit Fort Geneva wasn't a winner either. They were 1-2 just like we were, and watching em, I couldn't imagine who they'd beat.

We led 14-7 at halftime, and Buster tried to be upbeat, but considering the opposition, he knew better. We were slopping our way through a game against a lousy team, and we should've been able to hold on and win.

In the second half the Fort Geneva coach finally got a clue and all of a sudden we were running into each other, calling time-out in the huddle, twice getting called for delay of game. Late in the fourth quarter they take a 17-14 lead. With just a few minutes left on the clock, we take over first and ten on our own 20. I keep looking at Coach and I know he sees me, but he won't look my way. He knows what I want. We're not gonna wishbone our way close enough to give Snoot a chance to tie the game with a field goal, and I want us to try something from the new playbook.

But, no. Soon we're under a minute to go, and I'm mad. I'm still looking at Coach, hands on my hips, scowling. Now we're fourth and one and have to go for it. I raise both arms at Coach. He ignores me. Elvis gains a yard for the first down, but we've only got time for just one more play.

Coach finally looks up at me and nods. "Time-out!" I scream, and Brian comes scampering off the field. I pull him close and say in his ear, "Rainbow 46 Gold."

"Are you kidding me?" he says.

I shove him back onto the field and I can see the guys get psyched up in the huddle when he tells them. Waiting for the end of that time-out was like waiting for Santa Claus. On the snap the Falcons start chasing Brian around in the back-field, knowing that as soon as he goes down it's game over.

Elvis streaks downfield wide open, but unless Tee and Rachel figured out the play, I don't guess anybody else in the stadium was even thinking about him. All of a sudden Brian stops and fires the longest pass of his career. Elvis catches it in full stride and the place goes strangely quiet as he scores.

We were even for the season and in the con-ference with five league games to go, four of them on the road. Now if I could just get one stubborn old coach to change his ways.

28

Bev's recuperating at home, I'm seeing her regular, and practices are even getting fun again. We're running the new plays every day, nothing from the wishbone anymore, and the kids are psyched up cause we're tied with a couple of other teams in the middle of the league. The top two are 2-0, a few others and us are 1-1, and a couple are 0-2. We haven't played well yet and maybe it's silly to think we could actually compete for first place, but at least we weren't out of it yet. With just fifteen guys, most people thought we soon *would* be out of it, but for now we could enjoy the dream.

On the bus to our game that Friday night, Coach Schuler was in an unusual mood. He told the guys to stay aboard when we arrived so he could give his pregame speech. "We're a new team with new life now," he told them. "Season's even and we can determine our own destiny. We don't care what anybody else does. If we can win again and keep winning, we can go places. We're gonna take the wrapper off the new offense and show it tonight. You know this team has scouted us and thinks we're an old wishbone ball club. If nothing else, we'll surprise em. Let's see how long it takes em to adjust.

"I'm asking a lot from y'all, most of ya playing both ways. But like I always say, you got to play the hand you're dealt. This is us. Let's see how far we can take us."

The kids were inspired and played one of the most complete football games I'd seen in ages. Snoot was connecting on his kickoffs, his punts, his field goals, and his extra points. He even caught a few passes and made a couple of tackles. Brian threw well, the Shermanater was a terror on defense, and Elvis—well, Elvis was something else. He'd given us glimpses before of what he was capable of, but I don't think any of us had ever seen anything like what he did that night. Any time he had the ball he was a holy terror, juking, dancing, stutter-stepping, eluding tacklers when he had to, lowering a shoulder into em otherwise. And that speed! "Man among boys" is a cliché, but that's what he looked like.

And this time, the other team was good. We got em back on their heels early, didn't let em score til late in the second quarter, and led em all the way. We won 40-6, so the ride home was fun.

We rolled into Athens City about midnight and

Coach told the guys to take Saturday off. They already had Sunday off, so they went away whooping and hollering. Just before I left I saw Coach on the phone and he held up a finger to ask me to wait a minute. When he hung up, he asked if I'd ride with him to the rehab center. "Tonight?" I said, looking at my watch. He nodded. I called to make sure Rachel was in and safe and said sure.

On the way to Fairhope, Coach finally admitted he had taken my advice and left Helena alone for several days. When he'd called to check on her that night, the woman at the desk had said she'd like to talk to him in person. She was an older woman who introduced herself as Mrs. Knuth. She sat with us in soft chairs away from the desk but close enough to get to the phone.

"Now, Mr. Schuler," she said, "we have volunteers who come most every day to visit people who otherwise don't get visitors. They often come after their own workdays, so part of my job is to assign them, keep track of who's here, and document when they leave.

"Now you didn't discuss with me any strategy with your wife, but we all know her situation and that you had been a regular visitor. You were so predictable that we never assigned any volunteers to her."

"She probably would have been awful to em anyway," Coach said.

Mrs. Knuth nodded. "When first you missed a day, then another, I thought you might be away on business. But I follow the papers. I know your profession and I know you've been working your team out since last you saw your wife. I assumed you had either become discouraged by her response to you or you had decided on some new course of action."

I could tell Coach was about to tell her she was exactly right, but Mrs. Knuth waved him off. "You need not report to me," she said. "But I feel obligated to report to you. You see, your wife has made some progress. She had a very rough time of it early and, as you know, tried to escape a couple of times. And you remember we once caught her on the pay phone trying to order alcohol from a liquor store. As if they would have delivered it here.

"But as she dried out, her counseling and group therapy began to concentrate on her mental rather than alcohol-related issues. Often times those are difficult to separate until the patient has been sober for some weeks. Well, Mr. Schuler, her very silence in group therapy has been encouraging. At first she was so agitated and complained so vigorously that she was removed from the sessions during the first few minutes each day, though she was brought back the next day for another try every time.

"When she was finally silent and sat there, staring or listening—no one was quite sure which—well, we took that as a sign of progress."

"I would too," Coach said, looking to me for agreement. I had nothing to compare it to, but I nodded anyway.

"Sir," Mrs. Knuth said, "I must tell you what happened at the beginning of my shift some weeks ago. I thought your wife might have told you, but I realize now that she did not. It was a quiet evening and the only visitors were volunteers. I was reading but keeping an eye on the corridor, because when one of the patients heads my way, I must be sure to trip a lock on the front door that keeps them in. I saw your wife coming my way in her robe and slippers, but she looked as if she had combed her hair and seemed to be walking, while very slowly, with some dignity.

"She greeted me pleasantly and then leaned idly on the counter. I said, 'Is there anything I can do for you, Miz Schuler?' and she said, 'So you know my name.' I said, 'Of course I do, ma'am.' And she said, 'You know I'm Coach Schuler's wife.'"

Coach recoiled as if he'd been punched. "She said that?"

"She did, sir. Frankly I was afraid she was going to go into one of her rants about your son or say some of the things she often says to you when you visit. But she just said, 'You know he's going to abandon me.'"

Buster's eyes filled and he cupped his face in his hands. "Abandon her?"

"That's what she said. We have to be careful how we interact with patients and not expect them to make sense, so I didn't want to annoy her, but I knew she had become more lucid lately, so I countered her. I said, 'Well, frankly ma'am, if I were your husband, I would have thought that would please you.' She looked me full in the face and smiled faintly. She said, 'The only reason I mention it is that I'm wondering how one gets visitors.'

"I was shocked, of course, and I said, 'You'd like visitors?' She said, 'I would. And I would behave.' I'm telling you, Mr. Schuler, it was the most encouraging thing we've heard from her since she's been here."

Buster was still fighting tears. "You assigned her some, I hope."

"Of course. A middle-aged woman and a teenage girl were just coming out of someone else's room, and I asked if they could pay one more visit before they left. Your wife seemed quite pleased to walk them to her room. When they emerged half an hour later, they reported that they had read Scripture to her, prayed with her, and that she had told them too that you were her husband."

Coach shook his head and asked if he could leave Helena a note. Mrs. Knuth produced a pad of paper, and he wrote, "My Darling, I was here late after our away game and was sorry to miss you. I love you and will look forward to seeing you Sunday afternoon. Love, Buster."

"Mr. Schuler," Mrs. Knuth said, "I can't guarantee she will be any more hospitable than the last time you were here."

"I understand. But it helps so much to know what you've told me."

"You wouldn't prefer to see her tomorrow?"

He shook his head. "I hope I'm giving her something to look forward to."

I didn't know how much I should tell Bev about what was going on at the office. I spared her the worst of it, knowing she would find out everything when she finally came back to work.

The church was still praying for her, a course, and I'd rather been sitting with her Sunday than

Buster Schuler, but what're ya gonna do? I was disappointed when Coach told me he wanted to go
to the rehab center by himself that afternoon, but
I understood. The reason I wanted to go was probably the reason he didn't want me there: he might
make some progress with his wife. Good thing I
stayed home. Rachel asked Elvis over. He needed
to get some laundry done and she was gonna help
him with history.

I was trading off napping and watching football when he showed up, so when I stood to
greet him I was lightheaded. This was the first
time I'd let a boy see Rachel in the house, and I
didn't know what to say. Well, I knew what I
wanted to say, but I just said, "Son."

He said, "Coach."

"When you finish your washing and studying,
come watch the game."

He smiled like that was the furthest thing from
his mind. I was only being polite anyway.

It was hard to keep my eyes open, watching a
blowout, hearing Rachel explain the washer and
the dryer and that she was just showing him, not
doing it for him. Then, from the kitchen, I heard
just their voices. Sounded mostly like history to
me and she did most of the talking. I imagined him
just looking at her, trying to see if she'd gaze back.
Wouldn't surprise me to know she was sweet on

the kid. He was well behaved and good looking, but she had stuff to get settled with him. I wanted to tell him that Coach had contacted authorities up in Indiana and that somebody was bound to shake up his old foster family, but that wasn't my place, and anyway, nothing had come of it yet.

When the ball game was over, I drifted off and didn't wake up till Rachel cleared her throat and asked if it was okay if she walked Elvis to the highway. He was standing there with a canvas bag over his shoulder. His laundry, I guess. "Usually the boy walks the girl, right?" I said, knowing that sounded dumb.

"Daddy," she said.

"Should I come looking for ya if you're not back by school tomorrow?"

Elvis laughed, but Rachel didn't. I waved em off. I knew she'd come directly back. I'd begun wondering where she was a lot, but it was time to start letting go. I hadn't quit being her dad, but if I couldn't trust her by now, I never could. And I did. In the worst way I wanted to believe that all the times she was gone in the evening, she was still doing church and school stuff and not running off to see Elvis without telling me. I figured now that they were kinda out in the open and becoming at least friends, she'd tell me if she was seeing him more regular.

I was trying to keep myself awake so I'd sleep that night and be able to get a full day's work in Monday and still get some time with Bev. So I put a schematic of the factory on the kitchen table and got out my geography class stuff too. I got my lesson planned and started studying a section of the plant that had been busy during our heydays but now was just a place for storage. I could find another place to store stuff if we got serious about retooling that area for another kind of manufacturing. I wasn't able to noodle it long, though, before Buster Schuler pulled up out front.

29

Rachel had draped a bulky sweater over her shoulders. Elvis strode along in a short-sleeved sweatshirt, toting his laundry bag and a couple of books.

"Aren't you cold?" she said.

"This is cold to you because you grew up here. In Indiana this would be like springtime."

"Want me to carry something?" she said.

He handed her his books, pulling them back when she reached with both hands. "Left hand," he said. "You're strong enough, aren't you?"

The book spines just fit in her palm and she held them at her side. With his free hand he reached around her waist. She stopped briefly and gave him a look, then wrapped both arms around the books.

He reached for her again, and when she hesitated he wrenched the books back. "It's not like I need you to carry em," he said. "I just wanted to put my arm around you."

"I'm still getting to know you, Elvis."

"I'm not asking you to sleep with me."

Rachel stopped and he turned to face her, scowling. "Not attractive," she said.

In the fading light Rachel saw his face darken. "Sorry," he said. "But, I mean, come on."

"So that doesn't mean anything to you?"

He shrugged. "It's not like some kind of a commitment."

"Then I don't want to."

He shook his head. "So now I've done something wrong? You don't want to walk with me?"

"Not if you're gonna get pushy."

"Rachel! What century are you from? You don't want to know what I did with my girlfriends in Indiana."

"You got that right," she said.

"I don't mean *that*," he said. "But this? This is junior high!"

"Then you won't miss it."

He sighed. "You're kidding me, right? You think this is a big deal."

"Bigger than *you* think, looks like."

Elvis stared at his feet. "So I guess I'll see you around."

She squinted at him. "That's it then? You got your laundry done and help with your homework, but you can walk the rest of the way yourself?"

"Man!" he said. "What is it with you?"

Rachel stepped closer, knowing she was making him uncomfortable. "Make me out the prude if it makes you feel better," she said. "But don't think I'm gonna run home and cry over you."

"You wouldn't miss me?"

"That's the point, Elvis. How would I know unless I get to know you?"

"Lots of girls *want* me to ask em out. I can tell."

"There you go, big guy. Why waste your time on me when so many don't even *care* if they know anything about you."

That stopped him. "Well, wh—what do you want to know?"

"*Some*thing. *Any*thing. All I know is you can really play football, you grew up in a foster home, and that you came here to—"

"I didn't grow up in a foster home."

"You lied about that?"

"I had real parents until I was ten."

Rachel stood waiting. "That's what I mean. I'm listening."

"That's all. Got shipped to different foster families. Left when I was of age." Elvis looked miserable, like he wished he hadn't even offered that much.

"Would you sit a minute," she said. "Come on, right here."

She took his laundry bag and laid it on the grass near a tree. She sat on one end and pointed at the other. He set his books down and sat while she slipped her arms into her sweater and buttoned it up. "Tell me if you get cold," she said.

"I don't get cold," he said.

"I told you about myself," she said. "Didn't I?"

He nodded. "About your mom dying, yeah."

"So tell me about *your* parents." He looked away and shook his head. "C'mon," she said. "Friends tell friends stuff. Even stuff that hurts."

"You didn't," he said.

"You don't think it hurt to lose my mother? What kind of a person do you think I am?"

"You didn't say it hurt. You don't act like it hurt."

Rachel could barely speak. "It still hurts," she managed. "Of course it does."

"You remember her like some queen, and you're going to see her in heaven someday."

Why was he being cruel? "That's what I believe, Elvis," she whispered. "I couldn't go on otherwise."

"And you've got this great dad who's made everything all right."

"He's been more than I could have asked for. I'm sorry if you didn't have the same."

"Yeah, well, me too."

They sat silently and Rachel avoided looking at him. Finally she said, "So, your parents. What—?"

"I gotta go," Elvis said, standing. He picked up his books and reached for the bag. She moved awkwardly and let him take it. He hesitated. "I'll see ya," he said.

"Elvis," she said, "I want to be your friend. I really do."

He pursed his lips and nodded. But he walked away without looking back. As she hurried home, brushing away tears, Rachel realized she had told him the truth. She was not crying over him. She was crying for him.

30

I had to bite my tongue to keep from laughing at how Coach wanted to talk about everything except what he knew I wanted to hear. I mean, the man had just seen his wife for the first time in days, and I was dying to know how it went. All he wanted to talk about was the new offense.

"Calvin," he said, "I got to hand it to you, son. This passing game fits our boys and the fact that we got only fifteen of em. I believe we can win us some ball games."

I nodded, expecting more. "Uh-huh."

"We could win the conference, Sawyer, and I'm not just saying that. If we stay healthy and get some breaks—"

"Come on, Buster," I said. "You sound like every coach ever interviewed. Keeping fifteen guys healthy the rest of the season will be enough of a miracle."

"Not for me," he said. "I'm here to win, win it all."

"Good. But you didn't drive over here to thank me for the new offense. How's Helena?"

He shook his head. "I can't figure her out."

"Took you thirty years to see that modern football is about passing. So, what, she make you pay for not showing up for a while?"

"Got the cold shoulder. She says, 'Thought you were never coming back.' I said, 'Isn't that what you wanted?' She said, 'Go ahead, abandon me and blame it on me.' I told her I'd do whatever she asked." His voice got thick all of a sudden. "She said, 'You won't give up coaching football.'"

"She would ask you to do that?"

Coach nodded. "I told her I'd given it up for twelve years and I would give it up again if that would make her happy."

My eyes must've been bugging out. "Don't tell me you're quitting. You couldn't be, coming over here and bragging me up about the new offense. You can't break your contract after you threatened to sue the county if they breached. You said, '*We* could win the league.' Tell me you're not here to try to give me this team."

"Cool your jets, Sawyer. You are without a doubt. I told her I'd quit if that made her happy and I meant it. I was scared to death she was gonna call me on it."

"She didn't pick up on it?"

"She said she wanted me to quit only because I wanted to, and I told her I didn't want to. She said, 'I want you to hurt as bad as I hurt.' I've

learned not to argue with her, Cal. I know better'n to start competing over who hurts the
worst. I told her, 'Helena, I'll do whatever you
want. Quit coaching. Quit coming to see you. Or
keep coaching and keep coming to see you.'

"She looked disgusted like she couldn't stand
me, but she just said, 'I know you're going to do
what you want to do anyway, so do what you
want.' I said, 'Well, then, I'll see you tomorrow.'
And she said, 'Suit yourself.'

"On my way out I see Mrs. Knuth and she tells
me that Helena actually showed her the note I
had written her, not knowing that it was Mrs.
Knuth who delivered it to her box. Mrs. Knuth
said, 'Isn't that nice?' and Helena told her, 'He's a
fool.' But you know what, Sawyer? She says
Helena went back to her room and still had the
note with her, slipped it into her pocket on her
way down the hall."

"That's good, isn't it?" I said.

Coach nodded. "Coulda been worse."

He was gone by the time Rachel got home, and
it was a good thing. Something had happened
and she was ready to talk. "I won't be seeing Elvis
much anymore," she said. "He was just using me
to get his laundry done and get help with his history."

"You're not even gonna be friends?"

"I don't think he wants a friend."

"Maybe he's shy. You ought to try to draw him out."

She took off her sweater and leaned back against the door to her room. "Daddy, we don't talk about the bad times too much, do we?"

"The bad times?"

Her shoulders slumped. "Yes," she said, as if I'd just said the stupidest thing she could imagine. "I'm sure you remember."

"God brought us through it," I said.

"We just concentrate on that, don't we?"

"Try to stay positive, sure."

"But Daddy, it wasn't easy. I had awful days and lots of them."

I nodded. "So did I. Still do sometimes."

"We should talk about those, because sometimes I think we're pretending there's only one way to remember Mama, and it's just the good stuff."

I stood and stretched. What had brought this on? "Your mother was the finest—"

"See, Daddy? I know that! And I'm not trying to remember anything bad about her. But we're so used to saying that God brought us through and that we're gonna see her in heaven again someday—"

"And we are."

"I know, but let me finish! We say all that so much that it makes me forget what I went through."

"I'd rather not remember, honey."

"Me either, but that's just it! It isn't real. I mean, I know it's true about God and Jesus and heaven, but who can believe us when we talk about Mama dying and act like it was the best thing that ever happened to us?"

"The best th—?"

"You know what I mean! Sure, we'd rather she was still with us, but we act like it's okay because we'll all be together again someday."

"I believe that, Rachel."

Suddenly she was sobbing. I reached for her, but she covered her eyes with one hand and held up the other to keep me away. "I believe it, Daddy! But I was so young! I understood my mom had died and yet I didn't really understand, and sometimes I still can't! It was like someone had sucked the air out of the world and I couldn't breathe. I kept expecting to see her, and lots of times I thought I did. I dreamt about her. And I wanted to talk to her about how hard it was!"

"I did the best I could, Rach—"

"Daddy, you're the best and I love you and I

don't know what else you could have done. But I remember years, *years* of a blackness inside me, a hole I couldn't climb out of. And I couldn't shake the feeling that it was my fault."

"Rachel!"

"I know it doesn't make sense, but I didn't know it then, and I couldn't talk to you about it. But if I had been a better girl, if I had obeyed more or been more quiet or more helpful or—"

"Rachel, don't!"

She finally let me embrace her. "Daddy, I know. I wasn't responsible and there was nothing I could have done, but when you're that young you don't know. I said the right things enough times that I believed them. I know Mama is better off. I know she's with Jesus. I know I'm lucky to have a dad who loves me. But I don't think other people realized what we were going through. It's not their fault either, but I don't want to pretend it wasn't awful."

I was rocked. She'd always been such a good kid that I thought she was tougher than I was, that she had dealt with things better than me. Maybe I hadn't handled her the way I should have. I wanted to ask her what had brought this on from walking with Elvis Jackson. But she was through talking.

31

Rachel awoke at 5:30 in the morning and wrote a note to Elvis Jackson.

"It hurt me to feel awkward around you yesterday, and I could tell you were uncomfortable too. Can't we talk? Doesn't our argument seem petty now? I want to be your friend, but that takes two. Though it hurt, you struck a nerve when you implied I was unrealistic about my mother. You're right. I've hidden the truth. I don't know what happened to your parents and I don't need to know unless you want to tell me. But it's clear you have not glossed over your pain. It's made you angry, but my dad tells me that most people's strength is also their weakness.

"Well, that must work both ways, because if what you've pushed down inside you and won't talk about has made you angry, it's also made you driven and persistent. I can't see your eyes when you run with the football, but I imagine that the look on your face when you're refusing to be caught and tackled is the same as when you refused to tell me about your parents and when you accused me of pretending I wasn't suffering.

I'll make a deal with you. I'll tell you the truth about what it's been like for me if you'll promise to do the same.

"You can take your time. For all I know you haven't ever been able to tell anyone. You were young, and if your relatives wouldn't take you in, they don't seem like the type of people you'd open up to. And since you kept getting passed to different foster families, well, obviously that wasn't the right kind of atmosphere where you could talk with people. And you said you ran from the last family, so . . .

"What do you say, Elvis? I'll be in the courtyard at lunch. If you don't want to join me, it's okay. And like I said, I'll do the talking this time. You'll learn you can talk to me. It'll be just between us, and I won't ask you again to tell me what you're feeling. I don't know if this makes any sense, but I sure hope I see you at lunch."

Rachel would pass Elvis in the hall after first hour and hand him the note. Paying attention in calculus was impossible. What if he went a different way to avoid her? What if he wouldn't look at her, like yesterday? Well, if it came to that, she knew where his locker was. She could stick the note through the vents and hope he saw it in time to decide what he wanted to do at noon.

Rachel's heart thundered as she headed for second hour, the note folded small in her palm. She spotted Elvis from a distance and thought he saw her too, but as they got closer, he flushed and she couldn't catch his eye. He was fumbling with his books. Scared as she was, Rachel was not going to let the moment pass. She angled toward him and stood in his path. When he stopped, forcing a smile, she thrust out her note—just as he handed her one. Both notes dropped to the floor. They both knelt to grab them and banged knees. She said, "This reminds me of when we met."

He laughed. "Don't remind me. Gotta go."

"Oh!" she said, realizing she had picked up her own note. They traded and she ran to second period. She felt like a junior higher, using her textbook to hide the note as she unfolded it at her desk.

When she saw the simple printing, she pressed a hand to her neck and a sob rose in her throat. "Dear Rachel: I'm sorry about what I said. Will you forgive me? I just want to be friends too and you don't have to feel any pressure. Let me know. Love (as a friend) Elvis P. Jackson."

Rachel put the note away, only to slip it out again twice more before the end of class. Each time she unfolded it she was overcome with a feeling that Elvis was in some ways stuck at the age when he'd lost his parents.

She knew nothing would be longer than her classes before lunch. Elvis would come, she knew it. But lunch break was so short. She wanted to say enough but not too much. Above all she wanted to give him a glimpse of her real self and get him used to telling the truth about his deepest feelings. She pressed her fingers above her eyes and realized this would be new to her too.

Though Elvis had quickly become one of the stars of the football team, Rachel noticed he didn't seem to have any friends. She had eaten lunch with him a few times, finding him by himself eating a snack, never a meal. Though he worked at Tee's, and Rachel knew he wasn't paying rent, he had apparently decided not to spend his money on lunch either. Once she asked him how he could get enough fuel and energy for football practice with just a bag of chips for lunch. He'd smiled. "I can't," he'd said, "without this," and he held up his carton of chocolate milk.

"Yech!" she said. "Corn chips and chocolate milk?"

"Two chocolate milks," he said, and though he

grinned as if he enjoyed repulsing her, she knew he had to be self-conscious. "Lunch of champions," he added. Rachel tried not to look disgusted. She wondered how he could look so healthy and strong and clear-skinned. "I make up for all this after work every night," he said. "Tee fixes me whatever I want, and I always want the same. Rare steak and mashed potatoes." Rachel had wondered what he did for breakfast, but it was none of her business.

Today, as she sat in the courtyard with her lunch and an open book in front of her, Rachel couldn't eat. She couldn't read either. Josie came out from the cafeteria and invited her in. "Tomorrow," Rachel said. "Thanks anyway."

"C'mon!"

"Can't today."

"Well, sor-*ry!*"

Rachel laughed it off. If Elvis showed up soon, Josie would see why she was unavailable. And here he came.

Rachel smiled and waved, but that seemed to embarrass him. He carried one chocolate milk, and she guessed he had already eaten his chips and drunk the other carton. "Do me a favor, would you?" she said, as he sat across from her in the grass. "Throw this sandwich away for me? I had too big a breakfast, and I'm not gonna eat it."

"You sure?"

"Unless you want it. I hate to waste it."

"If you're gonna throw it out," he said.

"Please, really."

He unwrapped it while she pretended to finish reading. She had made the sandwich from left-over chicken, lettuce, and a little butter and may-onnaise. He seemed to shudder with the first big bite, and he ate fast. "I can hear you," she whis-pered.

"Sorry," he said, his mouth full. He took a gulp of milk. "Great. This is great!"

She shut her book and smiled. "I'm glad you came."

He looked away, his face red. "So you forgive me?"

"I do," she said. "And I want to talk to you about, you know. But we don't have much time." He wiped his mouth with the back of his hand and nodded.

"I figured out why I sounded phony about losing my mom," Rachel said.

He raised his index finger. "I didn't mean phony, but—"

"Sure you did, and you were right, but Elvis, I've been doing that for so long, I didn't even know. I think I talk like that because of my dad. Not that he makes me but just because I know it might hurt him if he knew how hard it really was for me."

"He doesn't seem like that kind of guy," Elvis said. "The way he looks at you and talks to you, he seems all right."

"But we usually only talk about my mom having been so wonderful and being in heaven now."

"I know. It bothered me because I thought you were just being, what's the word . . . ?"

"Unrealistic?"

Elvis nodded and looked away, busying himself with the lunch trash. "I wasn't saying it wasn't true, because I guess if you believe it, that makes it true. I just couldn't believe you could, I don't know, take it so well with what you've had to go without and all that. Maybe you *are* okay with it after all these years."

Rachel stacked her books and sat up straight. "I want to admit something to you, Elvis, but can I argue with you too?"

He smirked. "You already proved that."

She looked at her watch. "We're not gonna be able to finish this now, but—"

"I was hoping we'd have to talk again."

She felt her face flush. "I just want to say that you were right. I don't only remember good things about my mom's death, but for so many years I've said what people want to hear and what my dad wants to hear. I believe it cause it's true, but you hit my problem right on the head. I've kinda pushed down my other feelings about all that. They try to come back now and then, but I just start smiling and talking about how much God loves us and has taken care of us, and I keep ignoring the bad memories and the stuff that really hurts. And I don't think that's good."

"It's not honest, anyway," Elvis said.

"True. But I disagree with something you said—that if I believe something, that makes it true."

"Seems like it."

"Even if it's not true?"

He cocked his head. "It's not like I've thought it through. It's just that there's stuff I used to believe and I don't anymore. It's not true to me."

"But it's true to other people?"

"If they really believe it."

She stood and gathered her things. "We better get going. My next class is in Corridor D."

"I'm in C. I'll walk you."

"So, let me ask you, Elvis. Is something true if you believe it but not true if you don't?"

"Uh-huh."

"So my mom's in heaven with God and I'll see

her there someday if I believe that. But if I don't believe it, she's not there?"

They stopped at Elvis's class. "You might be too smart for me, Rachel."

"No," she said. "But I might be more logical. By your reasoning, if something's true because you believe it, then it's not true if you don't."

"I guess, yeah."

"So if I get killed in a car wreck tonight, I'm only dead if you believe it?"

Rachel thought she had drilled home her point, but Elvis clouded over as if she had punched him in the face. "Don't even say that! Why would you say something like that?"

She was flattered. He didn't want to think about something awful happening to her, but he had to see that whether he believed it or not had nothing to do with whether it was true. "I'm sorry," she said, smiling. "I'm just saying—"

"You're saying *nothing* to me!" he said. "Just forget it!"

And he left her standing there.

32

Rachel stopped in to see me after my class and asked if I would drive her to Tee's Diner after practice so she could talk to Elvis.

"I thought you weren't gonna—"

"Daddy, please. Will ya?"

"Course."

"But I don't wanna be seen waiting for you. How bout I visit Bev and you pick me up at her house?"

I nodded and started to walk her out, but she wasn't finished. "Daddy," she said, "what happened to Elvis Jackson's parents?"

I had to think about that one. "I know what he told Coach and me," I said, "but unless he wants to tell you himself, I don't guess I ought to."

She told me about their notes and their conversation. I looked at the floor. "You were trying to get him to tell you about his parents?"

"Eventually. I know it's too hard for him now, but if I can be honest about Mama, he'll open up. But I said something wrong. I was just trying to show him he was being illogical about what's really true or not."

"Let me just tell ya, you chose the wrong example."

"They were killed in a wreck, weren't they?"

I nodded. "You can't let on that I told you that."

I had to run to catch up with the team as they left the field house for practice. "Glad you could make it," Coach said. "Should I make you run laps?"

"Probably," I said. "It'd only be fair."

"Hey, how's that secretary a yours doing?"

I'd've been hung out to dry if I called her a secretary in the wrong company, but I didn't need to get into that with Coach. I brought him up to date. "She got a case against Memorial?" he said.

"Probably," I said, "but she's not the type to go after em. She'll say everybody makes mistakes."

"Quite a mistake," he said. I nodded. "Anyway, glad you're here, Sawyer. You wouldn't a wanted to miss my Longleaf Pine speech."

I chuckled. "Heard that one three years in a row."

"You wanna give it?"

"It's all yours, Coach. I wouldn't want to steal that thunder."

"It inspired you, though, didn't it? C'mon, tell the truth. Did I waste my breath on that one?"

"Nah, it was all right."

"Just all right? I always thought that was one a my best."

I smiled, remembering how some of the guys snickered behind his back.

"What? Now, come on. That speech carried me to a lot of championships."

"Then I know you'll do your best with it today."

The guys were finishing up a scrimmage when Coach called em around. "Take a knee!" he said. "Helmets off. I wanna tell ya about one of my favorite trees. That's right, this is a tree story. I've long loved this tree, not cause it's so beautiful, but because if you know something about it, you gotta respect it and learn from it."

"Learn from a tree?" Sherman Naters said.

"Why don't you wait till the end of my story till you decide whether it's got anything to teach you. I been talking bout this tree for years, but it wasn't until nine years after I left Alabama that the state legislature proved they were smart as I was and named it the state tree. Who knows what tree I'm talking about? Anybody? Nobody? Come on, you don't remember this? I heard about it in Kansas City forevermore, and they didn't teach you kids about it? Who can guess?"

Yash raised his hand. "Some kind of pine."

"Yes, sir! Some kind of pine, all right! What kind?"

Nobody spoke.

"Coach Sawyer, tell em what kind of a pine we're talking about."

After all my bragging about memorizing his speech I couldn't remember. And he had just told me. All I knew was that it had real long needles. "Long-needle pine!" I said.

"Oh, Coach Sawyer, I should make you run!"

"Longleaf Pine!" I said.

"More specific."

I shook my head.

"The Southern Longleaf Pine, gentlemen! What's so special about this tree? I'm gonna tell ya! The Southern Longleaf Pine can get big around as four feet and stand 150 feet tall. That's a big tree, but you know what it looks like before it's five years old? Anyone? Before it starts shooting up and developing foot-long needles and cones big as a cob a corn, it looks like a little lump a grass. That's right. The top is just needles, and all the growth those first few years is happening under the ground. Know why I'm telling you this? Huh? Anyone?"

"Cause we're out of our trees?" Snoot said, and everybody shook laughing.

"Well, you are, but that ain't it," Coach said.

"Bear with me. I'm serious now. If that tree can hide itself and do all that secret growing and establishing a foundation that can withstand 150 feet of height and four feet of diameter, how about you?"

Boy, did that bring back memories! Coach hadn't forgot a thing. By the time I was a senior, we coulda said that 'How about you' line in unison with him. "Well?" he thundered now. "How about you?"

"How bout us?" Brian Schuler said, looking around, fighting a grin. "Ain't we something?"

Guys giggled and elbowed each other, but Elvis Jackson shouted, "Shut up! You guys stupid or something? The point's obvious. We're little more than nothing now. Nobody even sees us building. We started out losing and then we were even, then we lost again and won again, and now we're one game up on the season and the league. It feels a whole lot better at 3-2 than it did at 1-2, doesn't it? But we're the only ones who know we're heading toward the league championship, then into the playoffs, then the state championship. We're nothing but a clump of fifteen needles right now, but come the finals we're going to be towering over everybody else. We're going to be 150 feet tall and four feet around. We're going to be the big old Southern, what'd-you-call-it,

Coach? Man! This would have been so much better if I could have remembered the name of that tree!"

The team laughed so hard most of em were crying, including Coach. "The Southern Longleaf Pine, Jackson," he said. "And I couldn'ta said it better myself, cept I woulda remembered the name."

I stood in the long shadows watching the end of that practice and remembering the day when Buster Schuler would've tore some heads off before he would let anybody laugh at one of his inspirational stories. But he had gone past that. He not only let em laugh, he laughed with em. Course, it helped that Jackson got the point and pretty much taught it to everybody else before missing his exit there. But what had happened to Coach? First he'd let me doll up a new offense, and now he was allowing boys to get the point and get motivated without his bullying em?

We always ended practices with suicides, a series of sprints that really tested who was in shape and who wasn't. There was a way of faking how hard you were going, of course. Any coach worth his salt could tell. Sometimes you made guys run more when you thought they were dogging it. Other times you let em off cause they'd played hard and practiced hard and you didn't wanna run em into the ground before the next weekend.

Strange thing that day, though. Nobody dogged it. They seemed to enjoy it. Elvis always outran everybody, but Brian and Yash would give him a run for his money, and they usually wound up working harder trying to see who came closest to him. Today they did that and so did everybody else. I swear everybody was faster, working harder, and seeming to have fun doing it. Course even Jackson had to turn it up a notch, cause he would not be beat, no matter how psyched up everybody else got. Heck, I even got into the action. I forgot how old I was, how gimpy the knee was, and how final-exam tired I was. I used to be able to run pretty good and still had a little spring in my step. Course I took off about ten feet ahead of the guys, then turned around and ran backwards till they almost caught me, taunting em, making em holler about me cheating. "Come on, ladies! Can't catch an old man?"

After all that, as Coach and I were picking up the gear, the guys raced each other to the field house. That wasn't something we told em to do. In fact, it wasn't something we expected. After a good hard practice and a long round of suicides, the guys usually dragged their tails in.

"You see that, Sawyer?" Coach said, heaving a bag of balls over his shoulder.

"I see it, but I don't believe it."

"Something's happening with this team, son. They're coming together."

"I think it was the speech, Coach."

"Okay, Sawyer."

"I *do*. I think you got em believing they can be like the Southern what-was-the-name-of-that—?"

"Shut up."

We liked the feeling in the locker room, and after the boys cleared out, Coach and I sat talking. "You know what, Calvin, I been seeing a little progress with Helena."

"Seriously?"

"She wants to see you."

"She does not."

"I'm not lying. She can still be cantankerous, but there's some kinda softness coming back, something I haven't seen for years. That Mrs. Knuth says Helena is still sometimes telling people—when I'm not there a course—that she's my wife. I mean, more people. I'm not sure what that says, but it sure doesn't seem like she's gonna keep hounding me to quit."

"Why she want to see me?"

"We've been talking a bit about the past. I keep

trying to steer her away from the bad stuff, you know. But she remembers you, and I talk about you a little. She remembers Rachel."

I should've told him I thought she'd already seen Rachel, though she probably didn't know it. I'd let Rachel tell him, if she wanted to.

"She's curious about other people too," he said, "and ones I'm sure she'd like to see. But she's embarrassed about where she is and doesn't want to see em till she starts getting out a little. But she knows you know where she is anyway, so . . ."

"I'll come soon as I can," I said.

"I've got some other news for you, Sawyer. News from Indiana." He grabbed a manila envelope out of his desk drawer and slid out a letter and a form and picture. "Is that a face or what?"

It was a little girl with big, sad eyes, kinda greasy hair, smiling bravely. The form said her name was Jennifer Lucas.

"Jackson's foster sister," Coach said, his eyes bright. "Look at the letter. They got her outa that trailer."

"Where to? Another foster home?"

"They've got her at some kinda central home."

"Ugh. Like an orphanage?"

"I guess. But that's better'n where she was."

"We hope."

"Listen to this. 'We appreciate your interest, Mr. Schuler, and you may rest assured that we will do all we can to insure the safety of every child under our jurisdiction. You may also let young Mr. Jackson know that we will keep confidential his general whereabouts, as he is now of age and entitled to his privacy. However, I would consider it a personal favor if you would inform him that Jennifer asks about him and would undoubtedly be encouraged to hear from him. I would be happy to pass along any messages and he may feel free to call the following number without fear that anyone will determine his whereabouts.'"

"Jackson see this yet?"

"Thought we'd tell him together," Coach said. "But I'm sure he's already run off."

"Yeah. To Tee's. Rachel's gonna see him there tonight. I'll have her tell him we wanna see him during his afternoon study hall tomorrow."

"You can come early with all you got going on?"

"I'll make it work."

I drove to Bev's feeling like I'd downed a cold drink on a hot day. Besides the news for Elvis, the team was up, Coach was encouraged, and Bev was slowly getting better. I was still raising a kid on my own and watching the slow death of a business, a school, and a town, but nobody ever promised everything would be rosy. Anyway, I was in love.

Rachel was there, waiting for me to take her to see Elvis. I didn't expect to see Kim, but it was okay cause she seemed to be easing up on me. Bev was asleep, so Rachel went to the car and Kim and I talked in the living room.

"You're doing more than could be expected, Cal."

"More than *you* expected, you mean?"

"I'm sorry I've been so hard on you. It's just that you mean so much to her."

"Well, she means a lot to me too, Kim. I'm just sorry it took something like this to make me realize it. I don't know if I was her whether I'd have waited that long for me to get a clue."

Rachel seemed put out when I got to the car. "I don't want to miss him, Daddy. They close early and he gets outa there as soon as he can."

Driving over there I told her to tell him Coach and I needed to see him the next afternoon.

"I'm not sure he's even gonna talk to me," she said.

"He'll talk to you."

"You don't know everything."

She hadn't said it as mean as it sounded. I gave

her a look, but it wasn't like she said something that wasn't true. I didn't come close to knowing half of anything. "Who could shut you out, honey?" I said.

"He's pretty mad."

"He can't think you said that on purpose. How could you know about the wreck?"

"How did *you* know?"

"He told me. Told me and Coach."

"Then he probably thinks that's how I know."

I pulled up just south of the diner.

"Speaking of Coach, Daddy, there's something I need to tell you."

"Shoot."

"Bev and I saw Miz Schuler at the rehab center."

"I figured."

"She didn't know who we were and we didn't tell her. She said we looked familiar and that she bet we were from Athens City. We just told her we were friends and that we wanted to read some Bible verses to her and pray with her."

"Yeah?"

"Then she said something weird and Bev and I just looked at each other and didn't know what to say. On the way home we decided we wouldn't tell anybody, but there's not much I don't tell you."

"Cept that you and Bev had become buddies. Did you promise her you wouldn't tell me what Miz Schuler said?"

"No, but you have to promise not to say anything."

"To Coach, you mean? Is this something he should know?"

"If it's true, he knows. I don't know, maybe *you* already knew this. Maybe he told you. For all I know, she could have just been babbling."

I was curious, but I wasn't going to make Rachel tell me.

"Bev was reading Luke 1:45 to her, something Bev says she likes to read to women when she doesn't know where they're coming from as far as what they believe and all."

"Remind me what it says."

"Oh, let's see, it's that one about Mary that you hear at Christmas. 'Blessed is she who believed, for there will be a fulfillment of what the Lord told her.' Something like that."

I nodded.

"That really got to Miz Schuler somehow. She looked real sad and dazed. I figured maybe she was disappointed in God, like that promise wasn't for her, you know? But pretty soon she interrupts us and she says, 'The Lord gives and the Lord takes away.' I thought I knew what she was talking about."

"Jack."

"Sure, but she wasn't. She said, 'God took my baby girl.' Scared me to death, Daddy."

"Her baby girl?"

Rachel nodded. "Bev says, 'You lost a baby?' And Miz Schuler says, 'Before she was even born.' That's when Bev and I looked at each other and Bev asked if she could pray. Miz Schuler didn't say anything, didn't bow her head or close her eyes or anything. She just kept staring, and Bev prayed for her. Then we left. Did you know anything about that?"

I shook my head. "And it's not the type of a thing I could ask Coach about either."

"Should I have told you?"

"It's okay."

I told Rachel I was willing to wait, but she said, "I hope Elvis and I will talk awhile, Daddy. If we do, maybe I can get him to walk me home. If I can't, I'll call you."

"I'll be sound asleep soon, hon."

"Well, if I don't call in half an hour, I won't need a ride."

I couldn't really sleep without Rachel safe and sound in the house. I sat by the phone, still dressed and nodding off. Finally, she called. "I just wanted you to know you could go to bed, Daddy. He's gonna walk me and we'll talk on the porch."

"Everything's all right, then?"

"I didn't say that, but this is a start."

33

Rachel had found the door locked at Tee's but the lights were still on, so Elvis had to be there. She knocked and knocked until he emerged from the back. He stopped dead and frowned, then unlocked the door and backed away, dragging a chair out from a table. He sat and looked up at her. "Thank you," she said. "I'll seat myself."

He said, "I've still got a lot to do here."

"Then let me help you. I'm not done talking to you, and I need you to walk me home so my dad doesn't worry about me."

"And you think all you have to do is say the word and I'll do that?"

"Elvis, I'm sorry for whatever I said that made you mad. But you have to understand that I don't do this stuff on purpose. I asked you to tell me about your parents the other day and you blew me off. I used a stupid story to make a point today and set you off again. I thought I knew how to talk to people. Most kids like me and don't get all bothered by what I say, even if it's something dumb. So can you give me a break? If

I insult you, can you just assume I didn't do it on purpose? Cause I wouldn't."

He looked down and she thought she might be getting through. "Elvis, I see something in you that you don't see. You've got this shell around you that keeps you from, I don't know, seeing stuff."

He sighed.

"I know that sounds silly," she said, "but it's like your world is small. I mean, this is a small town, maybe smaller than where you came from, but you're all tied up inside yourself and you're missing stuff you could be excited about."

"You're back to 'Everything's beautiful' now?" he said. "You admitted losing your mom wasn't some Sunday school story you could tell all your life."

"You're right and I *was* being phony, even if I didn't know it. But look at you. Do you have any friends?"

"What's that supposed to mean?"

"See? I'm not trying to put you down. It's just that I see this guy who could be so cool, who people would love if you'd give em a chance. You've got so much going for ya, but you've also got this attitude. I know more about you than anybody in town, but I hardly know you at all. You won't let me in. Does anybody know how you got here? Where you're from? That you didn't have parents? Okay, you had parents until you were ten. But see? You're looking at me like I'm saying something to hurt you, and I just want to know you." She stopped and shook her head. "Come on, give me a towel or a broom or something and let's get this place done so we can talk at my house."

Rachel talked as they worked, feeling as if she was building a fragile wall that kept falling around her. "All I'm asking is that you give me a chance, Elvis."

"A chance? You didn't even want me to touch you!"

"I thought we were past that! I told you, I don't take that lightly. If you'd think about it, look outside the personal little fort you've built, you'd let me know enough about you that I'd believe you really want to be my friend. Who knows? I might even hold your hand." Elvis scowled. "C'mon! That's a joke. Give me a laugh, at least a smile. You're not gonna treat me like some girl from back home, because I'll bet they didn't know you either. Am I right?"

He was wiping down the counter. "Yeah," he said.

Half an hour later, as they walked to her house, she said, "Okay, I'm starting, but one of these days, it's gonna be your turn. You wanna know the truth about my mom? I was only five, but I knew it was coming. She was real sick, and then she went into the hospital. I don't know how I even knew about people dying or getting better, but I wasn't hearing the answers I wanted when I asked my dad or my grandmaw when Mama was coming home.

"They'd say they didn't know or they weren't sure or they wanted her home as much as I did. I never believed that. I wasn't good at putting things into words, but nothing was like it used to be. Grandmaw or my dad putting me to bed just wasn't the same. They didn't hug the same. They didn't smell the same. They didn't read me the right stuff or sing me my song.

"Every night they tried harder and must've got hints from her. I don't know. They probably told her I wasn't sleeping well or that I was getting up in the night, and they'd all of a sudden start reading me the same stories Mama read me or singing the same song. But that wasn't what I wanted. I wanted my mom back and I didn't want to wait any longer." Rachel looked at Elvis in the darkness. "You sure you want to hear all this?"

"If you want to tell it," he said, emotion in his voice.

"I got to see Mama about once a week, and she

looked worse every time. Somehow I knew she wouldn't be coming home unless she started to look better. I'd say, 'Mama, you're white!' and someone would tell me not to say that. I'd say, 'You got more tubes than before,' and I'd be told not to say that. I'd say, 'I want you home,' or 'Sing me *Sunshine*,' and I'd get shushed. Finally I got so mad at everybody telling me not to bother Mama that I just started crying real loud. I was hysterical."

Rachel's eyes stung. "Grandmaw and one of my aunts were saying, 'Don't make Estelle go through this. Take her out.' Daddy picked me up and I was yelling, 'I just want Mama to sing *Sunshine* to me!' He was crying when he set me down in the hall and held onto me so I wouldn't run back in, but next thing you know, Mama was calling for me. I said, 'She wants me! Daddy! She wants me! Let me go!' And he made me promise to be quiet if he took me back in.

"I would have done anything, *anything* to not get dragged away from her, no matter how sick and tired and pale she looked. My dad took me back in, holding my hand, and Mama reached to me from the bed, saying, 'Come here, sugar.'

"I looked around to see if it was okay, and even though the big people all looked at each other and shook their heads, Mama kept reaching. Daddy lifted me up and held on so I wouldn't put too much weight on her or get tangled in the cords. I didn't care about the medicine smell or how I could see her veins through her skin. I was with my mama again and I was doing more than just giving her a quick kiss or letting her hold my hand.

"She put her arms around me and tried to pull me close, but she was so weak. Daddy was still holding me so I wouldn't hurt her. And then she started singing. 'You are my sunshine.'" Rachel's throat caught and tears streamed. "'My little sunshine. You make me happy when skies are gray.'" She whispered now. "'You'll never know, dear, how much I love you. Please don't take my sunshine away.'"

Rachel couldn't go on. She wanted to tell Elvis how her mother was never able to do that again and how even though Rachel had promised, she couldn't help crying and screaming again when her dad finally had to pull her off her mother. She had taken those words to heart and believed with everything in her that she was her mom's sunshine and that Mama didn't want anyone to take her away.

Rachel stopped walking and tried wiping her face with her hands. Elvis had turned away and his shoulders heaved. "May I use your sleeve?" she said.

He turned, sobbing, and offered his arm. She bent and wiped her face on his shirt and he embraced her. He cried and cried on her shoulder, then backed away and wiped his own face.

Finally they walked on. "See?" she managed. "Truth hurts. It's easier to just remember that when my mom died she was finally not sick anymore, she was with Jesus. It was what I'd been taught and needed to believe so bad. That was sure easier than what I just told you, which I haven't even talked about to my dad since the day it happened. I don't know if he even remembers it."

They reached Rachel's house and sat on the front steps. "Let me tell you something," Elvis said. "I'll bet you anything he remembers everything about it and that it hurts him just as much as it hurts you."

They sat inches apart for several minutes and finally Rachel leaned over until her shoulder touched his.

34

I never really sleep till Rachel's home. I heard her
and Elvis on the front porch till late that night. I
couldn't make out their words, but she did most
of the talking. That girl can talk to anybody. Wish
I was as good at it. Wish I had her faith too.
Rachel really believes God answers prayer. I do
too, course, but not like her. Even keeps a prayer
list. I'm on it. So's Elvis and the school and the
town, even American Leather. I don't know how
she keeps it all straight and I worry when she
doesn't get the answers she wants. She just keeps
it up anyway.

I dozed off and on for a couple of hours and
thought about going out there and telling them
to call it a night, but finally Rachel came in and
Elvis left.

It didn't take me long to conk out. Next thing
I knew the alarm was going and it didn't seem
I'd moved a muscle all night. Man, I needed that.
Ginny had things under control at the office, and as
usual I arrived to dozens of notes asking about Bev.

"Mr. Charles for you," Ginny said over the
intercom.

Chucky Charles. I grabbed the folder labeled "Dixie States Association of High Schools," not that there was a thing in it I didn't know by heart. Chucky was their commissioner, a big man with huge hands who liked smacking his friends on the back. I'd received my share of good-natured whacks over the years. I picked up and asked him how were things in Little Rock. Unlike usual, he wasn't small talking.

"Calvin, am I a straight shooter?"

"Nothing but, Chucky. Fire away."

"I ought to do this face to face, but I can't get down there and can't expect you to get up here before you might hear it from somebody else. I can't have that."

"Uh-oh," I said.

"Yeah," Chucky said, and he swore. "We're going a different direction starting next fall."

I couldn't speak. This was it. This was the company. They say your life flashes before your eyes before you die. Well, I saw hundreds of faces of people I'd worked with.

"I know we're a big part of your business, Cal."

He didn't know the half of it, and I sure wasn't gonna tell him now. "Worldwide, Inc.?" I guessed finally. They were hurting everybody.

"Yeah. And you gotta admit I told you we were being courted."

"Too late to counter? We can't sharpen the pencil, look at some ways to—?"

"You can't compete with em, Cal. I wouldn't ask you to. They gotta be losing money on us the first two years. And even when their standard pricing kicks in during the third year, it's so much lower—"

"They manufacture in—"

"Korea, yeah. I went over there, Cal, because we don't make changes like this lightly. I had to be convinced they could match your quality. I wouldn't have switched otherwise. It's a bottom line thing, bud. I got people to answer to."

The longer I sat there the harder it hit me. We hadn't taken Dixie for granted. They were the core of our business. He was shutting us down and didn't even know it. "I appreciate you being straight with me," I said.

"Never had complaint one with you guys, Cal. You know that. You fixed problems on the spot. And I'll never forget you driving those balls up personally during the shipping strike."

"So, nothing we should learn from this?"

"Well, yeah. You know you got to go overseas, pal. Handwriting's on the wall."

"I know. Thanks for telling me yourself."

"Only wish I could've come there. But I just

came outa the board meeting, and you know this is gonna get out quick."

"You have to announce it?"

"Better than just letting it get around, hey?"

"Yeah" I said. "Wish you could give me some time so I could tell my people myself."

"They know about individual accounts and care that much?"

"They know about yours, Chucky. Everybody here was proud to be your supplier."

"You'd better do it today then."

"Gonna miss you."

"Well, Cal, thanks. Anything goes sour with Worldwide, we'll come crawling back in three years."

To what?

Ginny didn't know me well enough to tell I'd just got the factory's death blow. She brought some mail while I was staring at the ceiling, trying to imagine breaking the news to the company. "Find me the number for Mr. Seals in Malaysia, would you?" I said. "International Athletic something or other. And before I call him could you get Marion Grant on the phone for me?"

I ran a hand through my hair, waiting to talk to my chief financial officer. I wouldn't just roll over, but I'd been through this before, trying to keep the place breathing as business went overseas. It didn't take a genius to know we were out of options. The intercom crackled. "Mrs. Grant is in a meeting, sir."

"Tell her it's an emergency."

"Tell me it's not Bev, Calvin," Marion said a minute later.

"She's better today."

"Thank God. What's up? Ginny said it was an emergency."

"As in Dixie High Schools."

"Oh, Cal. No."

"I wouldn't kid ya."

Her sigh made me feel better, but not much. "You know we're remarkably profitable, Cal, but we haven't got enough to carry us a quarter if we can't replace that business. And where do we find—"

"We don't. Can you imagine how many new accounts it would take to—"

"No," she said. "You're right. Dare I suggest the O word?"

"No choice but overseas anymore, Marion. I know this won't be scientific, but can you tell me what the numbers say if we outsourced the rest of the business at half the production cost?"

I heard her tapping her keyboard. "We could make that work," she said, "but we've always known that. Our reserves would be eaten up with severance packages."

"I know."

"You considering that?"

"If I have to let everybody go anyway? Might as well make some money on the accounts we have. I wouldn't lay people off *because* I was going overseas, but if I laid em off cause business was down, somebody's gonna get our accounts anyway."

"We're going to have a public relations nightmare."

"Not if I give the profits back to the workers."

"Cal, don't be rash. Everybody knows you're fair, but you mustn't feel obligated to—"

"Sure, I do! I'm not saying I'll give it *all* away. But, Marion, these people have, have—" I couldn't go on. The emotion of years of fighting washed over me. "They've hung with me."

"Of course," she said. "Let me do some more crunching here."

When I hung up Ginny knocked and poked her head in. "Excuse me, but could I ask what the emergency is? It's not Miss Raschke, is it?"

I shook my head. "Just business. I'd appreciate your confidence in this."

"You mean not tell people something's going on?"

"That's what I mean."

I wasn't gonna sit there doing nothing. I can stand being a victim for only so long. My mind was reeling with what I was supposed to do about everybody who ought to know. I had to tell Bev; I sure didn't want her hearing it somewhere else. And what about Rachel? She'd been praying for American Leather.

Maybe if I cashed in on the deal I could donate money to the county to keep the high school open another year. That would get Rachel through. I was mad at the people who had signed her petitions. She didn't know it was mostly parents of the kicked-off football players making sure no one got the money. Anyway, if you could believe the newspaper, the fund wouldn't begin to fill the hole the school was in. I had to face it. Business was going belly up, school was closing, town was dying. Only thing we had left was a ragtag football team starting to show promise, but I was probably kidding myself about that too. Had we beat anybody good yet? Could we win the conference and get into the play-offs without getting our helmets ripped off?

I called Mr. Seals in Asia and woke him up, but he came alive quick. "Have you thought about a trip over here with an associate, Mr. Sawyer? Can I pencil you in for—"

"Let me cut to it," I said. "I need some numbers. I'm gonna fax you info and you're gonna keep it confidential or every contact I got in the business will know you're not trustworthy."

"You can count on me, sir," he said, sounding hurt.

"I assume I can," I said. "I'm just trying to impress on you how important this is."

"I got it."

"I wanna know, if I start having my cowhide supplier send you the raw goods, dye, tackiness, and texture built in and ready for cutting, what the bottom line is."

I could tell he was scribbling and I could hear him breathing. "Um-hm," he said. "Okay. Yes?"

"I'd have to lay off my staff, cept for sales, and finance severance packages, unload my equipment, which—as you know—is probably worth something only to one other company in North America. Then I'd have to sell my building and property, which is fast declining in value cause the loss of this business is gonna kick the last crutch out from underneath a crippled town."

"Yes . . ."

"But I basically become the middleman, my

sales guys brokering the pretreated raw goods, you assembling em to our specs and quality satisfaction . . ."

"Absolutely."

"Then you ship to our accounts and handle all the billing and collection."

"Got it."

"What I need to know is my profit per unit."

"You understand it will vary with quantity."

"Of course. I'd need those breakdowns."

"And we're doing everything?"

"Even customer service and account management," I said.

"Turnkey. Which carries a cost."

"I understand. How long would it take to get a figure from ya?"

"I'd say twenty-four hours from when I have your numbers in hand, Mr. Sawyer."

"Fine, but I want a notarized document verifying that it's not a quote, not a guesstimate, not a first offer. We're not negotiating. If I don't like the number, I'm not gonna come back and ask for a higher one."

"I don't understand."

"Course ya do. You give me your best deal right out of the box or I take my business elsewhere."

"You don't want to haggle?"

"No, sir."

"Never heard the adage, 'The first offer ought to embarrass both parties'?"

"Heard it. Like it. Probably started it. But that's not how I wanna play this one. You know well as I do that you got neighbors right there in the Pacific that'd be happy to take a run at your offer. I'm not giving business away."

"I respect that," he said, "but I have a caveat too."

"A what?"

"Call it clarification. I need you to tell me on good faith that you're not just fishing. Our best people will come up with an offer I believe you'll find most acceptable, but I would like to know— since you've been forthright with me—that this represents serious interest on your part. You're not just satisfying your curiosity."

"I'm not making any promises, if that's what you mean."

"Yet you want an iron-clad offer."

"That's right."

"Just so we understand each other," he said.

"Well, if you want to understand me, Mr. Seals, I still hate the idea of an American like yourself taking all this business into a depressed economy and taking advantage of people who will work for next to nothing. If I didn't feel like I was beating my head against a wall and accomplishing nothing but having bricks fall on me, I wouldn't even consider this."

"I wish I could convince you that we are a legit-imate business that benefits Americans by keeping costs down—"

"But you know you'd probably just start to rile me, so—"

"Exactly."

Marion Grant is a warm but no-nonsense lady, and she looked surprised to see me buzzing around energetic-like after hearing death in my voice on the phone. "I'm not laying anybody off," I said.

"Calvin, slow down," she said, printouts in her hand. "Emotion has no place here."

"That's the trouble," I said.

"Perhaps, but we'd be remiss if we did anything rash."

"I just did," I said, and I told her about the fax to Mr. Seals.

"That doesn't sound rash at all," she said. "And if we get an acceptable offer, we can couch the announcement in favorable terms. While the plant is closing, business will continue and the profits will, in part, serve to benefit our former workers."

"I'm gonna do it by length of service."

"Tenure, of course."

"Some people will make as much as if they were still working."

"Calvin, that's not sound."

"I'll sleep on it."

"At least."

"But I won't change my mind," I said. "You know me."

She snorted. "Who but you would have hung in this long?"

"I'll take that as a compliment."

"Same way I praise my grandson for his energy."

35

I wasn't in the habit of taking calls from Kim. I worried she was calling about Bev, but she started by asking how I was doing. This was the worst time for a chat.

"You don't wanna know," I said.

There was a pause. "You're right, Calvin. I don't, as long as Bev still has a job when she's better." If she only knew. "Just wanted you to know," she said, "we have one motivated patient today. This girl wants to get well and get back to work."

"Well, that's good, but it'll be a while, won't it? What's the latest from the doctor? "

Kim ignored the question. "What have you been doing to make her so perky?" she said. That stunned me. Bev hadn't told her about us.

"Couldn't tell ya," I said. "Just trying to be a supportive boss, you know."

"Liar."

"It's the truth."

"Okay."

"And you might not want to tell her this, Kim, but Ginny has really been working out well here. Bev should take her time and not worry about a thing, and if Ginny proves irreplaceable, well, I'm sure we can find something for Miss Raschke."

"Go soak your head, Calvin."

"Anything else?"

"Not till I get some details about you two."

"What's Bev say?"

"Not enough."

"Well, you're not gonna get a thing outa me."

"Cal!"

"You didn't call just for that."

"Actually I did. No details?"

"Thanks for calling, Kim."

"Give me *some*thing."

"Bye."

I was dead in the water till I heard back from Seals, and I figured the longer I hung around the office the more likely someone would see from my look that something was up. I wouldn't deny we'd lost our biggest account, but it was way too soon to be playing taps for American Leather. We had to finish supplying the football season, even for Dixie High Schools, and I could truthfully say I was working to do right by my people—even if I couldn't tell em what that meant yet.

I left for my meeting at school with Coach and Elvis, telling Ginny where to call me in case we got a fax from Malaysia. It went totally against my grain, but I dug my cell phone out of the charger—where it'd been for at least three months. Most folks in Athens City still avoided em like sushi. If I had to carry one, it sure wasn't gonna be where anybody could see it. And I set it to vibrate instead of ring. Let people think I was running to the head if that thing started humming. Your reputation could be ruined by one custom ring in public, especially if it was some melody from a New York musical.

Elvis came in to Coach's office looking scared. "I'm studying," he said, sitting across from Coach and me. "I don't know what else I can do. Coach Sawyer knows I got the best tutor here."

"You're teetering academically," Coach said, "but you're eligible. That's not what this is about." He slid the envelope from Indiana across the desk and let Elvis take the stuff out himself.

The boy moved his lips as he read. Then he straightened up and laid the picture of Jennifer Lucas on the desk next to the letter. "You understand what they're saying?" Coach said.

"Pretty much," he said. "They got some kind of, um, restraint—"

"Restraining order to keep the dad away. Yeah."

Elvis's hands were shaking. "I almost brought her with me," he said.

"Count your lucky stars you didn't pull something like that," Coach said. "You'd been up to your neck in it, boy."

"But I told her I was going to, then I had to leave before she knew I was gone."

"That been working on ya?"

He nodded and his chin quivered. "I almost didn't make it as it was. She would have slowed me down."

"You stay on sixty-five all the way?"

He nodded.

"They'd had you before you got outa Indiana," I said.

Coach nodded. "And Lord help ya if you'd crossed state lines with a minor. Mercy."

Elvis covered his eyes. "I couldn't call her. Not at home."

"Well, you can now."

"She's going to cry. She'll want to come here."

"No way."

"I know. So what's the point?"

"She wants to hear from you."

"It'll just make it worse."

"Maybe a letter."

"Yeah, I'll do that." He looked at the stationery. "This address?"

"They'll get it to her."

"Why'd you do this, Coach?"

Schuler waved at him like it was nothing. "Cause I said I would. I keep my word."

Jackson dropped his head again. "I don't."

"What do you mean?"

"I gave her my word I'd get her out of there."

"She's out. She's safe. Be glad and don't muck things up."

"But I promised her."

"You shouldn't a done that."

"But I did."

"You didn't have the right. You promised something you couldn't deliver."

"Story of my life."

Coach stood and looked through the blinds into the empty locker room. He turned back with a sigh. "Don't be doing that now. Keep your head up. She's gonna be all right."

"You don't understand."

"Don't understand? You don't know who you're talking to, boy."

"She's the age I was when I got stuck in foster homes," Elvis said. "She'll be praying every night that somebody will take her, wondering why I lied. She'll turn out just like me."

"And how's that?"

"Can't trust anybody."

"I ought to be offended," Coach said. "You don't trust me?"

"I'm starting to."

"I should hope you are. I tell you something, I do it."

"That just makes me feel worse."

"Jackson! You'd have never seen that girl again if you'd tried to bring her with you. You'd be incarcerated in Indiana somewhere and she'd probably be back with that same family. You did the right thing. You got out, you told somebody who could do something about it, and you made her life better."

"She won't see it that way."

"Someday she will."

I leaned forward. "What'd you mean you almost didn't make it?"

He shrugged. "Hitchhiked. Got sunburn. Blisters. Ran out of money."

"What'd you eat?"

"Not much, once the money was gone."

"You steal?"

He shook his head. "Almost. I was already scared a picture of me was circulating. I couldn't risk it. I was at a convenience store where this guy I was riding with was buying food for his dog. I almost slipped something in my pocket, but there were mirrors and, for all I knew, cameras. I rode in the back of the pickup with the dog, and the guy opened the dog food and poured it in a bowl before he started driving again. Stuff was like meat-flavored marbles."

"You ate dog food?" I said.

Elvis gave me one a those teenage looks. "No. I asked the dog what it tasted like."

"Git back to class," Coach said.

"Thanks for doing this," Elvis said.

Coach waved at him again. "You write to that girl now."

"What can I tell her?"

Coach cocked his head. "About what?"

"About what we're going to do for her."

"It's been done, son."

"You're leaving her in an orphanage. She's not going to get adopted. She'll wind up in another foster home."

"There's good foster homes, Elvis."

"Maybe. Guess I just wasn't lucky."

"There's only so much you can do."

Elvis looked shocked. "Man, that doesn't sound like you," he said. "Didn't see that one on the wall in the locker room."

"Git."

"Coach, really. I don't want to sound like I don't appreciate—"

"Go on now."

I held the door for Elvis and he whispered, "Isn't there something else we can—"

"Scuse me," I said, grabbing my pocket. "I gotta run. We'll talk later."

"Where you going, Sawyer?" Coach said.

"Be right back."

I waited till Jackson was out of sight, then grabbed the phone. "Mr. Seals is trying to get hold of you in a bad way," Ginny said. "I didn't figure you wanted him to have this number."

"You figured right. Let me have his and I'll call him in a little while."

I slipped back into Coach's office. He was in his chair, facing the wall. "Kid's a piece a work, ain't he?" I said.

He spun back around and banged his hand on the desk, and on that big ol battleship-gray metal job it sounded like thunder. "He's getting to me with that little girl," he said. He scratched his ear like he does when he doesn't want people looking at him. But I couldn't help it.

"You've got a daughter, Sawyer." He pointed to the picture. "Isn't she sticking in your craw?"

"High schoolers think we have unlimited means," I said. "They think everything's possible."

"We do have unlimited means compared to them," he said. This from a guy living in one room of his little brother's house, tapped out by the co-pay on his wife's treatment.

"Yeah, I've got a daughter," I said. "What your excuse?"

He tipped his head down and peered up at me. "I know what it's like to be a parent," he said. "I remember."

"I'm sorry I said that, Coach. That was stupid."

"Just don't forget about that little girl," he said.

"I don't guess you'll be letting me."

I had an hour before class, so I sat in a corner of the smoky teachers lounge and called Mr. Seals. As I was waiting for him to come to the phone, Jacqui from the copy center peeked in and waved at me. I nodded and wished I hadn't. She hurried over. "You on hold?" she whispered.

"Sort of."

"Hadn't seen you for a while. Wondering what you were up to."

"Oh, just senior club activities, you know. Shuffleboard and bingo at the home."

"You're senior class sponsor?" she said.

"No, I meant, me, you know, senior—just a minute, Mr. Seals."

"I have a problem, Mr. Sawyer," he said.

"Just hold a second, sir." I turned to Jacqui. "Long distance."

"You live in a home? I thought your daughter was a junior."

"I was just kidding. I'll talk to you, hm?"

I turned back to the phone. "Mr. Seals!"

"Sir, I don't understand the figures you submitted. I was under the impression you were talking about shifting your entire operation here."

"That's what I'm studying, yes."

"And this represents the extent of your business?"

"Too small for you?"

"Well, it might be, I mean, for us to give you the most competitive per unit rate. I was expecting something substantially larger."

"And why was that?"

"Mr. Sawyer, you must realize that I'm not a telemarketer. I don't do cold calling, hoping to find an interesting business. We do our homework. We have your annual report. We study the trade journals and the appropriate Internet sites. According to my research, the prospectus you faxed us today represents little more than half the business you grossed last year. Am I reading it wrong?"

"If the copy is legible, you're reading what I sent."

I wondered if I'd lost the connection.

"Hello?"

"I'm here, sir. I, uh, just want to say that we will

do our best to come up with as attractive an offer as we can. But if we were basing this on what we thought were the parameters of your operation last year, we could have been much more competitive."

"Mr. Seals, if the parameters of my operation were close to what they were last year, I wouldn't be looking to sacrifice a hundred jobs to slave labor."

36

Practice that afternoon was another eye-opener. "I could get used to coaching just fifteen players," Schuler said.

"It ain't the number, Coach," I said. "It's the kids."

He made a noise and moved away from me, and the boys, looking crisp, ran through a bunch of plays. I caught up with him. "What? I say something wrong?"

"Naw. I just thought you were gonna say it wasn't the number, it was the coach."

I bowed from the waist, hands raised. "That goes without saying, great one."

"Sawyer, you are without a doubt."

After practice Coach and I stopped at Tee's before going to see his wife. Elvis kept glancing my way while clearing tables. Finally he motioned me to come talk to him. "Okay if I come over and see Rachel tonight?"

I was gonna see Bev after visiting Helena. "Long as you stay outside till I get home, probably about nine."

He nodded. "She there now?"

"She doesn't know you're coming?"

"No."

"Don't you think you ought to arrange this with her first?"

He looked down. "She gave me kind of a standing invitation to finish a talk."

"Uh-huh. Well then, be sure you stay standing."

He quickly looked up at me.

"That was a joke, Jackson."

Coach and me were the last ones out of Tee's, and Elvis was still working. We got to the rehab center a little after six-thirty and I waited outside Helena's door while Coach greeted her. She sounded different but awful tired. "It feels so strange to be fully conscious," she said. "I'm getting tired of this place."

"They tell me we can start taking you out on day trips in a week or so."

"That long?"

"We'll start slow and take it easy."

"Did you bring Mr. Sawyer?"

"He's here. You wanna see him now?"

"Of course I do."

I don't guess he wanted her to think I was standing right there listening. He stepped out and put a finger to his lips and we stood there for a second. Then he pulled me in. "Here he is, darling."

"It's been a long time," she said, and I almost didn't recognize her. She'd aged twenty years in twelve and people could easily mistake her for Coach's mama.

"Miz Schuler," I said, shaking her hand. Her firm grip surprised me. "Coach tells me you're coming along real fine."

"For an insane old drunk, hm?" she said, but she was smiling.

"Oh," I said, "he may be insane, but I've never seen him drunk."

Coach said, "She wasn't talking about—"

Helena threw back her head and laughed. "I like that, Calvin! I don't remember your being funny." She lowered her voice but still spoke loud enough for Coach to hear. "Explain it to Buster later." She turned to him. "Would you mind terribly if Calvin and I had a few minutes alone?"

He looked as surprised as I was, but course he said sure and asked if we wanted anything while he was gone. "Some kind of clear soft drink," she said.

"Cal?"

I shook my head and he left. Helena pointed to a chair next to her bed and I sat.

"You've been good to Buster, and I appreciate that."

"I owe him," I said.

"You do? Why?"

"Coached me. Taught me. Was a good example. Had a big influence on me."

"That so?"

I nodded and she looked toward the window, but the blinds were shut. "Me too," she said.

"Ma'am?"

She turned back. "Buster's had a big influence on me too."

I sat there awkwardly. I wasn't about to quiz her. "Good man," I said idly, the silence hurting my ears.

"Your daughter was here recently," she said.

"Yes, ma'am."

"It's lovely that she's a volunteer. We had a good long talk. First time I saw her I didn't know who she was. She looked familiar, heaven knows. I still see some of the little girl in her. Do you, or are you too close to her?"

"Oh, I still see it," I said. "See her mama in her is what."

Helena nodded. "I heard about Esther. I was so—"

"Estelle."

"Of course. We were so sorry. Buster sent a note, I believe."

I nodded.

"Unfortunately, I was going through my own

particular pain. Just know we were thinking of you." She rubbed her eyes with the heels of her hands. "Doing nothing can certainly be exhausting."

"Coach seems encouraged with your progress."

She smiled weakly. "Progress here is measured in lucidity. Everything happens in stages. I don't even remember coming here. I don't want to think about what I put Buster through. Pieces of it come back to me now and then, but mostly from Kansas City. I must have hit rock bottom for him to bring me all the way here."

"You're feeling better though?"

"That's the problem, Calvin. They detox you. In my case, they dried me out. But I was still on lots of medication. Gradually they wean you off of that. I was very aware of the stages. I don't know if you know anything about this, but there's a bargaining stage. Very ugly. Very deceptive. My life revolved around getting out of here and getting medicated again. That's the polite way of saying it. You know what I mean."

"Yes, ma'am."

"Then, as your body slowly adjusts to sobriety, there's the remorse. They tell me it's necessary and helpful, but I find it depressing and draining. Do you understand?"

"Tell me."

"You start to see where you are compared to where you've been. I should be happy to be sober, and in many ways I am. They tell me what's important now is getting your mind off yourself and starting to look outward. Put your attention on other people and their needs."

"Makes sense."

"No question, but it's awfully hard to look in that mirror and see what I've done to myself and to so many others. There's no making up for it, no going back. But there is a way to hide from it, a way I know all too well."

"And you don't want to do that."

She swung her feet off the side of the bed and straightened her gown. "My heart doesn't want to do that. My head sure does."

Buster knocked. "For you, darling," he said, handing her a glass. "Need a few more minutes?"

"Just a few, Buster. Thank you."

I felt bad for him. It seemed she talked more to me than she had to him.

"Your Rachel is so lovely."

"Thank you, ma'am. And a good girl."

"That's obvious. She's been keeping me up to date on Beverly. She going to be all right?"

"Looks that way."

"I loved her."

"Excuse me?"

"I didn't know she was your assistant, but from the first day she came in here, I was captivated. So loving, so precious. I realize now she must have known who I was, but that never came up. She talked to me like I was someone she cared about, and even if she did know me from years ago, she sure didn't know me now. She encouraged me, read the Bible to me, prayed with me. Well, prayed *for* me. Rachel didn't say much that first night, but she had that look, you know, of real compassion. I didn't feel pitied or like some object of fascination. I don't know why, but it seemed to me those two, particularly Beverly at first, didn't do this out of some obligation. It is something she enjoys doing because she truly cares about people, even strangers."

"And that wasn't even planned," I said.

"Oh, I know. I requested a visit and was just lucky it was those two. They came back each day for a while. Then I learned what happened. If I wrote Bev a note, would you deliver it?"

"Of course."

"I'm afraid I burdened her."

"Ma'am?"

"I let her pray but I didn't join in. And I blamed God for a tragedy I endured."

I nodded.

"Oh!" Helena said. "Did she tell you about that?"

"Bev? No. I didn't even know they were volunteering here then."

"I'm sorry, Calvin, but would you help me to that chair?"

I helped her off the bed. She pulled a box of cards and a pen from her dresser and began to write, talking between sentences. "If I was to start getting out of here and was to turn my attention to someone else, where would you suggest I begin?"

I was in over my head. "Well, I don't know. I—"

"Come now, son. Who could I help the most?"

"Coach," I said before thinking.

She looked up and put down her pen. "And what would I do for him?"

"Tell him what you told me, about him being a big influence on you."

She seemed to study me. "Let him back into my life, in other words."

I shrugged.

"No, now you go on. You know what you're talking about. But this has to be more than things said. We're talking about a project here, something I do. I leave this place temporarily and I do something for someone else. Buster's a good choice. But what do I do for him?"

"Come to a game," I said. "He'd love that. Rachel would sit with you. Bev too, when she's better."

What was I thinking? Her face went blank and she picked up the pen again. "A game," she repeated flatly, then finished her note. She didn't look at me as she slipped the card into a small envelope. "That would be a mighty costly way to do something for Buster," she said, still looking away. "You may send him in now."

I reached for her hand, thanking her for her time. But she just handed me the note.

37

Elvis was sitting on her porch steps when Rachel walked up. "You got time or you got homework?" he said.

"Both," she said. "Scoot over."

"Something's not adding up with you," he said in the darkness.

"Still? I don't know how to be more honest. I went from what you called 'everything's beautiful' to the ugly truth."

He sat shaking his head. She waited him out. He began slowly, "It's just that what you said about how you really reacted made sense. I mean, I don't care who you are or how you're raised, you can't help but be that way when something so awful happens to you."

"Yeah?"

"But now it's been, what, like twelve years and you seem fine with it."

"I wouldn't say fine," Rachel said. "I've learned to cope. And let's face it, Elvis, I have a lot of things going for me. My dad mostly, but my church, my friends—"

"Hold on. That's what I'm talking about."

"But, El, I can't stay angry and scared and crazy because I lost my mom. Who can live that way? What kind of a person would I be?"

"An honest one."

"No! If you think the 'everything's beautiful' is the lie and what I suffered is the truth, you've got it wrong. Everybody's got something they could be angry about. Maybe not losing a parent or both parents, but what kind of a world would we have if nobody ever got over it?"

"You're *over* it?"

"No! I still have my days. And lots of times I have questions. But nobody but God wants to hear that. I can ask Him 'Why me,' and don't think I haven't. But I don't expect Him to write it in the sky." She deepened her voice. "Miss Rachel, I took your mama so you would be a grief counselor someday. I'll make it up to you in eternity."

"Not funny," he said.

"I'm trying to make a point. I didn't lose my faith in God, and I do feel like He's bringing me along to where I'll be okay."

"That's what I don't get. You still believe in God."

Rachel felt stupid. *So that's what this is about!*

"Nothing's gonna change that," she said.

"Nothing?"

She shook her head.

"What if your dad died too?"

"Don't say that."

"Couldn't take that, could you?"

"Don't be mean."

"No! *I'm* making a point now. What kind of a God do you believe in? Somebody who is supposed to love you but takes your mom away? Sometimes I think how dare you be happy and cheerful and a little Goody Two-shoes? Is it that much easier to lose only one parent?"

"Wow," she said. "You've got it bad."

"I grew up like you, you know, only worse."

"What do you mean?"

"We were Christians. The best little Christians you ever saw. Church every Sunday. People getting saved all the time. Is that what you are? Saved?"

"Kind of an old-fashioned term," Rachel said, "but yeah, I received Christ, was saved from my sins. Yes."

"We called it accepting Jesus," Elvis said.

"Same thing, I think. So you did that?"

"No."

"Didn't buy it? Didn't like church?"

"Actually I loved it."

"But you didn't believe in God?"

"I bought the whole package. I just never got saved."

"Why?"

He shrugged and looked away. They'd come this far. He was driving at something.

"What happened, Elvis?"

He hesitated, then pulled a cheap wallet from his back pocket and removed the plastic photo insert. She leaned so the porch light shone on it. "That your dad?"

"Yeah."

He was a good-looking man with short hair, prominent ears, and a toothy smile. "What'd he do?"

"Mechanic. Huge football fan. Bears."

"And your mom, right?"

"Uh-huh."

"Pretty."

"Yep."

"She work?"

"Part-time. Grocery store and she did some people's hair, but mostly just friends and at our house."

"She's the one who named you?"

"Didn't have a clue what I'd go through, I guess."

"There's other people named Elvis."

"Nobody you know."

"There's that football player, the quarterback. And another singer. Costello."

"You know either of em?"

"No."

"See?"

He was stalling, but she didn't want to push. "This your sister?"

"I told you I didn't have any brothers or sisters."

"That's what I thought." She stared at the picture of the dark-haired little girl, then turned it over. "Jennifer," she read.

"Jenny Lucas. She's older now. Ten."

"Related?"

He shook his head. "Foster sister I guess you'd say. Last people I stayed with ran a bunch of kids through their family, but she was the one who was there when I got there and still there when I left."

"Close?"

"Used to be. Probably never wants to see me again."

Rachel froze. "You do something to her?"

"I lied to her. Told her I'd get her out of there, take her with me when I left. Chickened out."

"You couldn't have taken her, El. You'd have never got away with something like that."

"Tell her."

"Were they Christians?"

"Said they were. Went to church. I didn't

believe it. The guy was a hypocrite. Nothing like my real parents."

He stuck two fingers deep into the wallet and gingerly pulled out a yellowed, crumbling newspaper article. He unfolded it and placed it in her hands as if it was his most prized possession.

"Couple Killed in Crash; Son Spared," it read. "George A. Jackson, 31, and his wife, Eloise W. Jackson, 32, of rural Kankakee Banks, Indiana, were killed on U.S. Route 30 Saturday afternoon in a head-on collision with an eighteen-wheel cab and tractor trailer. Their 10-year-old son, Elvis P. Jackson, was thrown from the vehicle but suffered only minor injuries.

"Eddie Burns, 56, an over-the-road veteran and employee of Peak Cartage, Muskegon, Michigan, was uninjured and not charged in the incident. 'Looked like they pulled out to pass before they saw me,' he told police. 'I didn't even have time to hit the brake. I seen that little guy fly out of that car, and I never expected to find him alive.' The shaken Burns said he had never before been involved in a fatal accident.

"George Jackson was an auto mechanic at . . ."

Rachel swallowed and began to fold the paper. Elvis carefully took it from her and she covered her face with her hands. "Elvis," she whispered, shaking her head. He put everything back into his wallet. She wiped her face. "Do you remember it?"

"All I remember is following a truck and driving toward the sun. I don't remember my dad pulling out to pass. You'd think I'd remember the sounds or something. We were on our way to a gospel singing convention, one of those all-night deals with the southern quartets."

"I love those," she said.

"I used to," he said. "I'd try to stay awake as long as I could, but they always wound up carrying me out to the car and I'd wake up in my own bed."

Rachel leaned over and embraced him. "I can't imagine," she said. "Losing them must have been so hard." He didn't seem receptive, so she backed off.

"Thing was," he said, "I was just starting to get it."

"Get what?"

"The Jesus thing. I had started asking a lot of questions and both my mom and my dad tried to explain it. I told them I wasn't saved and they said they knew that but wanted me to really know what I was doing and understand. They said there was no rush and I said but what about all those scary stories about people who wait till it's too late and then they get killed or something? My dad finally told me that if I understood grace and what Jesus did for me, I was ready. I should make a decision and go forward in church and pray and get saved. But they always had an invitation, an altar call, at the quartet concerts. I wanted to do it there. I wanted to surprise my mom and dad."

Rachel said, "Didn't almost getting killed like that make you want to do it all the more?"

Elvis stood and walked down the steps to the yard. He turned around, his hands deep in his pockets. "I was in the hospital. Our pastor came after church the day after the wreck and he and the doctor told me about my mom and dad. He started right in with how he knows I have this hope because I'm a Christian and God will see me through. I wanted to ask him what kind of a God takes a kid's parents, but you don't ask questions like that."

"Sure you do. Elvis, nobody expects a kid to go through that without grief and anger."

"The next Sunday the pastor told everybody I was brave, that I had cried, sure, but I was going to be okay. But, Rachel, the last place I wanted to be was in church where everybody kept saying I should be grateful I was alive, that I could be used to tell everybody how good God was. They said my mom and dad must have been so good

God wanted them early. What did that make me? If there's a God who takes little kids' parents, why would I want anything to do with Him?"

"So you don't."

"I don't want to put down your faith, Rachel. I mean, you're really into it. But you're serving a God who took your mom from you—or at least let her die."

"I didn't say I understood Him, El. Who does?"

"I don't *want* to understand Him! If that's how He is, I don't want Him to exist. Guess I'm with those who say God didn't create man. Man created God."

"So I'm a fool," Rachel said.

He shrugged. "Your beliefs give you some kind of comfort."

"Yours do the same for you, Elvis. God doesn't run the world the way you want Him to, so you decide He doesn't exist, and poof, He's gone."

"I guess."

"One of us has to be wrong," she said.

"Why can't we both be right? God exists for you because you believe in Him. He doesn't exist for me because I don't."

"Because that doesn't make sense."

"And what does? God taking my parents the day I'm supposed to get saved? Having no relatives, *none*, who would take me? Sending me to

foster homes where they pretend to be wonderful and they're worse than no parents at all?
Letting a little girl live in a place like that and
sticking her with a guy like me who winds up
dumping her just like everybody did me? You
believe what works for you and I'll believe what
works for me."

Rachel stood and looked down at him in the
yard. "How's it working, El?"

"What?"

"How's that working out for you?"

He stared at her. "For a nice girl, you can be
kind of mean, you know that?"

"I'm not trying to be. You choose not to believe
in God because you can't make it make sense any
other way. But it's not working, is it?"

"I'm not happy, if that's what you mean. But I
don't expect to be. That way I'm not disappointed."

"You're so disappointed you can't stand it."

He showed her both palms. "Well, there you
are. End of discussion."

"Don't say that."

"I've got no more to say. Do you?"

"Well, I was just wondering. If you really think
stuff is only true if you believe it, why don't you
quit believing your parents are dead?"

He looked at her like she'd lost her mind.

Rachel was sinking. Why had she gotten into this? "I'm sorry," she said. "I'm just trying to get you to see—"

"Either they're really dead or they left me too."

"Elvis, forget what I just said. I'm not good at this."

"You're right about that."

He walked away. Why was this so hard? Everything she tried made things worse.

Rachel jogged to catch him. She reached for his hand, but he wrenched away. "Don't," he said. "Just leave me alone." He jogged off, and Rachel felt she had failed again.

38

I patted my pocket on the way home from the rehab center. "Scuse me for a minute, Coach," I said, pulling out my phone. I called Bev but talked low cause I wasn't ready to make clear to Buster what was going on between us. "Just checking in on you, Miss Raschke."

"Oh, you are, are you? How's my sweetheart?"

"Fine, and you?"

"Aren't we formal? You on your cell phone?"

"Yes, ma'am."

"Surprised you know how to use it. You're with someone, aren't you?"

"That's correct."

"Who?"

"Coach Schuler and I are on our way back from visiting his wife."

"How is she?"

"Fine, ma'am. More on that later."

"Tell me you love me."

"More on that later too. Glad to hear you're doing fine."

"You rascal."

"Yes, ma'am, looking forward to your getting back to work one of these days."

"I'll bet you are. I love you, Calvin."

"Thank you, ma'am."

"With all my heart."

"All right, then."

"I wish you were here so I could kiss you."

"Me too, ma'am."

"I want you to hold me and—"

"Okay, then, Miss Raschke, I'll check in on you again."

"When, Calvin?"

"Bye, ma'am."

"When, Calvin?"

"Sooner than you think. Bye."

The light was on in the front room when Coach pulled up to my house. "I'd better not find Jackson in there," I muttered.

"Hm?"

"Nothing."

"I heard most of your conversation with Helena, you know," he said.

"I figured."

"Guess I should be encouraged."

"I'd say."

"Long road ahead," he said. "But she's worth it."

"Attaboy."

"She tell you she miscarried a coupla years after Jack was born?"

"No."

"We never told anybody. It was a girl."

"I'm sorry, Coach."

"Tore me up, but it just about did her in."

"Never went through that," I said. "But I understand it's hard."

"Made her almost smother Jack. I was afraid he'd be a mama's boy."

"Never seemed that way."

"No, but you can see why it was hard when he—"

"Yeah. Sorry bout what I said to her about coming to a game."

"I was touched. You know me too well."

"But I wasn't thinking, Coach. Expecting her to watch a football game that would bring back all those mem—"

"You meant well."

I found Rachel sitting on the ottoman, her head in her hands. I stepped over her and sat in the chair. "I hurt when you hurt, baby," I said. "Talk to me." She climbed into my lap and cried on my shoulder. We told each other about our evenings.

"Well, we both seem to have the right idea," I said. "But we don't close so well, do we?"

She laughed through her tears. "What am I gonna do, Daddy?"

"Nobody's gonna explain God. Best we can do is try to show what He's like by doing what we think He wants us to."

"But can I show Elvis that?"

"Sounds like you tried."

"I'm not gonna quit."

"I believe that."

I'd had Ginny call every employee from both shifts to a meeting at the plant at 8:00 the next morning. Almost every one of em showed up. I was in a suit at work for the first time in years. We put the answering machines on in the offices and shut down the lines in the shop. Everybody crowded into one end of the old brick building. The stillness was so strange. I stared at men and women who came to work every day in sneakers, jeans, and T-shirts. Some of em had goggles hanging around their necks. The turners and stitchers wore adhesive tape on their fingers, even after years of building up calluses.

"You know I don't call everybody together for good news," I began. "I could do that at the company picnic." Man, I was looking into some pale, stony faces.

Someone hollered, "Is this about Bev Raschke?"

"No. She's doing better and she sends her greetings. Early this morning I told her what I'm about to tell you, so let me get right to it. We lost our biggest account yesterday. Dixie's done with us at the end of this season."

People started mumbling and I held up a hand. "Stay with me now. We all know that should put us out of business, and maybe it will. But you know I won't go down without a fight, and I know you won't either. I'm looking at every angle to see what we can do, and, hear me now, that does *not* include more layoffs. Now, hang on! I'm not saying we'll still be open in ninety days, but if we are, it'll be with everybody I'm looking at right now. Either we all make this happen, or it's over for everybody.

"Some of you may not be able to live that way, and if you feel you have to move on and find something solid, no offense taken. But if I sell this place and split the profits, it'll be with everyone who stayed to the end. Do I want to sell? No! Am I looking at adding product? Yes. Do I have a clue what's gonna happen? No.

"I'll promise you this. You'll know within twenty-four hours of anything happening. My top priority is taking care of the people who have taken care of this business, and that's you. Yeah, I could sell it and close it and wish you the best.

But you know me better'n that. If anybody benefits from what's happening, we all do. Fair
enough?"

They applauded.

"Questions?"

"Would you send manufacturing overseas?"

"I won't deny considering every option, but I'll
tell you this: If it comes to that, somebody's
gonna pay through the nose, and you're all gonna
get a piece of it."

"We trust you, Mr. Sawyer!"

"Yeah!"

"Yeah!"

"All right," I said. "I appreciate that, and I'm
asking you to stick with me. Squelch rumors.
Don't believe what you read in the paper. And
don't believe anything about American Leather
unless you hear it from me. Okay? You know,
Gideon went to war against an army of thousands with just three hundred men, because they
were the only ones with the guts to fight and
win."

"Yeah!"

"And let me tell you a brief story about the
Southern Longleaf Pine. You know, that majestic
tree—"

"Hey, boss! You ain't the only one what played
for Buster Schuler!"

"Then you know this a good one! Now, shut up and listen!"

Bev got a kick hearing me recount that meeting. And course she was more eager than ever to get back to work and help. But she was being told she needed several more weeks of bed rest. I spent most of my mornings with her, through lunch, then worked with accountants, bankers, consultants, efficiency experts, and suitors—a fancy name for the vultures that start circling a dying business. Mr. Seals and his International whatever were history. We weren't big enough for em now that Dixie had left us. Didn't break my heart. I just hated to see the sea of money rolling out with not much to show for it.

Helena Schuler finally started getting out of the rehab center once in a while, and where did she wanna go? Straight to Bev's. And she wouldn't be driven there by anybody but Rachel, who had finally got her license but was technically too young to be responsible for her. That meant I had to be along, which I didn't mind, cause it gave me another reason to go to Bev's.

Problem was, it was always ladies' day when Helena was there, cause that meant Kim came too. They would shoo me out and gather in Bev's

bedroom or around her easy chair and do whatever it is women do when men aren't around.
Plotting something if you ask me, but I was
accused by more'n one of em of being sexist
when I suggested that. So I shut up.

Rachel kept trying to reach out, as she called it,
to Elvis. One of her schemes was to fix him a
lunch every day. I said, "He can come over and
make himself a lunch from my groceries, but
you're not gonna be preparing a meal for him
every day and call *me* sexist." Fortunate for me,
the other ladies agreed. That was another thing I
learned about being in love with a woman who
knows my daughter and my coach's wife and
whose best friend kicked me in the seat till my
eyes opened up: a man has no secrets. They all
know about my every thought and decision, and
they all got opinions. Mercy.

Before you know it, they all know Elvis's history and they're weighing in on that. It's all
Coach and I can do to keep the boy focused on
his school work, cause he ain't gonna be going to
college for the academics, if you know what I
mean. Anyway, all he wants to do is carry the football, and the way he practices and lifts and trains
and, best of all, plays, there's nothing we want
more than to let him have at it.

The kids stay motivated, and Buster's at his best

and getting better as his wife's doing more than giving him the time of day. Four weeks and four games later, Bev's serious about coming back to work, at least part-time. Everybody, even Coach, knows we're seeing each other, and the football team's got the whole town talking. Heck, the whole state. Seriously. Even the kicked-off kids are coming back to watch.

We win four straight conference games to go 6-1 in our league (7-2 overall) and two teams knock off Dickinson for us, so we're in the play-offs. Elvis is setting offensive records people haven't even dreamed about, and we're getting talked about on TV again.

Bev tells me she'd like to come to our first play-off game. It's gonna be at Beach, and course I've told her what their smart aleck coach said to Buster after they whipped our cans in the opener.

"Are you sure it's all right?" I say. "You supposed to be out? It could be cold and I don't think their stands are any softer'n ours."

"It's a Saturday afternoon game, Cal," she says. "And Kim and Rachel will watch out for me."

"How about Miz Schuler?"

"That's not gonna happen. Don't think we haven't suggested it. I think it's a miracle she even cares what happens with his team. And I sure wouldn't want to be reminded of what she saw twelve years ago."

I nodded. "Looky there," I say, pointing at the TV. It was a reporter strolling our end zone again.

The graphic shows Athens City ranked in the top twenty in the state, and the reporter is saying, "Do not adjust your TV. The half-strength, high-scoring Athens City Crusaders are defying all odds by striking down one Goliath after another. Two months ago we reported that after twelve losing seasons the football world had given up on Athens City. Well, don't tell Coach Buster Schuler and his miracle squad of just fifteen players. In their final season of play, the Crusaders have their eyes set on the state championship. And like we said, when a legend comes out of retirement, you'd better take notice, Alabama."

They show clips of our team winning here and there, us charging out onto the field, Buster walking taller, shoulders back, chest out, determined look on his face. Man, he looked like he believed we could beat anybody.

The reporter continues, "People in every corner of Alabama are asking one question: can lightning keep striking Athens City? Everywhere they go, stands are full, people are signing petitions to keep the doomed school alive, and kids are asking the players for autographs."

It was true. It was all we could do to keep our kids' minds on the games what with the TV cameras, out-of-town newspaper reporters, and all the talk about the school. They interviewed Fred Kennedy on TV and he just smiled real nervous and said, "We're grateful the team is doing well and giving us something to remember about Athens City. The closing of the school is, sadly, a done deal. I'm not a popular guy, appearing to ignore hundreds of names on petitions, but this is not about money anymore. We're not going to accept the Jack Schuler Scholarship money, and even if we did and it was ten times what we know it to be, Athens City High is history at the end of this school year."

Seemed like most of the time we were home, Elvis Jackson was there. It was clear nothing was going on between him and Rachel. They didn't so much as stand close to each other in public. For sure he wasn't gonna pass up the free lunches, even if I still insisted he make em himself. It was just them studying, him doing his laundry, and him fixing a lunch, every time I turned around.

One night after he left, I asked Rachel, "You all right with me and Bev?"

"Are you kidding? I love her, Daddy."

39

Our little band of Gideonites showed up at Beach Saturday, November 10, and I swear there are as many Athens City fans as Bearcat fans for the first round of the play-offs. Biggest kick for me was Kim and Rachel bringing Bev. She looked a little tentative, but she also looked as happy to be there as I was.

Buster gathers the team around after we're all warmed up, and he tells em what the other coach said to him after they beat up on us at our place, opening night. "I told him we were gonna eat their guys with a spoon in the play-offs. And here we are boys. I wanna eat guts, not crow."

That psyched the kids up, but when they ran onto the field, I said, "Coach, you remember what he said back?"

"Course I do."

"He was right, you know."

"What're you saying, Sawyer?"

"You're not gonna do it with a Stone Age offense."

He smiled. "Don't tempt me. I might whip these guys with the wishbone."

"Don't you dare."

He didn't, but he sure got excited. He was running up and down the field, keeping pace with Brian and Elvis and Yash. How these kids stayed strong, playing both ways all those weeks, I'll never know. That day we grabbed the early lead and kept pulling away. It was sweet.

I was proud of Coach after the game. Their coach shook his hand, giving Buster a look that said he knew he deserved a tongue-lashing. But Coach just said, "Your boys played hard and you coached a good game. Good luck to ya."

Tired as she was, Bev hosted one of her ladies' bashes that night. So I had Coach over to our place, and Elvis showed up to do his laundry. "No date, no parties, no movie with the guys?" Coach said.

Elvis shook his head.

"You don't hang with anybody, do you?"

"Too much on my mind. Just want to pass history and stay eligible."

"What do you hear from Jenny?"

"She only wants me to write. No calling anymore. I couldn't stand hearing her cry anyway. She just kept saying that I promised. I don't know how many ways to apologize. There's nothing I can do now. I swore I'd get up to see her when school's out, but she doesn't believe me, and why should she?"

"So, you'll surprise her."

"If I can stand it. She'll hang on and never let me out of her sight. She said two kids got adopted last month, but both of them were about five, and she didn't even get interviewed."

"You know, Jackson," I said, "we all care about her."

"Lot of good that does her."

"The women that Rachel is with tonight—"

"Pray for her, yeah, I know. They've got a picture of her on the wall, the whole bit. It's made a big difference, hasn't it?"

"I wouldn't underestimate God."

"Too late," Elvis said.

The next Saturday we really shocked the state by winning our sectional. It was our eighth straight win and seventh on the road, but I was worried. I should be more than satisfied to have got this far, but for the first time since we started winning, it looked to be taking a toll. Our guys looked tired. I know they're teens, and I know they're resilient, but we were way past where we deserved to be, now one of the last eight teams in the state, and I'm finding myself more worried about how they're gonna deal with disappointment than with trying to stay on track and win it all.

The quarterfinals were set for Friday night, November 23, another road game. Bev had been back to work for a week by then, and it seemed most of our time was spent squelching rumors about the company. We were both happy to confirm the rumors about us. Everybody wanted to know when the big day was, but I hadn't even asked her yet.

I worried about her strength, wondering if maybe she should be working only half days for a while. She worried about my stress. I tried to tell her I could handle it.

What could I do but weigh every option? "Right now it looks like we sell lock, stock, and barrel to some broker on the last day of the year and split the profits with the employees."

"You're gonna go down as the most generous man Alabama's ever seen," she said.

"That's my goal, all right."

She laughed. "I know you just wanna stay in business."

"I'm so tempted to try the ball glove thing."

"Does it make sense, Cal?"

"Course not. It would take the rest of our reserves. We'd go belly up anyway, then there's nothing for anybody."

She sat wearily, looking into my eyes. "I've loved you for ten years, Calvin. But never more than now."

I like to talk, but I'd learned to just shut up and kiss her when she said something like that. "There *is* something I need to tell you," she said. We'd had so much fun the last few weeks, I could tell when she was serious.

"I'm listening," I said.

She held my hand in both of hers, and I could see the pulse in her neck. "I didn't tell you everything that went wrong at the hospital."

My brain almost shut down. If she was gonna tell me she was still sick, or worse, that she was gonna—but she must've seen the fear in my eyes. "I'm okay," she said. "But there was some permanent damage done too."

I wouldn't have even been able to ask her what. I loved her so much by now I couldn't bear to hear she'd been hurt any more. "Permanent?" I mouthed, but no sound came out.

"I don't like talking about this stuff either, Calvin," she said. "Plain as I can say it, when the doctors perforated my colon, my abdomen was filled with stuff, you know, that neither of us wants to talk about."

"Yeah, awright, I get the picture."

"Well, there was some scarring of the fallopian tubes."

"Uh-huh."

"You know what I'm saying?"

"I think. I mean, I know what those are, but no. What're you saying?"

"The lab report called it 'scarring/destruction.'"

"Of your, um—"

"My reproductive organs," she whispered.

I didn't know what to say. I wanted to tell her it was all right cause no matter what happened with us I didn't count on having another baby in the house. I can't tell you how many times I've thanked God I kept my mouth shut. It was all over her face how hard this was on her. She told me, "I'm not saying starting a family was something I still hoped to do anyway. It's risky at my age and you and I would have to work through the whole idea, you having almost raised a daughter already."

I nodded.

"But I sure would've liked to have had the choice."

"Course," I said, holding her.

"A few years ago I pretty much resigned myself to never being a mother," she said. "I figured my time was past. But there's something about knowing it's not even an option anymore. I love kids so much."

"I know," I said.

"Anyway, I would've felt dishonest not telling you, Cal. I didn't want to misrepresent damaged goods."

I pulled her closer. "Don't ever say that again, Bev. Please. I would never think of you that way."

Bev, the other two women, and Rachel had started taking turns writing to Jennifer Lucas. Elvis told Rachel he appreciated it, but he was still worried folks were gonna figure out where he was by the return addresses.

He oughtn't to've worried though. He was looking for help with the little one and he'd mostly quit contacting her for all the grief and guilt it raised in him.

People say a couple in love ought not to try to work together, but that didn't prove true with Bev and me. We'd been working side by side for so long, it only seemed natural. Course I was more attentive than I used to be. Other words, according to Kim, I finally had a clue. Bev was more than my assistant now. She was becoming a partner. I knew she had my best interest at heart, and so I included her in all the discussions and decisions. She liked to kid me that if I'd done that all along, we wouldn't be in the mess we were in now. She was probably closer to the truth than she knew.

One night before Thanksgiving we were sitting on the couch in my living room, and Rachel was in the kitchen, doing her homework and waiting for Elvis to come and do his laundry and lunch thing. I said, "Bev, you know the history of this knee, don't ya?"

She said, "If I say yes, will you spare me the story?"

"I think you're up to speed on it."

"Whew!" she said, hugging me.

Nothing an old jock'd rather discuss than his career-ending injuries. "I just wanted you to know when the time comes why I don't get on my knees."

"When the time comes for what?"

"C'mon, Bev. This is hard enough for an oblivious kind of guy."

"Can't you bring knee pads or a cushion or something?"

"What're you, serious?" I said.

"I just want to be sure you've planned ahead, thought it through."

"Me?" I said. "Have you?"

"Only for ten years or so."

"So you're primed," I said. "You're ready."

"Say I'm ripe and you'll be sitting here alone."

"I'd just like a hedge against rejection."

"Like I'm prepared to reject you," she said.

"You know I want all your tomorrows."

She pulled back to get a better look at me. "That wasn't bad," she said. "Really, coming from you, bad knees and everything, that was all right."

"Thank you."

"You're welcome, but don't stop now, cowboy."

"Hm?"

"Bring it on home."

"I'm asking," I said.

"Preach it."

"Bev, I love you with everything that's in me, and I mean it. I can't even imagine living without you anymore."

"And so?"

"And so I want you to be my wife."

"When?"

"Two months from Friday. That would be Wednesday, January 23, 2002."

"That's not a minute too soon, Calvin, but you know I've got to ask."

"Why that date?"

"Exactly."

"Not that I plan on forgetting my anniversary, but who could forget 1/23?"

"Let me tell you something, Calvin. First off, the answer is yes. Second, you're never gonna forget the day you marry me."

Well, it didn't take long for that to get around, and it somehow encouraged people at American Leather. Nobody thought I'd close the factory just before I got married. Fact was, I wanted the football season and the business stuff behind us before the wedding.

If getting past the first two rounds of the playoffs made us a big deal, you can't believe what winning the quarterfinals did. Now we had a problem of overconfidence, of all things. It's one thing to get a little swagger in a team, but put a hopeless little bunch into the semifinals and they think they can beat the Super Bowl champs. We were beat up, hangdog, limping, and wishing we hadn't had so much for Thanksgiving dinner the day before. But you'd've thought we'd already won the state title. Course there was the matter of two undefeated teams first. The Palm City Panthers at their place the next Friday night and, if we somehow survived that, guess who? The Rock Hill Raiders on Pearl Harbor Day.

"I think that's the only thing we got going for us," Coach told me. "We're gonna have to surprise em at dawn to have a prayer. They still ain't been outscored for one half, going on three years now."

"You're doing something I've never seen you do before," I said, "and I don't like it."

"Don't worry," he said, "I know. And I won't do it around the kids."

"What?"

"Looking ahead. We even get as far as December 7, we should thank the Lord for the day we strapped on our pads."

"Amen," I said. "These kids have had an unforgettable season already."

"Way more than we deserve," Coach said. "Same way I feel about Helena."

He could change subjects faster'n a kid with stolen cookie crumbs on his lip. "Say what?"

"The way Rachel and them have befriended her, Cal, I'm just so grateful. You know, she's on pace to get out of there before you get married."

"Seriously?"

He nodded. "My little brother's wife isn't too excited about having her in the house, but we'll find something."

"Bev and I ain't gonna need but one house. Take your pick."

He laughed. "Been a long time since you been married, hasn't it?"

"Pardon?"

He could hardly talk over his giggles. "You'd better consult your fiancée on that one, Sawyer."

He had a point.

"Almost gave my house away, did you?" Bev said later.

"I didn't know which one I was giving away," I said.

"Do the math, Cal. Move a husband and a step-daughter into my little house and I gotta move out."

"Well, that won't work."

"Good thinking."

The night we bought her ring she told me, "I'd like to take a few days' vacation week after next."

"What's your boss gonna say?"

"You're a laugh a minute, Calvin. Is it okay?"

"Course. Going somewhere?"

"Kim and I thought we might take Helena somewhere."

"Rachel's gonna feel left out," I said.

"We already told her. She can't get off school."

"You'll be back in time for the championship game?"

"When's that, again?"

"Stop it."

"Course we will, Cal. You expect to be in it or you want me to save seats for y'all?"

"Truth is, sweetheart," I said. "Coach and me been watching films of this Palm City team."

"I was just kidding."

"I'm not. They been averaging almost forty points a game."

"Uh-oh."

40

It was a strange week, leading up to the Palm City game. The press somehow got hold a my number at the plant and we had to finally tell Ginny to not let any more of their calls through. That made it hard, cause Buster had done the same thing at school, so nobody could talk to anybody.

More calls than I can remember were getting through to Bev, and I knew she was having to make personal arrangements for her trip and taking Helena and all. A couple times I had to pick up when she was on the other line, and once Ginny told me it was the lawyers again.

I said, "Again?"

She said, "Not the business ones or the bank ones or the finance ones. The other ones."

"We got more lawyers?" I said.

She said, "Miss Raschke's lawyers."

I pretended I knew what she was talking about and left a message for Bev. "Your lawyers called about the prenup."

"Very funny," she said.

• • •

All week at practice, Coach is stressing offense, offense, offense. I'm going, *What is this? Palm City's gonna steamroll us if we don't have some kinda strategy on defense.*

"What's the old adage?" Coach says.

"I know."

"Tell me. Say it."

"'Best defense is a good offense.'"

"Bingo."

"But you can't let em run over us and expect to—"

"Sawyer, get a grip. You've seen the films. We've got one kid on defense that can compete with their offense."

"Naters."

"Right. I don't want Jackson or my nephew or Yash or anybody else trying to play over their heads when we need em so bad on offense."

"It's your call."

"You disagree?"

"And what if I did?" I said, laughing. "Let me call the paper and tell em I have a better idea than Buster Schuler how to play Palm City. They'll say, 'Scuse me? The same Buster Schuler that coaches the miracle team, the fifteen guys who are still in it with two weeks to go? You must have the wrong number.'"

"You ought to take that on stage, Sawyer," he said. "Vaudeville. Really."

Well, course he turns out to be the genius again. It's cold on Friday night, November 30, in Palm City. We can see our breath, and we can also see the Panthers are monstrous. A lot a experts are picking them to mop the field with us and beat Rock Hill for the state title too. Our kids were standing there with their eyes bugging out. Those other kids looked like adults. Bigger than adults. I'm glad nobody asked me, cause I wouldn't have given us a chance.

Oh, they were good. They scored and kept scoring, but our kids—man, you should've been there. The place was going nuts. I'm lying if I didn't see most of the workers from American Leather there. There were people from the hospital, the bank, everybody we ever see at Tee's. Yeah, there were a few parents of kicked-off players probably not there, but I'd be surprised if many of our students didn't show.

We were matching em strike for strike. They were hurting us on the line, and our kids were staggering off the field. But it takes more than size and strength to stop a dang good passer and receivers like Upshaw and Jackson. Only thing is, Palm City was a little better by late in the fourth quarter, and when we needed a touchdown trailing 35-31, we just couldn't punch it in. Snoot kicks a short field goal to put us within one at 35-34, but I didn't see how we were gonna get the ball back. I was actually thinking that this is like winning, coming within one point of a team like that. Athens City ought to be proud.

Well, Snoot kicks off a squibber, one of those short on-side kicks you pray the other team'll bobble so you can fall on it. Doesn't happen, but we smother the return guy at their 30. First play from scrimmage they're just playing safe like we would do in the same situation, and the Shermanater goes berserk, blasts into their backfield, and somehow the ball is loose. I was so happy for Brian when he fell on it. It hadn't been easy for him, being Coach's nephew, having the season of his life, and taking a backseat to Jackson's miracle year.

So here's our chance. But course Palm City isn't about to give in. They stop us twice and then it's third and ten on their 30 with just a few seconds left. Coach calls time-out and tells Brian to try a short screen pass to Jackson and tells Jackson to be sure to get out of bounds to give us one more play. We've got one time-out left, but what if we don't call it in time?

I grab Buster. "Coach, I can't believe you. Our whole season's on the line right here. We have got to throw deep."

"That is exactly what they're expecting us to do," he says. He spins and grabs Brian by the face-mask and it's just like twelve years before. "This team needs you. Now you be a Buick!"

With the snap of the ball, I'm dying, jumping, wanting something to happen. Brian gets off the short pass to Jackson, but Elvis is still in the backfield. Unless he gets lucky, he's going nowhere. But he doesn't even head for the sidelines. He's hammered at the line of scrimmage. Brian is screaming for a time-out. We all are. I'm just sure that clock's gonna run out. But we finally get the whistle with the clock showing one second. But fourth down at the 30? What're we gonna do?

I'm looking to Coach to see what he's gonna say and I see him go pale. I follow his eyes and see Jackson is still down. The ref signals to us that we can go out there. We find Jackson moaning and holding his right wrist. "Let me see it," I say. He lets go, then flinches when I barely touch it. "Sharp or dull pain?"

"Sharp."

I look at Coach. "Busted?"

Coach shakes his head. I can see the game, the season, and twelve years ago on his face. "Why didn't you listen to me?"

"Sorry," Elvis said, and it sounded like he really meant it.

"Help him up," I tell the others.

"What's Snoot's best kick?" Coach asks me.

We're on the 30. Add ten yards for the end zone and several for him to set up. "Half of this."

"Snoot!" he hollers. "Start stretching that hamstring."

As we pass Snoot, Elvis says, "Bail me out."

Snoot Nino's a good kicker for a little guy. But he's not a long kicker. High school kids don't kick forty-plus-yard field goals as a rule. But here's what it sounds like.

The stands are silent. Then come the grunts on the line as the center snaps the ball to Brian, the holder. You hear the ball smack his hands just as the gun sounds to say time has run out. Once this play's over, the game's over, the season's over for somebody.

Then comes the sound of shoe on ball, and that's when I knew. Somehow that little guy got the distance. Everything would be perfect if it could just stay on line.

And then I heard all the cheering from behind us, on our side. I just stood there, shaking my head. We were going to the state championship on our own field in seven days. And our best player had a broke wrist.

● ● ●

If you've ever lived through one of those crazy situations where a whole town gets behind a team, you know what it was like for us that week. The David and Goliath stories got so old I'd've choked on one more. Banners, signs, chants, a pep rally, front page stories.

Coach gave the guys Monday off, so they hadn't been on a field for three days when they showed up Tuesday. Talk about your walking wounded. Elvis sat on the bench with his wrist in a tight, elastic cast. When people came by, he shied away, making sure nobody even brushed him.

I liked that he was there—moral support and all. But the guys were dragging. I don't think we had a player who didn't have some kind of wound. They could run a little, but they couldn't walk, if you follow. Worst of all was the look on their faces. It was sad, really. I wished they could've enjoyed what they'd done. The whole season was unreal, course, but that win Friday night—I mean, come on. That alone would make a season.

But these guys were done. They really were. There was nothing left. Even the Shermanater, who everybody looked to when the tank was empty, had a glazed look. They were scared. They were spent. And I don't think they had another game in them.

I expected Coach to jump all over em, but after watching em limp through a few drills, he just called everybody over to the bench where they sat on the ground in front of Jackson.

"Well, we've had a heckuva ride, boys," he said. "I've told you since the first day you stepped onto this cursed field that coaching is really done before a game. Once we're in it, I'm just there to steer. I can't do it for ya. And I can't get you excited either. Now you're hurt, I know. We're wounded. One of our limbs has been amputated. But there he sits. He's not a quitter, and neither are any of you. If I'm wrong, let me know and I'll just phone in the forfeit to Rock Hill.

"Life isn't fair. Every one of you has proof of that somewhere in you. I gave you the worst handicap when I fired most of your teammates. And I dare say we wouldn't have come this far if we'd had those cowards with us. In the crucial, turning-point play you might've let up 1 percent and counted on somebody else to do what only you could do, and we would've lost. Think of the games we could've lost if any one of you had let go your grip on the rope.

"Well, here we are, and it ain't fair. It wasn't fair to line you fifteen rascals up against a team like Palm City. But what did you do? You showed me. You showed them. You showed everybody. We went from being this novelty shorthanded team that won more games than we should have to now having a legitimate shot at a state title. Think of it.

"But now there's just fourteen a you, and—let's face it—that one we lost was more than one-fifteenth of this team. Two weeks in a row, a challenge like this? I ought to be ashamed of myself for asking it of ya. Well, here's my take on it. We got ourselves into this and we can get ourselves out of it. I'm dead serious. You had enough, I'll let em know. You think Rock Hill wants to face you? They win and everybody says, well, a course! They got nothing to gain and everything to lose.

"I gave you three days off and you still limped out here like you was through. I don't blame ya. I really don't. We can call it quits right here and I'll still say I'd rather have coached this team right here than any other group a guys that ever strapped on a helmet for me. I'm gonna let you go home now, and I want you to think about it.

"Because whoever shows up on this field tomorrow afternoon is who I'm gonna put on the field Friday night. And if you're here, I don't care what you look like. I don't care where it hurts. I don't care if I ought to have my head examined for going to the well one more time.

I'm gonna use you as if you're ready to go. Just so you know.

"If you'll suit up one more time for Athens City, come Friday when it's all over, the score won't make a bit a difference. Win, lose, or draw, you'll still be the best team in Alabama to me. Now go on."

At the crack of dawn Wednesday, Coach and Rachel and I saw Helena and Bev off. Kim was driving, and they all thought it was cute to never tell us exactly where they were going. "North," was all they would say. Well, shoot. You can't go far south from Athens City.

"Don't worry about us," Bev whispered as I kissed her good-bye. "Helena has to be back to the center by Friday afternoon, and you know I wouldn't miss the game."

When I dropped Rachel off at school I said, "You know, don't you?"

"Know what?"

"Where they're going."

"Maybe."

"So, what's the big secret?"

"What's it worth to ya?"

"What's it gonna cost me?"

"Wow, Daddy. That makes me wish I really knew."

• • •

The team that showed up for practice Wednesday and Thursday didn't look any different than the one that had limped out there Tuesday. But they were there, at least. "Is this team beat already?" Coach asked me in the locker room Thursday night.

"They look it, don't they?" I said.

"Finished, I'd say. I don't know what else to do. They know the plays. They know how to win. It's just whether they believe they can do it one more time."

As he and I left the field house I realized we didn't look any more confident than the boys. But what can you do? Put on a happy face? The game was gonna be won by the team that wanted it the most. Well, maybe that was overstating it. That might've been true last week. We could want it bad as we could and there was still a team on the other side of the ball.

Dan Ferris, the principal, was waiting outside. "Got a minute, gentlemen?" he said.

"On our way to dinner," Coach said. "Wanna join us?"

"Thanks, no."

He stood there until the last player was gone, then we followed him back inside to the weight room. Dr. Ferris kept running his hands over the tops of his ears like he was smoothing down hair that wasn't there. "We customarily announce the, uh, scholarship after the last game of the season. The problem is, the county board has never wavered on their decision. I have known, and I sense you two have as well, that there was really no recourse for Athens City High. Our students will be merged with Rock Hill next fall, and there are, of course, tremendous financial benefits to the school population. In anticipation of that, the state has decided—"

"Scuse me, Doc," Coach said. "All due respect. Could you just give me the bottom line. I'm exhausted and hungry and I got to start focusing on tomorrow."

"Of course, certainly. There is no scholarship fund. We're broke. All our reserves have been frozen by the state to go into the new situation next year."

Coach slapped his palms to his knees and stood. "That's it, then. Thanks for letting us know."

"I'm so sorry."

"Don't be, Dan. I never liked that scholarship idea anyway."

"But it being named for your son was meant to be—"

"I know. It's all right. Okay? We done here?"

41

Rachel sat at the kitchen table with Elvis, taking a short break from studying. He held his hands in place like a goalpost and she flipped a tiny makeshift paper football through them with her fingers.

"She shoots, she scores!" he said.

"Okay," she said. "Halftime's over. Back to history."

He smiled, then fell serious. "Okay if I pick up my laundry tomorrow on the way to the game? I'd rather not try to lug it home tonight with this." He flexed his right hand and winced.

"You're not thinking of playing tomorrow."

"Scholarship's within reach."

"Championship, you mean."

He looked embarrassed. "Right."

It hit her all at once. "No wonder you didn't get out of bounds like you were told."

His eyes flashed. "A championship doesn't guarantee me the next level."

She shook her head. "I can't win. If you lose the scholarship, you're gone. If you get the scholarship, you're gone. You want me to apologize for my idea, something people are starting to believe in. Most people want to believe in something. Even you."

He smiled and leaned in, whispering, "I love a good fight. But you do make a guy want to believe."

"Elvis, I wish you'd dare believe there's something bigger than you."

He sat back. "Like you said, halftime's over."

42

Friday afternoon Elvis hung around after school, flexing his fingers, telling himself his wrist was stronger, that he could play. He wandered the stadium, watching the pep club hang banners and affix streamers. A couple of hours later, people would start lining up for the game.

He stood in the shadows near the concession stand and saw that Coach Schuler was also unable to stay away. He unlocked the field house, spent several minutes inside, then came out, leaving it open. Elvis waited till Coach was out of sight, then went in and put on his practice uniform. It wasn't easy alone, especially with a tender wrist.

He retrieved his old football on the way out, the American Leather logo now just a faint imprint. He thought of the day he got it, and he thought of his dad.

The sky was darkening and someone had turned on the stadium lights. Elvis jogged onto the field, feeling the pain with every stride. When he felt warm and loose, he ran up and down the field, gingerly switching the ball from hand to hand. He couldn't hold it in his right for long, but Rock Hill didn't have to know that. What would a tackle feel like? What if he landed on his wrist? Or forgot and used his right hand to push off the ground to get up?

The pep club was gone. A lone figure sat in the stands. Coach. Elvis walked up the stairs and sat a couple of rows down from Schuler and to his right.

"Looks a lot different from up here," Elvis said.

"You trying to play tonight?"

"Think of it, Coach. My dad went to one pro game in his entire life and it happened to be the Gayle Sayers game when he was five years old. One of my favorite memories was listening to him describe that game. He always told me I could play like that someday. Got one more chance."

"You know, Jackson, you and I are a little bit alike. Did you know I too was stuck with a first name I couldn't live down?"

"Seriously?"

"Why you think I go by Buster? You don't think that's my given name."

Elvis shrugged.

"You think 'Elvis' is a tough one, try going by 'Roscoe.'"

"Roscoe?"

"Tell a soul and you're history."

Elvis shook his head, smiling.

"But we are alike in other ways too," Coach said. "When I was a kid, my parents had to constantly keep an eye on me. One winter day I ran across the street to a neighbor's frozen pond. The ice couldn't have been more'n a couple inches thick. My dad had to stand at the edge and plead with me to get off. The more he pleaded, the more I wanted to stay on. He was just looking out for me, but I couldn't see it. My boy never learned that lesson either.

"Son, I don't know exactly why you're here. We all play for different reasons. But I've never seen anybody who can do what you do on the field. If you can learn what Jack didn't, you won't need his scholarship."

Elvis closed his eyes. "I didn't get it, did I?"

"There ain't a dime in my boy's fund. Town's broke. I just found out yesterday. Sorry."

Elvis couldn't breathe. He heard Coach stand and sensed he had paused behind him. But then he moved on and down the steps and disappeared in the tunnel.

43

Rachel's dad had told her after school about the scholarship. So that was it then. The petitions meant nothing. She was glad she hadn't known earlier. Elvis would have been able to tell something was wrong by the look on her face.

Rachel left the pregame FCA prayer warriors meeting early and, surprised by the chill in the air, sadly moseyed the mile and a half home to get her jacket. She couldn't wait till Bev got back. If she had to spend another minute with the vacuous Josie, she'd scream.

The Rock Hill team bus passed, and the players leaned out the windows, banging on the side and hooting at her. It would be so great to beat them.

The light was on in the front room when she mounted the steps, making her hesitate. Her dad had to already be at the stadium. She slowly opened the door and found Elvis angrily stuffing laundry into his backpack.

"What're you doing?" she said. "You should be at the—"

"Didn't you hear?" he said. "We both lost."

"Well, I'm not leaving town."

"Let's just say I don't have what you have."

"But you could, Elvis! You're here and it's all right in front of you."

"I'm glad I gave you and your school one last go round, but in the end, I got nothing but used."

"Cause you didn't get the scholarship? That's all there is?"

Elvis slung his bag over his shoulder and stuck his face in hers. "Get out of your fantasy world! The Crusaders are going to get destroyed tonight, and this town will disappear. And God, Schuler, and your silly little petitions aren't going to change that!"

He pushed past her and stormed out, slamming the door.

Rachel pulled on her jacket and walked back to school. Cars lined the streets a mile from the field. The band boomed in the distance. She arrived to a crowd like she'd never seen. Pickups ringed the place, backed up to the fence, tailgates facing the field, families, dogs, and cats jammed in to watch. Only Rock Hill was on the field, their fans singing, chanting.

She found a spot near the top of the stands where there'd be room for Bev and maybe Kim. And here came Josie. Rachel couldn't hide her tears. How long had it been since she had prayed in that end zone? And what had been the answer?

44

Coach tells me it's tradition that he and his assistant wrap players' ankles themselves before a championship game. Like I couldn't remember from my playing days.

The guys, pale and looking terrified, seem impressed. When everybody's dressed and ready to go, he gathers em and says, "Tell ya what: Supreme Court or not, I'm praying." He removes his hat and kneels. "Anyone who wants in, take a knee."

Afterwards, we head out to an ovation I'd only dreamed about. I wanted to tell the guys to enjoy it, cause it might be the last of the night. We lose the coin toss and kick off. Within a couple minutes we're down 7-0, and I gotta tell ya, we look like a junior high team against the Crimson Tide. It's like the Raiders are in our backfield. We don't gain a yard in the first quarter. Not one.

45

Elvis trembled with rage as he marched out of town to the Washington farm. If this was it, if this was all there was, he was going to do something. He would hitchhike all the way to Indiana, get Jenny out of that orphanage, and fight with his bare hands anybody he had to.

He climbed into the dark loft to grab as much of his stuff as he could carry. A full moon streamed through the hay mound door, making him pause. He stepped to the opening. "All right, God," he said. "You got something to say to me?" He waited a beat. "Didn't think so."

He felt around in the shadows for matches, grabbed a lantern, and slid up the glass top to light the broad wick. When the light invaded the loft he flinched, noticing something in the corner.

"What the—?" A slew of homemade pies and cakes covered the wood floor. Taped to each were handwritten notes, many written in crayon by kids.

"Sorry about your arm."

"Get better soon."

"Good luck."

"I'm gonna play like you someday."

A voice behind him made him jump. "Always nice to be needed."

Orville Washington was at the top of the ladder.

"How did you know I was—?"

"Got an inkling when the third pie turned up. Finally figured out why I kept getting mail addressed to you from the school."

"Where'd all this stuff come from?"

"People in Athens City take care a their own. By the way, as your landlord, I took a customary fee." He smiled and Elvis had to chuckle at the blueberry filling in his teeth.

Elvis sat on his cot, overcome. People in the diner? Fans? They cared this much?

"Hey, boy," Mr. Washington said, "you late for the game, ain'tcha?"

"Guess I am."

"Come on. I'll give ya a ride."

46

I wish I could tell ya this was one of them Disney movies where we pull off the impossible and some heathen hockey team gets humiliated by a bunch of thirteen-year-olds. Unfortunately, this was high school football in southern Alabama, and we were getting it handed to us. I mean, it was a disaster. Only time we had the ball past the 50-yard line in their territory was after they already had us down 27-zip early in the second quarter. They tried some trick reverse play on one of our punts and the ball came loose and who should fall on it but Snoot. I think he was sorry he did, with all the piling on. But three plays later, when we'd lost six more yards, he up and kicks a field goal.

That just irritated these monsters, and their scrubs scored ten more before halftime. Now we're getting killed 37-3, and that wasn't all. If you can believe it, it was worse than it looked. We had nothing going. We couldn't stop em and we couldn't move the ball. We were overmatched on every single play, and you could see it all over every kid. If I was a quitter, I'd've taken em off the field to protect their psyches.

Besides that, Coach and I were actually distracted. We were trying to stay in the game, stick with the plan, call plays, all that, but we were also peeking into the stands now and then too, cause I hadn't seen hide nor hair of Bev, and I know Coach wanted to know she was here so he could be sure Helena was safe and sound at the center. I caught a glimpse of Rachel, but she was with that airhead—scuse me, girl—she can hardly stand, and I couldn't even coax a wave out of her.

If ever a game was over at the half, this was it. We get in the locker room, and you can imagine what the guys looked like. Most of em seemed on the edge of tears and I wouldn't've blamed a one of em if they'd just broke down and sobbed. Coach looked like he'd been out there himself and got in the way of that killing Rock Hill football machine.

I passed out orange slices and the guys were guzzling water, but mostly they just sat staring at the floor. I mean, some things can be dealt with and some things you just have to suck up and take. Coach walked over to Sherman. "Coupla great hits, boy. That quarterback'll be sore for days."

He found Nino. "Snoot, nice boot. Really sent that one into orbit."

He clapped Upshaw on the shoulder pad.
"Yash, a nice catch under pressure. Fingers of
glue, son." The poor guy had picked up maybe
two yards on a throw over the middle.

"Gather round, boys," Coach said, the wind
gone from his sails. They shuffled over. "We're
gonna lose, make no mistake. This'll probably be
the worst rout in Bama play-off history. But this
year's been worth it anyway, and don't think it
hasn't. I've loved it and been honored to see you
boys come together as a unit, one body. You res-
urrected something that had been lost. You've
made me proud."

"You on empty, Coach?" We all look up. It's Elvis
in street clothes. "Is that all you've got?"

Straightening up, Coach smiles. "Y'all started
without me," Elvis continues. "Coach, may I?"

Well, Coach nods, and Jackson takes a deep
breath, looking at his teammates. "Look, I think
we all know why I came to Athens City. It wasn't
for this school or even this team. I never believed
fifteen players could get this far. And we get here
only to find out that none of us is getting the
scholarship, the school's still closing down, and
we're playing a team we can't beat. Doesn't seem
worth it.

"But for some reason the stands are packed, the
fans are still cheering, and I've got enough 'Get

well' pies to last a year. These people are here because they believe in Athens City tradition again, and we had something to do with it. I don't know about you, but being part of something like that is new for me."

Sherman Naters stands and starts pacing furiously.

Brian stands too and says, "When people remember football in Athens City, Alabama, let's make em think of the next twenty-four minutes. We got something left!"

"Rock Hill hasn't been outscored for a half in three years," Elvis says. "We win this half, we got our pride."

Now Sherman's pumping his arms and waving his helmet. "This game starts over right now! Heads up! Act like champions!"

I look at Coach and we shrug. They wanna pretend its nothing-nothing, why not? Coach says, "Awright then, if we're gonna put one more half in the books, let's do it right." He walks into the coaches' room, drags out an old trunk, and hoists it onto the table. I open it and find the crimson jerseys from the state title game of 1988. Who'd a thought?

Coach disappears for a minute, so I start passing out the jerseys. When I give Jackson number 40, he turns to Brian. "Think I got your number," he says. Then he mocks Brian's accent. "Tradition's real important round here."

We hear banging on the field-house door. "You guys got thirty seconds!"

Coach reappears and walks up to Elvis with his son's jersey out of the display case. "This one's seen some action, but it's got two more quarters in it. My boy's watching, Jackson. Give it all you got."

"Coach," Elvis said. "I just can't—"

"—turn this down is what you can't do."

"Gonna get blood on it."

"That's why it's crimson."

Brian helps him suit up, then it's all hands together. Coach says, "Don't get fancy. Just hit em. Let's show em some barnyard football."

When we get out there, one of the refs has already dropped his flag for delay of game and we were close to getting disqualified. "Pick up that flag now, John, and I mean it," Coach tells him. "They don't need any more help."

"Listen, Schuler, you can't change jerseys in the middle of a game."

"Course you can. Rule book just says you got to keep the same numbers."

"Well, a couple of these don't even meet that criteria."

"C'mon, John. This is the last game for our boys.

We ain't gonna win. If Rock Hill pitches a fit, tell em we forfeited. This is just for pride."

It's clear our fans are stunned at the new jerseys. And a bunch of em spot Elvis. I hear em chanting his name and I turn to see Rachel running down from the stands and up to the fence. Elvis hollers, "Pray for me!"

She calls out, "Why are you doing this?"

"I'm a Crusader!"

I'm telling ya, if I had an orchestra . . .

Rachel waves at me and points back up to where she'd been sitting. Course I spot Bev first, sitting there with Kim, and I'll be dogged if there isn't a little dark-haired girl. I want to quit right now and get up there to see what's going on, but that's when I spot Coach's wife. I shoot her a double take and grab Buster, turning him and pointing. He spies her and his hand comes up to his mouth and he sucks in a breath like he can hardly stand it. She gives him a shy little wave, and I thought I was gonna have to coach the second half.

Snoot and Brian have carried out the big green chalkboard from the field house and put it under the scoreboard. Brian draws a line down the middle and puts the team names at the top. When he puts a big zero under each team, our fans erupt.

"Coach! Coach!" We turn to see Abel Gordon and his dad. "We'll keep score!" Buster nods.

All right, I admit I had to check the paper to see if I was making this part up, but it happened. Rock Hill kicks off, and guess who runs it all the way back for a touchdown, carrying it in his bad arm? Okay, so maybe he carried it in his good arm, but anyway, it was almost too good to be true. Snoot kicks the point after, so now it's 37-10. But the chalkboard reads 7-0, us. Our guys are jumping around, smacking each other on the back. Rock Hill just looks puzzled.

"Team is back," Coach says.

A couple minutes later, Rock Hill puts up another seven. The scoreboard reads 44-10, the chalkboard 7-7. All of a sudden Buster is really into this one, strategizing, telling me who to have run a slant, who to line up in the slot, saying who'll be wide open, and course being right every time. "Chess match on grass," I say.

Elvis is wide open for a huge gain, and I see the Rock Hill coach and his assistant arguing, pointing at each other. Their coach bellows so I can hear him all the way from the other side, "You see that, Raiders? We are in a *war!*"

Elvis scores to make it 44-17 for the game, 14-7 us for the half. Rock Hill strikes back quick to tie the half at 14 and lead the game 51-17.

In the fourth quarter the Shermanater breaks through to lay a huge lick on their quarterback in their own end zone for a two-point safety, so now they lead 51-19 for the game but we lead 16-14 for the second half.

Rock Hill starts picking on Elvis, probably seeing he's hurt. But they try to pass his way once too often and he intercepts one and runs it in for his third TD. The game's out of reach, course, at 51-26, but now we're up 23-14 on the chalkboard.

Then it was like the Raiders got tired of toying with us. They break back for two fast TDs, and now they lead 65-26 with just minutes to go. It's hardly possible to score that many points in forty-eight minutes. We're deflated, cause after all our work we even trail the half now, 28-23.

We need a touchdown, but their defense breaks through on a blitz, and Brian is chased to our sideline and crushed right in front of us. Coach and I kneel over him. "Where does it hurt?"

"Everywhere. My hair hurts."

Coach says, "I'm proud of you, Brian. Let's call it a night."

"Coach, please. I don't want to walk off this field till the gun sounds. I can't throw, but maybe I can still run."

Elvis says, "What's Schuler's commandment number one?"

"Let the bone roll," Coach says.

With less than a minute to go, Brian keeps pitching out to Elvis, who keeps gaining yard after yard. Once I heard a Raider defender grunt, "Stay down!"

Rock Hill's coach is screaming, "We will *not* lose this half to a team of *fifteen players*!"

Our guys are racing to the line with no huddle, and Rock Hill, who should already be celebrating their third straight undefeated season and state title, are sucking wind and trying to keep from losing this half. With less than twenty seconds on the clock and us inside their 10-yard line, Rock Hill calls a time-out. Nobody's ever heard of a team ahead by thirty-nine points calling time-out. We hear Rock Hill's coach ranting, "I will *not* give them the satisfaction."

Coach tells our guys, "This is it. Maybe two more plays in Crusader history. Use what you've got and do it any way you can."

Our crowd's chanting, "El-vis! El-vis!"

Raider fans are shouting, "De-fense! De-fense!"

Brian pitches to Elvis, who gets blasted out of bounds and over the Rock Hill bench. Five seconds show on the clock. Even the Rock Hill coach is urging him to stay down. But he gets up. Rock Hill players are shaking their heads.

Brian pitches back to Elvis and he starts one more run, barely eluding defenders as the gun sounds. The world goes into slow motion. The roar of the crowd deafens me and I feel like I'm alone before the biggest high school crowd ever. The lights, the color, the action all swim together and somehow I've got the time to realize how ludicrous this is. Elvis can't get back to the line of scrimmage, and I'm yelling I don't know what, pumping my fists and hopping down the sidelines, trying to will him to get somewhere, do something. We've been slaughtered, but a touchdown will give us this half, and there's nothing in the world that matters more.

Out of gas and stumbling, Elvis is swarmed by Raiders. They look as whipped as he does. Somehow, some way he twists and keeps his arm free as they climb his back, drive into his knees, and grab him around his neck.

I'm dying, screaming, hopping. And as the best high school football player I've ever seen finally buckles under the bulk of all that weight and starts to crumble to the turf, he launches a desperate pass. At first I don't even follow the ball. I don't believe he's unleashed it. He disappears under hundreds of pounds of Raiders, and I'm guessing they think it's over too. But there's no whistle. The ball's still in play.

I search the sky and pick it up, a pitiful dying quail of an end-over-end toss that doesn't look to have a prayer of getting past the wide-eyed Rock Hill defenders. They quickly crouch and leap, trying to tip the wobbly ball away. But it somehow eludes em.

Brian Schuler is running like a madman, snaking through the secondary, eyes wild, mouth wide open, desperately looking over his shoulder. Inside the 5-yard line the ball drops just behind him. He slows and stretches and reaches and it hits his shoulder pad and bounces just above his helmet. Now he's fair game and a corner back drives his helmet into Brian's back and wraps his arms around him, just above the waist.

So now they're both flying across the goal line, the force of the blow pushing Brian's hands out in front of him. The ball drops into his arms as he's slammed to the ground. The whistle blows, the ref signals touchdown, and I drop to my knees overcome at the best loss I've ever suffered as a player or coach.

The Crusaders are all over the field, high-fiving, piling atop one another, and I run out to meet em in the end zone where they're hugging Brian and Elvis. Rock Hill has won 65-32, but Andy Gordon has scribbled on the chalkboard Crusaders 29, Raiders 28.

Rock Hill looks beat. State champs and they're dragging. Their fans are silent. A Raider pulls Elvis out of the scrum. "Don't you guys get it? You lost!"

"Not this half, we didn't," Elvis says.

The Raiders trudge off the field while our fans gather around the goal posts and start to climb. Soon the goals come toppling.

Rachel shoots past me into Elvis's arms. "I am so proud of you," she says. "Look who's here." Jenny Lucas jumps on Elvis and brings him to his knees.

That was about all I could take.

Coach was off looking to see where Kim had taken his wife. Bev grabbed me from behind and I had to remind myself she was still recuperating. "Guess you know I got a million questions," I said over my shoulder.

"All in good time, cowboy."

47

Turns out I'm marrying a lot more woman than I ever dreamed. Kim says it's cause I'm still basically oblivious. I tell her I'm not oblivious, I'm Protestant, and she says, "That was mildly funny the first time." My vote against her being in the wedding will likely go unheeded.

Anyway, if you could believe the rest of Bev's bevy, this was all her idea. Soon as she learned about Jenny and made her the point of all their meetings, they started conniving to do something about her. It took all kinds a legal rigmarole just to get permission to take her out of Indiana to visit strangers who cared about her. I guess all of us were checked out by the authorities, and one of the rules was that the girl couldn't be under the sole care of a lady still in treatment for alcoholism. Course it turns out Jenny hit it off with Miz Schuler as well as anybody, maybe cause Helena was older and seemed like a grandma.

Jenny just knocked us over. The fact that she was scared and shy and tired didn't keep her from stealing our hearts. She had those huge, curious eyes, and she was so glad to be with Elvis again, you could tell she was fighting to stay awake. She eventually lost the battle and Rachel put her in her bed.

Elvis wasn't much more comfortable with all us oldsters around, but he mustered enough courage to thank the ladies. Best of all, and he said this in front of us though he was talking to Rachel, "I don't want to get all dramatic and I don't want a big fuss, but Jenny wants me to take her to church Sunday."

Bev and me and the rest of us traded glances but tried to pretend we hadn't heard that. Naw, there shouldn't be much of a commotion when the best football player in Athens City history and its resident atheist shows up in church. "I don't want people expecting me to come running down the aisle or something," he said.

"At least not without a football."

That was Coach and he looked mighty proud of himself to have got a laugh. I heard Rachel whisper to Elvis, "People will let you move at your own pace. You're on your way, but God won't push you."

Course Jenny had to be back to Indiana by the middle of the following week, and that was hard. You sure had to feel for the little thing, especially when she had to say her good-byes. I'd hardly had much time with her, but I couldn't keep from crying. What must it be like to have all these new friends and then hear promises you've heard before and be expected to believe em?

We told her we'd call. We told her we'd write. We told her we'd come visit sometime and even bring her back down to Athens City. She hugged our necks so tight we wondered if we could peel her off, and I can still feel her hot tears running down my neck.

Bev hadn't been back from Indiana twenty-four hours before she told me we had to talk. "I don't wanna catch you when you're vulnerable or make you think this is the only way to make me happy," she said. "But you know I did my homework. You've just about raised your daughter, Cal, and this may be the last thing you even wanna consider, so stop me now if it's out of the question."

I knew what she was talking about. Course I did. But when I didn't say anything, she had to wonder. Maybe she was hoping I'd grin from ear to ear and tell her I was hoping she'd suggest this. "I mean it, Cal," she said, studying me. "This is no light decision, no easy thing. This is a long-term commitment."

"I made one of those recently," I said.

"And that may be plenty for now."

"No, I'm listening."

"Don't let me waste my breath," she said. "Because if I'm to let this go—which I'm willing to do, and I mean that—I don't want to invest any more emotion in it. I love you, Cal, and I'd be thrilled if it was just you and me and Rachel for the rest of the time we've got together. If that's what you want, I leave this right where it is."

I gathered her in and she lay her head on my shoulder. Her heart was racing. "What'd you find out, sweetheart? What'd they tell you?"

"Cal, I'm not asking for a decision right now, but I'm serious—I don't want to get into talking about this if there's not even a chance."

"And you wouldn't see me as the guy who stood in the way of your dream?"

"You are my dream, Calvin. And I know I'm naive. I know this couldn't be easy. There may be days when we regret it. We don't know what this girl brings with her, what she's suffered, how that'll play out. And sometimes I think I get enough mothering satisfaction just interacting with Rachel. The Lord knows that girl has accepted me already, and that can't be easy. But if this thing is not going to be, I need to know now so I can start shifting gears."

"I don't understand the maternal thing," I said. "I don't know how that feels. All I can do is try to imagine not having Rachel. Being her dad is who I am. I think back about what life would've been like with Estelle and no baby, and my mind won't even conjure it. And then when Estelle died, well, I couldn't've gone on without Rachel. I wouldn't be quick to deny you the raising of a child."

She shifted her weight. "I've gone forty-two years single and childless," she said. "I imagine I could keep going."

"Not single you couldn't," I said. "I'd have to sue you for breach of promise."

She put a finger to my lips. "Legal stuff comes later."

I had no idea what that meant, but I told her I was willing to hear her out about Jennifer Lucas. She pulled a folder from her bag and began running down the prerequisites for an out-of-state individual to adopt a child. "Parents have to be no more than forty years older than the child," she began.

I said, "Hey, that leaves out the Schulers."

"So does Helena's condition," Bev said, "but did she ever come alive with Jenny. And Coach loves her."

"Godparents?"

"That's what I was thinking." Bev's eyes were afire. "If we hadn't worked together all these years, I might worry about bringing a little one into a new marriage. And it still won't be easy. But it'll be worth it, don't you think? Or were you looking forward to an empty nest? Am I messing everything up, Cal?"

"Course you are! Kid or not, the nest ain't gonna be empty with you here."

We talked about it all afternoon, and it seemed Bev couldn't think a nothing else for days. She was obsessed with Jenny, and I was getting there. My mind was clouded by the business falling apart, but come Christmas I finally found out what Bev meant about legal stuff. While she was arranging for the adoption, I was resigning myself to the fact that American Leather was dying, while still—recklessly, I know—keeping one eye on the ball glove market.

Bev and I drove down to the shore for a Christmas Eve dinner, and she looked beautiful. We'd talked with Jenny on the phone that day and told her the news. She could move in with Bev by the middle of January, and we would become a family on the twenty-third. No matter how the business deal came down, I wouldn't have to work. But that wasn't me. I told Bev, "I gotta start reading the want ads."

"That sounds like a cue for my present," she said.

"I didn't bring it," I said. "It's under the tree."

"I meant my present to you," she said. But she had carried only a small purse. "Is now okay?"

I nodded and she pulled out a business-size envelope. It was from an insurance company and addressed to her. She had crossed out her name and address and written in, "To my darling Cal, with love forever. Merry Christmas 2001. What's mine is yours and what's yours is ours."

"What's this?" I said, studying it in the light of the table candle.

"I don't know, darling. Maybe you should open it."

Inside was a memo on the insurance company's letterhead, regarding Athens City Memorial Hospital, Inc. "Ms. Raschke, enclosed is your portion of the settlement with the above-named corporation. It has been our pleasure serving you. We wish to remind you that the details herein are, by binding agreement, confidential. With your acceptance of the enclosed, you absolve the corporation and its staff, in part and in whole, from any legal liability related to your case. For purposes of public knowledge, you are stipulating that the corporation admits no guilt or fault in the matter.

"While the award enclosed could never compensate for your pain and suffering or permanent physical damage, we hope that it in a small way helps allow you to put behind you a difficult season in your life.

"Cordially . . ."

I looked up at her, afraid to peek at the "enclosed."

"I, ah, never thought you'd pursue this, Bev. I really didn't."

"You know me well, Cal. I wouldn't have. I listened. I said I wasn't the type to bring action. I said everybody makes mistakes. I said there was no way someone did this with intent. They said, 'You almost died. That colonoscopy almost killed you. And before they repaired the damage, the poison in your system took away your most natural female ability.' I told em I understood but that I would not be making a claim against the hospital."

"So what's this?"

"They asked permission to withhold my wishes from the hospital while they pursued their own claim. They said, 'We're not about to pay for the further procedures necessary to keep you alive, which were the result of their error.' I told em that sounded fair enough and that I was sure the hospital would waive those costs."

"This is waiving costs?"

"Cal, their attorneys went in there with a handicap. I was a victim unwilling to file. But with my permission not to reveal that, as long as they didn't imply otherwise, they started negotiating with the hospital corporation's lawyers. They established the case for malpractice, just to make clear that they knew well what had happened.

"They tell me the corporation's lawyers advised the hospital to settle. I argued with em, Cal. I told em to get back in there and tell em it was unnecessary, cause I wasn't gonna file anyway. They said, 'You can do what you want with your part of the money. If it were up to us, we would treat this as a first offer and try to get more.' I said, 'Let me see that,' and they slid it across the desk. They said I could make a generous donation to the hospital if I wanted to. 'Give it all back,' they said. 'We don't care. But we'll be keeping our portion.' Cal, you can see I could give half of it back and still have more than enough."

I slid the check out from behind the memo and stopped breathing. I've been in a high ticket business all my life and I'd never personally seen so many zeroes on a check. "Bev," I said, "you can't take—"

"I didn't ask for it. They offered it because of

what they did to me. I like that hospital and I hope you'll think about a generous donation."

"Beverly, you can't give this to me. I—"

"I can and I have," she said, lifting her hands to show she wouldn't take it back. "There's nobody I'd trust more with it, sweetheart. Think of it. Think of the church, the hospital, the bank, the town, the factory, Rachel, Jenny, us."

"The factory?"

"You been having trouble getting through to that liquidator, right?"

"Yeah, what's with that?"

"I told him we were going a different direction."

"We are?"

"Ball gloves, Cal. You know everybody wants to do it. Everybody has a job, morale goes up, we have a new challenge."

"But it's bad business, Bev. You don't pour money down the drain just because you can. We can't compete with the other manufacturers any-more."

"You'll find a way to make it turn, Cal. It'll start making a profit sooner or later. And if it doesn't, who says it's money down the drain? People have jobs. Customers have quality. American Leather stays the best equipment manufacturer in the business. Everybody benefits. It helps the Athens City economy. The town stays alive."

• • •

Mrs. Raschke coaxed one more trip out of Clifford, and he was able to get down the aisle to give the bride away. Kim was Bev's maid of honor. Coach was my best man. Elvis and Rachel were witnesses. Jennifer was junior bridesmaid. Helena hosted the reception.

And the runners-up to the state high school football championship, all fifteen of em, stuffed an entire bag of marshmallows into the tail pipe of my car.

I didn't shake the last of them Crusaders till I was nearly outside Mobile.

Epilogue

The day after the wedding, Rachel left Elvis at Kim's to play with Jenny while she took a walk into town by herself. Later she would visit Coach and Mrs. Schuler in their new home, where Bev used to live.

She reached the high school football stadium and strolled into the end zone near the scoreboard. "Lord," she said silently, "when people talk about Athens City's last chapter, and the Crusaders' last half, and about Schuler's last stand, please help them remember it was You who showed up and showed off."